THE
FIFTH COLUMN

THE
FIFTH COLUMN

ANDREW GROSS

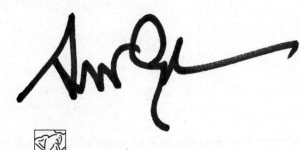

MINOTAUR BOOKS

NEW YORK

First published in the United States by Minotaur Books, an imprint of St. Martin's Publishing Group

THE FIFTH COLUMN. Copyright © 2019 by Andrew Gross. All rights reserved. Printed in the United States of America. For information, address St. Martin's Publishing Group, 120 Broadway, New York, NY 10271.

www.minotaurbooks.com

Designed by Omar Chapa

The Library of Congress Cataloging-in-Publication Data is available upon request.

ISBN 978-1-250-18000-1 (hardcover)
ISBN 978-1-250-26662-0 (signed edition)
ISBN 978-1-250-18001-8 (ebook)

Our books may be purchased in bulk for promotional, educational, or business use. Please contact your local bookseller or the Macmillan Corporate and Premium Sales Department at 1-800-221-7945, extension 5442, or by email at MacmillanSpecialMarkets@macmillan.com.

First Edition: September 2019

10 9 8 7 6 5 4 3 2 1

For Martin and Louis

THE
FIFTH COLUMN

1939–1941. *While there was already a war raging in Europe, at home there was intense, widespread opposition to President Roosevelt getting America involved. Isolationists still controlled Congress and the State Department, pushing the president to remain neutral. The America First Committee enjoyed widespread support. Charles Lindbergh, after Roosevelt the second-most-admired man in America, was an outspoken Nazi sympathizer, often butting heads with the administration. The National Socialist Bund, a powerful pro-German organization headquartered in Yorkville on New York's Upper East Side, a uniquely German neighborhood, defended Hitler and his transformation of the German Republic in fiery, public rallies. German families even spent summer weekends at pro-Nazi camps in New Jersey and on Long Island, where children wore swastikas on their arms, sang patriotic German songs, and gave Nazi salutes just like the Hitler Youth back in Germany.*

As Roosevelt supplied arms and equipment to the Brits and Russians, fears grew that Germans long buried in the fabric of our society were actually Nazi agents who would carry out acts of sabotage should America enter the war. On one day alone, in 1939, some 2,850 reports of suspected German espionage were reported to the FBI. Those fears flamed the highest in February of that year, when over 22,000 Nazi supporters in khaki uniforms, waving swastikas and singing German songs, packed New York's Madison Square Garden for a raucous, hate-filled rally. This story begins on that night.

1

FEBRUARY 1939

"Eli, just one more," I said to the man behind the bar, sliding my glass across to him. "The same."

"How about we think about calling it a night, Mr. Mossman?" the barman replied, likely detecting that rise in my voice that immediately gave me away when I'd had one too many. "What is that now, two, three?"

He was being kind. It was four, actually. Four Rob Roys. And he knew just how I liked them. A jigger of Cutty with only a wave of vermouth skirted around the edge. Pretty much scotch on the rocks for anyone else. Along with an ashtray full of Chesterfield butts. That's how I passed every Tuesday and Thursday eve.

But he was right—I ought to get myself home. I had a wife and a daughter there, the remains of a once-happy family, even if it was now more of a memory than a fact. For weeks now, after work—if you even called it work, what I did these days, teaching evening classes in U.S. history to immigrants applying for citizenship—I'd been stopping by this dark, smoky bar with its red neon sign flickering on and off—*Eli's, Eli's* . . . It was in a part of the city most people steered away from after dark, south of Madison Square Garden and north of Forty-second, where the Greyhound Line buses came in. I always instructed the Irish owner who manned the bar as I took a stool, "Just the one, Eli. . . ." Only to make the bus ride across town and the rickety Lexington IRT back to Yorkville more bearable (though I usually threw my wobbly ass into a cab) and to go over the stories of the day: the deteriorating situation in Europe; that madman Hitler threatening to take over the Sudetenland; the wave of America Firsters and our own isolationist Congress seemingly closing their eyes to the looming danger there. What every thinking person in this increasingly blind world could clearly see.

But invariably, the "one" had a way of always turning into two, and two, three—as the discussion heated. "Let those Europeans work it out for themselves," Eli would say. "Me, I don't want a single one of our boys dying over there for them. Not after the last war . . ."

And then the three might become four, or even more, until it was clear as the torment on my face why I was really there, drinking myself into a dulled state, and that it wasn't all over the gloomy condition in Europe.

That clearly, undeniably, I simply didn't want to go home. That home merely reminded me of the promise and hope rapidly fading from my life. That once I had been in the doctoral program at Columbia, instructing graduate candidates in nineteenth-century European history while I finished my dissertation. That once I had a smart and beautiful wife who thought of me as the center of her universe, but now looked at me with scorn and disappointment—if she even looked at me at all. And a daughter, Emma, the apple of my eye no matter what I had done to ruin things, who had seen me stagger home more sideways than straight far more times than she could even count to at the age of four. "Mommy, what's wrong with Daddy?" she would ask. "Is he sick?"

"Yes, honey, Daddy's just not feeling well," Liz would say, doing her best to cover for me.

Hearing my daughter's words and seeing her questioning look was the most painful part of it for me. Still, as bad as things had become with Liz, and whenever it was that our troubles had truly begun, tonight, it seemed, the whole city was in the same state of unrest. Maybe the world.

Tonight, over twenty thousand supporters of that maniac Hitler had gathered at Madison Square Garden to listen to finger-pointing fascists spew their hate and vitriol on the Jews and the international interests who were threatening our society. Thousands, dressed in khaki shirts and armbands or even in their business suits draped in Nazi flags, listening to anti-Semites like Fritz Kuhn, Father Coughlin, and Joseph McWilliams (known as "Joe McNazi)" rile them up into a hate-filled state; shouting their vile calumnies against the Jews and Bolsheviks who they claimed had infiltrated our government and were now running our country. Bernard Baruch. Henry Morganthau. Felix Frankfurter. And our president, Franklin Delano "Jewsavelt," and his Commie New Deal.

I'd heard there were over two thousand of New York's policemen trying to keep order over on Eighth Avenue, and thousands of protestors, the last line of sanity in this world, shouting back and pointing fingers at them for their treatment of Jews in Europe, shouting, "Fascists! Make Europe safe for everyone."

Now, three hours later, the bastards were still roaming the

streets around town in raucous bands of six or ten, singing Nazi songs, bustling into fistfights with hecklers who flung curses and garbage back at them. Railing against the "interventionists" who were trying to draw America into Europe's unrest. America is for Americans, they would say. Yes, it was all crazy. Not just in *my* soul, in my conscience tonight, but everywhere.

Eli, just one more.

Eli, in his white shirt, sleeves rolled up, and a matching apron around his waist, looked at me with a philosophical shake of his head, the wisdom that came from serving a thousand people like me with similarly empty souls: *Don't you have something better to do with your life, son, than sit here?* His look said, *You're smart. Educated. You're not like the usual riffraff who crawl their way in here this time of night. Go on home. You've got a beautiful gal waiting for you there, an adorable daughter. Didn't you show me their picture once?*

But then he just shrugged—that complacent, unjudging bartender's shrug that says, *I just give 'em what they want.* And he reached to the shelf for the open bottle of Cutty and filled my glass one more time. "Your poison, young man."

Yes, my poison.

This time I waved off the vermouth and took a gulp, no longer even feeling the bite of the alcohol, just the warmth of it going down and doing its job. Forgetting.

"You know what tonight is, Eli?" I asked him. I lit another cigarette.

"All I know is it's one woeful night to make a living," he said, turning his blue Irish eyes at the sparse crowd and at the bedlam going on outside.

You could still hear bands of them parading down West Forty-third Street, roaming the deserted, trash-lined streets, drunkenly singing their "patriotic" songs, kicking over trash cans, scrawling swastikas and anti-Semitic slurs on store windows. The cops all seemed to look the other way. All they wanted was for it all to go away. Hell, half of them probably felt the same way as the mob if you asked them over a beer. Last October, only five months ago, almost a hundred Jews—old men, women, rabbis, even babies—had been murdered throughout Germany, with hundreds more beaten senseless in the streets or protecting their homes and synagogues. Jewish businesses and religious sites trashed and destroyed; Torahs and Talmuds defaced. Kristallnacht, they called it—The Night of Broken Glass. All egged on and even sanctioned by the Reich. The very people these drunken idiots here were celebrating tonight. The world was horrified. It had been the deadliest state-sanctioned attack on Jews since the violent pogroms in Russia in the early part of the century. It made people—even the ones who had supported them initially—think, what had these Nazis unleashed? What dark demons of the soul had they let loose? How could we avoid war?

But as bad as it was outside, it only mirrored the turmoil playing out in my own soul. My once-promising career and marriage were now corkscrewing into a fiery crash like one of those downed Messerschmitts on the newsreels.

It had all begun about a year ago, when the head of the history department was changed at Columbia, my old friend Otto Brickman sacked—two-thirds of the way through my thesis on the punishing effects of the Versailles Treaty on Germany today, the damage fell on me. "All this talk about punishing Germany, it's just a bit too radical for now," said the new head, Townsend Rusk, a pipe-smoking, tweed-jacketed bigot who'd spent ten years in the State Department before taking a cozy position back in the classroom. "Too inflammatory with all that's happening in the world."

But what he was really saying was that there might no longer be a career path for me there. And it was clear it was partly related to my last name. That the full-time professorship I'd had the inside track on with Brickman would now be handed on a platter to someone else. Someone with a different name and background. And that it might be in my best interest to begin looking for a teaching career elsewhere.

There was still a quota around the Ivy League for Jews on the graduate level, and suddenly it was hitting me square in the face. Three years I'd put into that work, into my job there. And it was gone in a day. So, yes, maybe a drink or two as I looked around for a new position did kind of ease the sting and disappointment.

And then there was Ben.

Six months ago, word that my twin brother—six minutes younger, the one with the true brains of the family, we always said (and the guts to put them to use)—had been killed while fighting the fascists in Spain. He'd joined up after a spat we had at our family Seder the year before. "You hate the fascists so much, go sign up and fight them," I kind of dared him, after he took issue with my thesis argument, that Europe and the United States had forced Germany toward the Nazis by handcuffing them economically with the Versailles Treaty.

Ben, who was in his second year of residency at the Brigham and Women's Hospital up in Boston, looked back at me with that gleam in his eye that said he rarely backed down from a dare. "Maybe I just will" was all he said, going back to the noodle pudding, and not six months later he boarded a freighter across the Atlantic and joined the fight as a medic. My father begged him not to be a fool, not to be such an idealist, but he went nonetheless. In August, we heard he'd been tending to a wounded soldier in a hotel lobby in Valencia when a bomb planted by a Nationalist saboteur blew up most of the lobby. For almost thirty years there hadn't been a day when my brother wasn't a part of my life. He was the person I looked up to most. Judged myself against. Competed against. For me, it was hard *not* to shoulder some of the blame. Certainly, my father, who still hadn't come back from it, made me feel that way. I was the one who had never put much on the line for anything, but always found a way to get by. He was the one who put himself on the line for everything, and now he was gone.

That afternoon scotch soon turned into two or three.

And then came Natalie. Natalie, with the bright, curious eyes and the high-breasted points in her cardigans. An intoxicating sophomore who I kept focusing on more and more in class and I couldn't stop thinking about (or the bouncy bob in her sweater), until the flirty fixation became the elixir for all that was ailing me in life. This was at Marymount, where I'd finally landed a teaching job after Columbia—undergraduate women this time, a long way from Morningside Heights.

She would visit me after class, at first with a question or two, and pretty soon, I was locking the office door and had her skirt up and her legs over my head. By then, it was the alcohol doing most of the talking, a lot more than reason or sense. Not so long ago, I had the prettiest, smartest girl I could imagine who thought the world of me. She'd cuddled up to me after a strings concerto at McMillin Theater and said, *Charlie, let's start a family.* We met at Columbia—where she was in the doctoral program in musicology, finishing her thesis on Chopin. Now, she barely even talked to me. Could I really blame her? Once the thing with Natalie got out, I hurt her in a way that was beyond repair. Early on, she had begged me to stop. The booze. Blaming myself. For the sake of our marriage. If not, then for our daughter. *You'll get work elsewhere, Charlie. You know that. You will.* And for a while, damn it, I did try. When I started at Marymount, I took a look in the mirror and saw the haggard face of someone I didn't like at all. I stopped feeling sorry for myself. I even stopped the booze.

But then the news of Ben came, and the parts of my life that still hung together with tape couldn't hold back the grief and guilt that came with it. After the business with Natalie got out and I lost that job too (also maybe thanks to a few classes I hadn't shown up for and some end-of-semester exams that I had failed to correct in time), Liz threatened to take Emma and leave. "Daddy's just not well." Brickman, my old department head at Columbia, said I was pissing away my life. "I've seen that next rung down, Charlie, and let me tell you, it's not a pretty sight." Now I had a night job twice a week at John Jay College, teaching American history to immigrants aspiring to be citizens.

I stared at myself in the glass across the bar. I'd found that next rung down.

And Otto was right—it wasn't pretty.

"Here you go, Mr. Mossman." Eli pushed across my glass. I noticed it was half-filled. He was doing his part.

"Bottoms up," I said, throwing a good part of it down in a single gulp. "I never told you what tonight is, did I, Eli . . . ? I mean, why would you know?"

"No, you didn't." The barkeep came up to me.

It was February 10.

February 10 was Ben's birthday. And mine, of course. He would have been thirty today. As was I. I blinked my head clear.

I'd let everything slide so deep that I could no longer even see the light above me to crawl out toward. But maybe this would be a good time to try. It was time to own up to a lot of things, I realized. I looked across from me in the mirror at the man sitting at the bar. I knew I had to start fighting sometime. Otherwise I was lost for good. Liz saw it. Brickman saw it. Hell, even Eli saw it. *Go home to that pretty wife of yours, Mr. Mossman.*

Ben surely would have seen it too.

For years, I'd had these two imaginary figures perched on my shoulders—my own personal angel and devil. Fighting in the existential tug-of-war for my soul.

The voice of reason would always tell me: "Put that glass down, go on home. You're drunk. Go be with Liz and Emma. Before you hit that bottom rung. Look at all that promise you let slip away. This is your last chance." And on the other shoulder, the voice of temptation, my own little devil, in that ever-denying snicker of his: "Don't listen to that fool, Charlie. Have one more. Who'll know? You know how it makes you feel." *Promise* . . . the word felt more like a dagger turned in my gut when it came from him. "That bottom rung, you still got a long, long way to go, Charlie-boy."

A long, long way.

But this time I knew that Eli was right. For once the words penetrated like a beacon of light through the fog. I pushed the unfinished drink back across the bar and threw a few bills on the table. I swiveled off my stool. For once, at long last, maybe I would let Chuck win.

"Eli—" I started to say.

Suddenly I heard a loud crash from the front of the bar. I spun around. Someone had taken a metal trash can and hurled it through the front window, which caved in in a shower of glass. A woman screamed. Shattered shards rained in on a couple seated near the door; they leaped up and dodged out of the way. *"What the . . . ?"*

Four of those pro-Nazi revelers staggered in. By the looks of them, they'd had one too many. Two wore the typical uniform: khaki shirts with red-and-black armbands; another with red hair and a ruddy complexion was in a suit with a tie yanked down, a Nazi flag draped over his shoulders. He carried a half-drunk bottle of booze.

"*Eli's* . . . ?" The one wearing the flag snorted. "What kind of place is this, some kind of Hymie bar?"

"I'm as true-born Irish as any of you," Eli called out from behind the bar. "But I'll be serving the chief rabbi in Brooklyn before I will any of you, so get your drunken asses out of my place before I call the cops on you. You're not welcome here."

"*Your place* . . . Hear that, boys?" the drunken leader mocked. "Appears we've stumbled into some kind of class joint here. Excuse us then," he chortled. "Well, one day you'll all be gone"—he looked around—"if any of you *are* yids. You and that Hymie president of yours and the bloodsucking band of Jews he keeps around him. Your time is coming, right, boys? *Sieg Heil!*" They all shot out their arms. "All hail to the Führer!"

He kicked the shards of glass deeper into the bar.

"I'm Jewish," I said, my four scotches pumping me up with a shot of courage. I stubbed out my Chesterfield in the ashtray. "And what I'm thinking is you owe my friend Eli here a new window."

"A new window, you say?" The redhead snorted like he thought it funny. "He's lucky we don't turn the place into rubble if he's serving the likes of you."

"Just leave 'em be, son," Eli said to me, holding my arm from across the bar top. "They're drunk as a ship's cat, and a piece of glass is not worth getting yourself bloodied over. You'll only get yourself in trouble."

"No, I won't let them be," I said. I wasn't the most observant of Jews; I'd only been in temple twice in the last few years and only went to the family Seder so my daughter knew the meaning of the holy days. But images of Kristallnacht swirled in my brain—mixed with everything else that was spiraling out of control in my life. And somewhere I heard this voice pushing me to act: What would my brother Ben do here? He wouldn't have just "leave 'em be."

"Anyway, what can go so wrong?" I said to Eli. "It's my birthday, right?"

So I stood up. I'd wrestled in high school, and made the team at Tufts as a freshman. I could take care of myself pretty well. At least, that's what the liquor was letting me believe. But as I stared at the group who'd barged in, the contempt in their beer-sodden eyes, all the images of my own dissolving life—Rusk's snicker when he told me it might be time to leave; Natalie's tartan skirt above her waist as she eased back on my desk; the shame I felt from my own daughter asking if I was okay; my marriage in tatters—all swirled together into a dark cloud I could no longer hold back, and stumbling more than standing, propelled me.

"Hey, Jack," I said to the redhead who was doing all the talking, "here's what this Hymie thinks of you."

I lunged at him, draped in his red Nazi flag, his bottle headed toward his mouth, catching him on the jaw and sending him stumbling backward, the bottle crashing to the floor. He put his sleeve to his mouth and spit out a mouthful of blood.

"Say we teach the lousy Jew a lesson." One of the ones in khaki looked at the rest.

In a moment, the four of them were on me. Raining punches, knocking me to the floor. Kicking me. I fought my way up to my feet, flailing wildly. We all tumbled outside. One of them picked up a trash bin from the curb and swung it at me. It caught me on the side of the head and I fell, my brain echoing like I was in the percussion section of an orchestra. I put my hand to my head and there was blood on it. One of the guys in khaki stomped his black boot on me.

Every frustration and body blow of grief and disappointment from over the past two years seemed to come together in my drunken brain. I didn't know if it was me or the booze talking—but by that point, I didn't care. I lunged at the guy in the boots, figuring with all the cops around there'd be a whistle any second or at least a passerby interceding to break us up. But there was no whistle, no set of arms grabbing on to me, save theirs. Their fists and heels.

Bloodied, I bulled myself up from the street, my vision blurred and blood streaming down my forehead, hearing only the taunts of derision and mockery all around.

I spun with my fist cocked, and lunged for the first khaki shirt I saw.

"Hey, watch out, mister," I heard someone shout through my fog.

I clipped the guy flush in the jaw and saw him reel backward, arms cycling to catch himself. He fell back against the shattered bar window—the hanging red neon flickering, *Eli's . . . Eli's*—his head impacting with the edge of jagged, splintered glass. Slumping to the ground, he let out a muffled cry. Then he didn't move at all. His eyes rolled back in his head just as a tremor of panic knifed through me.

A woman in a red coat and hat screamed out, looking at me with horror. "What have you done?" She kneeled down over the fallen man. "Johnny? Johnny?"

Even the bunch of Nazis just stood there, jaws open, eyes wide, staring back at the pool of blood forming under the guy's skull. Until they all took off as one and sprinted down the street and around the corner, and disappeared.

I wiped my face clear and stared at exactly whom I'd struck.

Only then did my vision start to come clear.

I saw he wasn't part of the group I'd been fighting with. In fact, he wasn't wearing any German or Nazi markings at all. His khaki shirt was just a shirt, in a gray sweater vest, not a uniform.

Then I saw he was just a kid.

Sixteen, it suddenly came clear to me, most. Maybe younger. Not moving. Seemingly not even conscious.

And the woman who had shouted at me, likely his mother, kneeling over him, begging anyone who'd listen, "Someone please get help. Johnny, Johnny, can you hear me? Johnny!"

On the street, a police car screeched to a stop. I heard a voice in my ear. My little devil's voice. No longer that mocking snicker I was used to, but more of a quiet admonition this time, filled with worry himself, as the boy's blood pooled on the pavement.

"I guess you've finally found that bottom rung now, Charlie-boy."

2

JULY 1941

Two years passed. Not the kind of years anyone would ever want to spend.

Not the kind of years the world wanted to spend.

Europe was at war now. Six months after I'd thrown that punch at that kid outside that bar, Hitler annexed the Sudetenland in Czechoslovakia, and a year after that, unleashed his armies on Poland. By the time of my sentencing he had marched his way through Holland and Belgium and overrun France, and his Messerschmitts were raining a nightly incendiary hell on London.

Of course, I'd watched all this take place from the correctional facility up in Auburn, New York, serving two to four years for the charge of third-degree manslaughter.

And I was lucky to get away with that. The prosecutors had pushed for first-degree. I was drunk. I'd thrown the first punch. I'd shown malicious disregard for the victim, Andrew McHurley, a fifteen-year-old from Teaneck, New Jersey, who was out for a night on Broadway, having gone to see *Life with Father* with his mother.

They were merely on their way back to where the New Jersey bus lines picked up on West Forty-second Street. It wasn't hard to paint me as a person not worthy of much consideration. Someone who went around drunk, who had cheated on his wife; someone who had slid down the sinkhole of second and third chances in life until he couldn't fall any farther. Someone who'd had all the advantages of intelligence and a top education, and yet had chosen to throw it all away: His family. A once-promising academic career. His moral center.

About the only thing I did have going for me was Eli's testimony that I had been standing up to a pack of drunken, taunting Nazi-lovers, though by the time the police on the scene went to search for them they were long gone. By sentencing time, the public view of Hitler and Nazis had changed. Europe had been overrun; Jews were being openly persecuted and beaten. Britain was hanging on by a thread. FDR begged for support for the war in Congress. That was the only sympathy I had. Four years was reduced to twenty-two months for good behavior and for tutoring inmates in American history. And I was lucky to get that.

Upon my release, my father was far too ill to come for me, having never fully recovered since Ben had died. He and Mom had only driven up to visit me a couple of times, consumed with guilt and shame. So my uncle Eddie picked me up in his old Packard and we drove the six hours back to his home in Lawrence on the Island, much of the trip in silence.

I had no idea what I was going to do.

Columbia had tossed me out of their graduate program. No school I had worked for since wanted me back. I had about a hundred and twenty dollars in my pocket I had earned instructing inmates. Everything else I had handed over to Liz and Emma.

But two days after my release I stood looking up at the brownstone on Ninetieth Street between Park and Lexington. The number over the coffered front door read 174. It was hardly the nicest on the block: three stories, gray stone, Georgian in feel, with a staircase leading up to the front door with settled cracks running through it. There were high, rounded windows on the second floor with planters on the sill, where, in season, pots of tulips and daffodils might bloom. It was on a part of the block shaded by large oaks, hiding the house in a swath of shadow. On the sidewalk, two kids in white T's bounced a Spalding against the stone façade—Yanks against Dodgers, DiMaggio or Pee Wee Reese. An American flag draped languorously over the entrance.

She was still in Yorkville, I reflected, a part of the city on the Upper East Side between Eighty-sixth and Ninety-sixth, extending east to Carl Schurz Park and the East River. The area had been home to German-Americans for decades—and our home, when we were first married. And most of the businesses on the streets between Lexington and First Avenue had German names: Schaller and Weber meats. Old Bavaria Café. Gustave Bitner Travel Agency. Café Geiger. Rheingold beer.

Before the war in Europe, Yorkville had been home to many public pro-Hitler and America First rallies. Fritz Kuhn, who had established his German American Bund there, was now in jail on tax evasion charges. Father Coughlin, who had had his own highly followed national radio show, and once made a fiery Fortress America speech there, was off the air. Even Joseph McWilliams, "Joe McNazi," who once tried to organize a boycott against Jewish businesses, had been shut down. Now, from what I'd heard, any expressions of support for the Nazis were far more private, and conducted behind closed doors. Support for Britain in the war and the rounding up and persecution of the Jews had rallied public opinion, as had the German torpedoing of Allied merchant ships on the high seas. Above the door, the American flag rippled faintly in the breeze.

Anticipation stirring in me, I climbed the front stairs. I had been nervous during my trial, nervous at my sentencing; nervous as hell when they escorted me the first time, cuffed and in chains at Auburn, down a long block and into my cell.

But I felt even more nervous now. Seeing my family for the first time since I was out. Since I was free. Since we would have to see where we would pick up.

The outside door was unlocked; it was clearly the kind of neighborhood where you didn't have to be worried about such things. In the vestibule, a Persian runner led to the inside staircase. A low-hanging Tiffany-style chandelier hung from the ceiling. I scanned the intercom buttons and saw the name there. My heart dropped off a cliff. Rubin. Liz's maiden name. Not Mossman. Apartment 3A. I rested my finger on it, then hesitated, and took in a deep, unsure breath, trying to overcome my fears. I decided not to ring. Instead, I started up the stairs, with the bouquet of flowers I had bought on the street and the box in a brown bag marked *Simpson's Children's Toys, Every Child's Dream is Our Joy.*

On the second-floor landing, there was a framed drawing of an English hunting scene hung over an upholstered wooden chair, and on three, a mahogany table with a doily on it, a small vase of dried flowers, and on the wall, a framed landscape of verdant hills over a winding river with a castle on a hill. The Rhine, maybe. Everything had a fine, European feel to it.

I stood for a while in front of their apartment, my heart ricocheting with nerves. Maybe this wasn't the best idea. Showing up like this, out of the blue. I thought about going back down. There was no name on the door, just a pink heart-shaped sticker, which made my heart soften and my nerves suddenly go away.

Two years. Twenty-seven months, actually, including the trial. That's how long I'd been away from them. I'd gone away a man ashamed to look at himself in the mirror. Now . . . now I was different. I was. Sober. Remorseful. I had a lot to make up for. I was ready to face the family I had let down. Ready to make it up to them.

Rubin. No longer Mossman. I inhaled a breath.

If they were ready to face me.

Blowing out my cheeks, I pressed the buzzer.

I didn't hear anyone inside. Maybe they weren't here. I admit I felt the slightest lift of relief. Maybe they were out, or still at school. I knew Emma was in a summer program. Or at the park. Or maybe Liz didn't want Emma to see me. They hadn't come to visit me since March. (Sure, it was a six-hour bus trip up to Auburn, and a night over, hard for a young girl. But still . . .) I glanced back down the stairs, thinking it wasn't too late to leave, to do this another day.

Then suddenly I heard the patter of running footsteps coming from inside.

The lock opened and then the door was flung wide. And my daughter stood there looking up at me. A larger version of her than I recalled, up to my waist now. In a light blue gingham dress. Pigtails. Her million-dollar smile and bright green eyes shining happily at me. Completely washing away my fears. And I heard the word, the one word, I'd been aching to hear for almost a year.

"Daddy!"

3

"Hey, peach face." I bent down and hurled Emma high in the air.
Liz had brought her on three or four visits, but we were always
separated by glass. After a while they stopped coming. I squeezed
her and held her close. I hadn't had a hug like that in years.

"Mommy, Daddy's home. Daddy's here!"

I stepped inside and Liz came out of the bedroom. Our eyes
met, Emma still hoisted in my arms. Any nerves I was feeling
melted. It was like I was seeing her there for the first time, and
also seeing why I'd fallen for her. In a pretty navy dress, a lace
collar unbuttoned at the top. Her brown hair was in a bob, which
I knew from newsreels and the occasional Hollywood magazines
that made it to me was now the fashion of the day. She didn't approach me. She just stood there, clearly unsure herself, her hand
on the floral chair by the love seat in the tiny sitting room—tinier
even than our first apartment on Eighty-eighth and York, before
everything fell apart. She gave me a faint smile, the best she could

do. Who knew where we even stood now? The name next to the buzzer downstairs made that clear.

"Charlie."

"Boy, you're both a sight for sore eyes," I said. I cradled Emma in my arms. "You can't even imagine how much I've looked forward to seeing you, peach face. And look how big you are now." I put her back down. "Six. A real lady now." I rubbed my knuckles softly against her cheek. "You too, Liz. You both look great."

"I'm glad to see you're out," Liz said, neither sympathetic nor cool. "Eddie called me." There was a measure of hesitancy in her voice, an edge of distrust as well. And why not? I'd put her through the wringer. She'd had to raise Emma on her own these past two years. All I'd done was leave her in a big hole.

"I wish you could have come," I said. "It would have been nice to, you know, see someone there. It really is like in the movies. They give you your possessions back. In a brown paper bag. Your watch. Whatever money you came with or earned inside. Then they open the big iron door and suddenly there's a loud clang behind you and you're on the other side. Uncle Eddie was waiting for me. In that beat-up old jalopy of his. I guess Mom and Pop, they . . ." They hadn't been so well since Ben had died. "We hardly exchanged ten words on the way down. But it sure is nice to see my angel now!" I said, cupping Emma's happy face to my thigh. "Hey, I brought you something." I handed her the gift bag. The toy store owner told me it was all a boy or girl of her age wanted these days. It and the flowers for Liz had cost me a chunk of the money I came out with. "And Liz, here . . ." I handed her the roses. "I got these for you."

"Thanks, Charlie," she said with the slightest smile. "They're really lovely. I'll put them in some water."

"Do it later," I said. "Right now, I just want to take a look at the two of you."

"Look, it's a View-Master, Mommy!" Emma said, brimming with excitement. Plastic binoculars in which you inserted a disc of photo images and one by one, as it rotated, it made it seem like you were there. Live. The store said it was all the rage now for kids her age.

"I see, honey. That's nice, Charlie. It really is."

"They have discs for Africa, and Europe. And the Ten Wonders of the World . . . And the Far East," I said, "inside."

"I love it, Daddy. Millie Richards has one. Are you going to be around now, Daddy?" Emma asked.

"Didn't Mommy tell you? I sure am, honey. I am most definitely going to be around. I'm not going anywhere."

"Daddy's going to be back now, Mommy," she said. "See."

"We've had this conversation, Charlie," Liz said, with a bit of exasperation in her tone. "Emma, why don't you give Mommy and Daddy a few minutes together and play with your View-Master in the bedroom."

"You'll still be here, won't you, Daddy?"

"Of course I'll be here, honey." I winked at her. "Promise." Emma smiled and went inside.

Yes, we had had the conversation. Though it was behind a glass wall and in whispers. And I always had the hope that once I was out I could show her differently.

The real Charlie.

The window was open, but there was no breeze. "I see you're still in Yorkville," I said. "Eddie gave me the address."

Liz put the flowers down at the sink and shrugged resignedly. "Yes, we are. But as you can clearly see . . ." Her eyes drew me around the place.

It was even smaller than where we used to live. A tiny open kitchen off the sitting room and what appeared to be two small bedrooms. The furniture was sparse and unfamiliar—a love seat, a worn print chair, a plain coffee table with some art books on it; it all must have come with the place. On the wall, though, there was the little Monet reproduction of the cathedral in Rouen we bought in France on our honeymoon. About the only thing that looked familiar. I went over and put my hand to the frame. We stayed in this little place in the *place* overlooking it. We got drunk that night, enough pastis to last a lifetime. "I remember this. . . ."

"I had to get rid of a lot of stuff," she said. "None of it would fit."

I turned and let my eyes drape over her, like silk to a form. She was still beautiful. "You do look great, Liz. I can say that, can't I?"

"Sure, you can say it, Charlie. And you too. You've lost some weight."

"Well, I never heard of anyone who went in there for the food," I said, hoping for a smile.

She complied with the smallest one. "You want some coffee?"

"Sure. I don't want you to go to any trouble though."

"It's no trouble." She bent down, took out a kettle from under the stove, filled it with tap water, and placed it on the burner. It took three or four times for the flame to catch.

"We *are* still married, Liz." I so wanted to go up and give her a hug, but I knew she wouldn't let me. We had talked about it. The last time she came to visit, back in March. Four months, thirteen days ago. Without Emma there. "I saw the name downstairs. But I am still your husband."

"We've been through all this, Charlie. You know this. I've moved on. I didn't want to make it harder on you by taking it any further while you were still inside. Though everyone told me I should. But now . . . I know I said I would think about it, the last time I was up there, and I have. I have thought about it. I know the nightmare you've been through. But it hasn't been easy for me either."

"I know it hasn't, Liz. . . ." I went up to her and placed my hand on her waist. All I wanted was for one moment to feel attached the way we used to, to the life I had wrenched away from her so violently. From both of *them*.

But she pulled out of my grasp and reached for two coffee mugs from the cupboard. When she turned around, whatever softness that was in her eyes and voice a moment before were gone. "You destroyed our lives, Charlie." There was the flicker of a tear in her eye—not from tenderness, but anger maybe. "I can't forgive you for that. Everything's changed. I work in a dress shop now. My folks help out, but I have to support us. We live in this tiny place. With furniture that isn't even ours."

"I can help support you now, Liz. I'm not the same man who hurt you. I know how hard it is to see that now, to fully believe that. But I'm not. I haven't had a drink in over two years. Obviously, where I've been," I shrugged, "the choices of alcohol were just a tad limited. They didn't have my brand. . . ."

All I wanted was one small sign of what it used to be like between us. And she gave me a softened look—as if for a moment she could forgive me. But then she merely nodded and her eyes deepened almost like she'd aged ten years in front of me. "It's not going to work, Charlie."

"What?"

"Us. What I know you want."

"Liz, look, if there's one thing I've had an abundance of these past two years, it's been time. Time to think about what I've done. The choices I made. You read my letters. Both to you and Emma. And to that boy. You have to know, if I could go back somehow and take back that punch, I'd give everything up to do so."

"The punch . . ." She looked at me, and this time her eyes did fill with moisture. But it was more like the sorrow of someone saying, *Don't you even understand?* "But you can't take back that punch, Charlie. And you still don't see, it was more than just the punch. A lot more. For me. The *punch* was just the way it all just crashed to an end. You can say you're sorry to that poor boy's mother for that punch a hundred times . . . But not to me. . . . It was more than that punch." She reached for a scissor from the drawer to trim the stems, and found a vase. "Thank you though, for these. They're beautiful."

The punch was just the way it all just crashed to an end.

She meant Natalie.

"I've told you, Liz, that thing with Natalie was the biggest mistake of my life. By then, it was just the alcohol doing the thinking, not me. And that part's gone now. It's a condition of my parole. I'm back. The real me. Charlie." She was looking at me but there was virtually no connection in her gaze. Like we had never laughed together, never made love. Made a child. What could I expect? Her parents were professors at Michigan. Her brother was an attorney. They hardly wanted her burdened with a self-destructive lout like me.

She shook her head finally. "I'm not though. I'm sorry, Charlie. I'm not back."

I took in a breath, stung, and sat down. "Do you have a guy?" I asked.

She shrugged. "There's someone I occasionally see. He works for an advertising company. Emma takes up most of my time. And there's my job. At the shop."

"What about your work?"

"My work? I just told you."

"Your real work, Liz. Chopin." Her thesis was the most important thing in her life.

"This *is* my real work, Charlie. All that, that was a long time ago. Another world. But we're not going back to it. Look, I trust you've changed. I can hear it in your voice. I see it in your eyes. And I'm happy for you, Charles. I really am. You still have your own life to live. But trust . . . it just isn't something you can just pick up where you leave off, like a book you put down for a while. Like nothing's happened in between. You may want to, but I'm sorry, you just can't. You can't. . . ."

I picked up a salt shaker in the center of the table and tapped it on its side. "I understand," I said, nodding resignedly. "I know I have to live with what happened then. Everything that happened. And believe me, Liz, I see the image of that kid lying there on the pavement every day. Who won't get to live out his life. That's the sight I see every night before I go to sleep. Other than yours and Emma's. I know I have a lot to make up for. And I accept that I can't just show up, and do it in a day. But all I thought about these past months, you know, is maybe, just to have the chance. The chance to try and prove myself to you again. To the two of you. That would mean everything to me, Liz. I know how you feel. I saw the name you go by downstairs on the door. But you can't blame me for fighting for that. For my life."

She arranged the roses prettily in the vase and placed them in the center of the tiny sitting table. "You can't really love me any-more, can you, Charlie? I mean, really love me. Not just the idea of being a husband again. Or a father. And trying to put the whole thing back together."

"I will always love you, Liz. I'm sorry, I can't help that."

That seemed to touch her a bit, get past the shield she'd put up to push me off, and for a moment I saw a glimmer of the Liz I once knew. In her eyes. We'd been happy. How I had been a knight to her and she an angel to me.

Then the kettle sounded. Steam poured from the spout. It seemed to break the spell. She looked over at it and shook her head. "I'm sorry. But I can't. I just can't." There was finality to it this time. She looked at me as if it was a broken vase we were talking about, a family keepsake, and it was futile to put the pieces of it back together. "You still want that coffee . . . ?"

"I understand," I said, nodding. "But I need to see Emma. My parole officer says I can. As long as I'm sober. And we *are* still married. At least for now."

"You were always a good dad." She smiled. "Through it all. That's one thing I can't take away from you. She loves you to death, Charlie. And she's missed you terribly."

"And I could be a good husband again," I said. "Like before."

"Before . . ." She gave me the tightest, most begrudging smile, more a ray of fondness and remembrance than promise, and I saw there was no turning back. "Do you have a place to stay?"

"A friend from Columbia is letting me flop on his couch," I lied. I was sleeping in my car.

"That's good. That's good." She didn't even ask who it was. She said, "It's best if you come by in the afternoons, after Emma gets out of day camp. Mrs. Shearer picks her up at three and stays with her until I get off work. That's around six."

"Okay." I got up.

She picked up the box from the View-Master and placed it on the counter. "I'd appreciate it if when I got back from work you were gone."

4

Later, I did stop for a cup of coffee at a café on Second Avenue that the two of us used to go to. Old Heidelberg, it was called. Yorkville was always a vibrant neighborhood. It was known as Germantown. Stores and restaurants from the Old Country were on every block. In the summer, oom-pah-pah music played loudly in the outdoor cafés and German beer was aplenty. On the street, more German was spoken than English.

But now, with Europe besieged by war, celebrations of life back home had changed. I'd read from jail that the German American Bund that had sponsored the giant rally at Madison Square Garden that night had all but fallen apart, and its leader, Fritz Kuhn, was serving time in jail for tax evasion. The bombing of London, the harsh treatment of the Jews, not to mention Charles Lindbergh's anti-Semitic America First speeches, had driven all but the most ardent supporters of Hitler and National Socialism behind closed doors. To many, what was happening across the Atlantic was a European war, which would only result in the loss of American blood if we took sides and stepped in. Many remembered the last war, where over fifty thousand doughboys had been killed. A resistant Congress had forced Roosevelt to sign a Neutrality Treaty, though his lend-lease program of shipping arms to Britain tested the limits of it, and to many, presidential authority.

Our old waiter, Karl, was still at the restaurant and seemed surprised to see my face. "I haven't seen you in ages," he said, happy to greet me again. "Have you moved away?"

"Yes, for a while," I said, eager to keep it at that. "But now I'm back."

"Good. Good, Mr. Mossman. And how is that lovely wife of yours?"

"She's doing well," I said. The less said, the better.

I ordered a weisswurst with cabbage, something I'd dreamed of in prison and hadn't had in years. And I even thought about washing it down with a beer—for me, it had been a long time between them—and the frosty mugs of Wurtzheimer and St. Pauli Girl I saw carried about looked tempting. But I merely said water would be fine.

That last thing Liz said to me had stung. I'm not sure what I'd been thinking—that I was just going to come back after two years and pick up where we left off after destroying their lives. I guess I'd been harboring that fantasy somewhere in my mind, fueled by many months of hopeful dreaming in my cell. But hearing her ask me not to even be there when she returned from work put an end to it, as abruptly as a head-on car collision.

Still, it had been great to see Emma again, and we made plans for me to come back the following week.

When I finished the three sausages, I threw a couple of dollars on the table and hopped the bus down to Thirty-fourth Street. I walked across town to Penn Station. It was my first day back in Manhattan. Just being out among people, rushing to and from work, passing the department store windows, all the buzzing activity of being home again after being confined so long, made my head swell with the vastness of it. For two years my entire world had been in an eight-by-ten cell.

At Penn Station, I grabbed the 6:07 train to Lawrence. The hamlet sat at the western edge of Nassau County, virtually more in Queens than the Island. My uncle Eddie had lived there in a small two-bedroom for ten years, having moved out from the Bronx. He worked for the city as a claims auditor for the comptroller's office.

"I'm sorry, but you can't stay here, Charlie," he had said in the car on the ride down, looking over with an air of guilt and helplessness. "Lucile's mother is in the second bedroom and you know she's not so well these days. We have the basement, but . . . I'm just not sure it would be for the best."

My aunt Lucille had never been the warmest of people toward me, or my father and mother, and my recent trouble with the law and the state of my life didn't make that any easier. "Don't think twice about it, Uncle Ed," I said. "I've made arrangements."

He'd kept my '36 Buick roadster in his garage for the past two years, the only real asset I had.

"If you need a few bucks," he said to me, "I told your dad we'd try and help out. Fred and Dot," my parents, "they're not doing so well anymore, since the store closed." My father had a linen store in New Haven that had closed in the downturn; now he worked in one, behind the counter. The New Deal, so far, hadn't worked so well for them.

"Nah, I'm fine, Eddie," I said. "Thanks for offering." I had under a hundred bucks to my name and zero job prospects. I knew I had to sell the car as fast as I could.

The train rattled out of the city. It was dark now. I saw the familiar Sabrett sign as we chugged our way into the Jamaica, Queens, station. Lawrence was the third stop.

I needed a job; that was clear. When I knew I was being released, I wrote a few contacts: Otto Brickman, my old department head at Columbia, who was now at Hunter. The dean at John Jay. The rest of my bridges, I'd burned. *If you know of a position open, I'm a new man,* I told them, *and I could really use the work. Any work.*

Look, Charlie, Brickman wrote back, *I'd like to help, but there's nothing I can offer you now. Things are pretty tight these days.* Especially things for a convicted felon who's spent two years in jail, I knew he wasn't saying. And with a history of an affair with a female student. *Maybe I can find something for you grading papers. . . .*

The dean from John Jay was even less sanguine.

My parole officer said he should be able to line up something for me. Washing dishes or sweeping floors. The usual parolee kind of work, trying to acclimate back into society. Next to his usual clientele, I was at the top of the list.

The honest truth was I had nothing.

The train rattled into Lawrence station. I got off with a throng of businessmen straight from the office and women in dainty suits who looked like they had spent the day in Manhattan having lunch. I'd borrowed an ill-fitting sport coat from Ed, a pair of rumpled slacks, and a workman's shirt that made me look like I belonged on a breadline more than a job interview. A few cars were waiting in the lot as passengers flooded out on the street. Doors opening, wives welcoming them back with a kiss; it only brought home how far I had fallen. Others just dispersed onto the main street, their afternoon *Suns* or *Journals* folded under their arms. I waited on the platform till the crowd went their ways and grabbed one, the *Sun,* that had been left behind. The headline was: "26 German-Americans Arrested as Spies by the FBI. Fears of Larger Spy Ring Grow."

I took the paper and walked to an alley next to a liquor store across the street.

I'd left my Buick in the lot there. A handwritten note on the windshield read, *Please don't park here again. Private Property.*

I got in, then turned the car on and pulled out onto the street. I drove down Central Avenue to Nassau Expressway, past restaurants and filling stations. It led to Far Rockaway. It was dark, drizzly. The day crowd had gone. I turned into Silver Point Park and continued to the end, to the inlet where I could see Long Beach Island across the way, and beyond that, the sea. I sat in the car and watched the evening fall. Sea lights twinkled and the smell of marine life and fuel oil hung in the air. A barge went by. And a large freighter, who knows, maybe making the perilous crossing of the Atlantic, carrying supplies to Reykjavik and then on to England for all I knew. German U-boats were targeting American vessels now. Anyone who helped the Brits. I'd read that the crossing had become pretty hazardous these days.

Not to worry, I'd said to Liz. *A friend from Columbia is letting me flop on his couch.*

A lie, of course. All I could think of to save face. The truth was, no one had offered. Not even a couch to spend the night on. I might as well have been back in a cell. Lights flickered in the distance. A gull landed on my grille. It looked at me curiously and seemed to be saying, *Don't you have anywhere better to be?* I opened the newspaper and munched on the roll I'd wrapped up in a napkin and put in my pocket from Old Heidelberg. I read the headline by the lights of the seawall. The spy ring had set up offices at the Knickerbocker Building right in lower Manhattan. Their target had apparently been top-secret bomb sites from the Nordon Corporation, and those arrested included employees of the plant, even accountants and engineers.

Operating right in New York. Right under our noses.

"But fears of a fifth column," an FBI source said, "a network of German spies embedded in day-to-day life here, were largely overblown."

I put down the paper, put my head back against the seat rest, and closed my eyes.

You're broke, Charlie. And alone. A convicted felon. My life as a professor was just a twinkling in my memory now, like these lights I was staring at in the dark. In the distance. *Rubin,* Liz's nameplate had said. A husband without his wife.

But you are a father again.

I thought of Emma. Leaping into my arms. Throwing her arms around me. *Are you going to stay, Daddy?*

I sure am. I'm not going anywhere, peach face.

And that made me smile.

I grabbed a blanket I had taken from Uncle Ed's and curled up in the front seat. Daddy. How beautiful it was to hear that word again. Hear her laughter.

For once, the sight of Andrew McHurley on the pavement with his eyes rolled up wasn't the last thing in my mind as I drifted off to sleep.

Emma was.

My daughter.

My dreams were peaceful. Easing.

And for the first time in two years, free.

5

For the next couple of weeks I came by the brownstone to see Emma twice a week. Though each time I rang the buzzer I noted with dismay the hand-scratched name there that was not my own.

I hadn't had much luck finding work. I tried with the academic offices of every college in the city for a teaching position, and when those didn't pan out, the private schools, in town and in the Bronx, and then even the trade schools. I'd teach math if they'd let me. But the moment the conversation turned to where I'd spent the last two years, the discussions ended pretty quickly.

I came by the brownstone in the afternoons, around three thirty, like Liz had said, after Emma got home from the day camp at her school. She was always happy to see me, even if the dour Mrs. Shearer, the woman Liz had spoken of who picked Emma up from elementary school on Ninety-second and Madison every day and took her home, was not. She took care of Emma till Liz got back around six. Mrs. Shearer was a tightly strung, seemingly guarded woman of around sixty with graying hair tied tightly in a bun; pinched, narrow cheeks; and a face that seemed perpetually unsuited to a smile. She always seemed to do her best not to let Emma and me be alone—I could see in her eyes my daughter's questionable father who had been sent away for a violent crime— always saying it was time for her milk and a snack, or her home- work, practicing simple arithmetic or writing cursive, which I was always happy to help her with myself, or that she had to climb into her pj's before her mother got home.

I tried my best to soften her up. I even brought her gifts and flowers. "I'm not exactly Al Capone, Miss Shearer. I threw a punch. And someone died because of it."

"It's Mrs.," she corrected me frostily. "And from what I'm told, you were drunken, Mr. Mossman. And it was not just someone, as you say, but a child."

"Yes, and I paid my debt for it," I defended myself. "And trust me, I couldn't be sorrier for what I did."

"That may be," she said grudgingly, as Emma played with the View-Master, popping in a disc with images of the Wonders of the World. "Though I wonder if that boy's parents would feel similarly."

I had written the McHurleys a dozen times from prison, though they never answered. It was part of my making amends. But how many more times could I say I was sorry?

Still, I managed to enjoy the time I shared with Emma, and began to feel that we were picking up where we had left off before fate had come between us. She seemed delighted to finally have her father back. I helped her with work she would encounter when she was in school. With basic arithmetic and cursive. I played games with her. And we looked through the View-Master, describing an- imals in Africa and the pyramids in Egypt and the Great Wall in

China, sometimes with a bit more historical background than perhaps a future first grader might appreciate, which caused her eyes to glaze until she kind of cocked her head at me and said, though never wearily, "Isn't it time for a snack, Daddy?"

As July turned into August, Mrs. Shearer let me take her on walks in the neighborhood. To Carl Schurz Park. Where we always played with dogs. Or to Gracie Mansion, where the mayor resided, where once or twice we saw his black limousine coming through the gate. We usually stopped at Oscar's Fudge Shop on Third Avenue for a treat. In truth, about all I looked forward to in life were my twice-a-week afternoons with her.

One day, as we headed out for such a walk, the door opened to the apartment across the third-floor landing. A pleasant-looking woman stepped out, maybe sixty as well, holding two envelopes she was obviously preparing to mail. Her deep gray hair was in a tight bun and she was dressed in a simple beige suit, her collar buttoned to the top.

"Mein Schnitzel!" she exclaimed happily when she saw Emma, displaying a trace of a German accent. Her eyes lit up brightly and she bent down to give her a hug.

"Aunt Trudi!"

"And how is my little girl? So big and coming back from school." She gave me a polite but wary glance. Anyone connected to Emma always seemed to give me the same watchful look.

"I thought I knew all of Emma's aunts," I said with a smile. "I'm Emma's father, Charlie," I introduced myself.

"This is my aunt Trudi, Daddy," Emma said.

"I'm Gertrude Bauer." The woman stood up. "But everyone calls me Trudi." She put out her hand, seeming gracious enough. Everyone else always seemed so guarded around me. I wondered how much she knew of me. Then she came right out with it. "You've been away, I understand?"

"Yes. Too long," I said, choosing not to explain it further and not sure what she knew. "But not any longer, I'm happy to say. Emma and I have a lot of catching up to do." I squeezed her shoulder.

"Uncle Willie and Aunt Trudi teach me about life back in Swisserland," Emma said.

"*Switz*erland, my dear," Trudi Bauer corrected her.

"Yes, Switzerland. And how to make *schoggibirnen* as well. . . ."

"*Schoggibirnen* . . . ?" I questioned.

"It's a dessert. The finest in the world." Trudi Bauer beamed with pride. "Stewed pears. Steeped in chocolate sauce. My own family's sauce, I'm proud to say. It's Emma's favorite."

"I didn't know that," I said.

"But not with those run-of-the-mill tinned pears that are available in the stores today. I stew my own. In caramelized sugar. And the sauce. . . . One thing we Swiss know about is chocolate. Is that not right, my dear?"

"Daddy, it's *so* delicious," Emma said, licking her lips.

"Do you like sweets as well, Mr. Mossman?"

"Sweets? Who doesn't?"

"Well, you will have to come over with Emma and sample it sometime."

"I look forward to it," I said. "So you're Swiss? From where?"

"A little town called Chur. It's capital of the canton of Graubünden. Near Austria. But we have been here many years. Have you been to Switzerland, Mr. Mossman?"

"I'm afraid not. One day, perhaps."

"A place of great natural beauty. Hopefully, one day you'll

have the chance to see for yourself. Once all this madness in the
world calms down." Clearly, she was referring to the war, which
in Europe was two years old now, even though Switzerland had
remained out of it. "I've been telling Emma about the Alps. And
about Heidi, of course. Our national heroine. We've even taught her
a few words. Of German, I hope it's all right. Do you remember?"

"Eyes . . . ," Emma said, pointing her fingers to them. *"Augen."*

"And smile . . . ?" Trudi said, a finger to her lips.

"Lachlen," Emma replied.

"Läch-*eln*," she corrected her, "but good. And . . ." She put a
finger to her nose.

"Na-se." Emma smiled, pleased.

"See, she picks up everything quick as a hare. Anyway, schnitzel, you can come over later if your mother is okay with it, and I'll
read you from Tales of Hoffmann. Not the opera of course, but the
original romantic stories. . . ."

"Will there be cinnamon cakes?"

"Zimfladden. I can see if that can be arranged. You see, your
daughter is a natural bargainer, Mr. Mossman. Did you know?
And maybe a little Heine and Schiller, as well, my dear."

"Heine and Schiller? They're German, are they not?" I asked.

"Ah, so you know them. Not everyone does here. My parents
were from Freiburg in southern Germany. They moved to Chur
many years ago. Therefore we are German-Swiss, to be precise. In
Switzerland, we claim four languages as our own. Right, Emma? I
believe you can name them, darling?"

"French, German, Italian . . ." She rattled them off quickly,
tapping her fingers. "And . . ."

"And, my dear, the toughest one that always escapes you . . . ?"
Trudi Bauer coached her.

After a moment, Emma seemed to give up.

"Romansh, I believe," I answered. As an undergraduate, I had written a paper on the breakup of the Old Swiss confederacy in the sixteenth and seventeenth centuries; how it got its independence from the Holy Roman Empire. For that I took a couple of semesters of German too. "It's a cluster of many of the local dialects, I believe. No?"

"Very, very good, Mr. Mossman. That one always stumps people. But it was for your daughter to answer, not her father, was it not?" She looked at Emma and said with a forgiving smile, "Nonetheless, we will still invite you for *schoggibirnen* one afternoon to give you a taste of our native culture. Our real culture," she said, "not what has been taken over now by hoodlums and thugs." Her face twisted into a weighty frown.

It was clear Trudi Bauer was no fan of what was going on back in Germany. *Our real culture.* And how the continent was engulfed in war. It was also clear that Emma adored her. And she, her.

"I was just going down to the first floor to mail these. . . ." Trudi held out her letters when the buzzer rang at her entranceway. "Excuse me," she said. She closed the door and in her deep accent asked who the visitor was before ringing him in.

"Ach, I'm afraid I must go," she said as she came back. "A customer. In our business, they come at all hours, I'm afraid. . . ."

Below us, I heard the front door close and someone slowly climb the stairs. "We're headed out," I said. "We'll be happy to post those for you." There was a tray near the entrance that the mailman used for outgoing mail.

"Would you be so kind? Here . . ." She handed the envelopes to me. "It was a pleasure meeting you, Mr. Mossman. I have heard about you over the past two years and that you are a great student

of history. I admit, I am a bit nosy when it comes to my Emma."
She placed a hand to her head. "I couldn't be more partial to her
if she were my own granddaughter. It is nice to finally put a face
to the name."

"And you too, Frau Bauer," I said with a polite bow. "And I look
forward to the *shoggibirnen*," I said, pronouncing it as best I could.

"Very good!" she exclaimed in approval.

A man came up the stairs. He was around forty, tall, lean, in
a brown tweed suit and peaked cap. *A customer . . . ?* He tipped
his cap to Mrs. Bauer and to Emma and me, though he appeared
slightly uncomfortable to find us there. I could see he was balding.
A mole on his chin. A clipped mustache.

"I didn't expect you until five, Mr. Atkins," Trudi Bauer said.

"My meeting ended early," he replied, glancing at us. "I hoped
you would be available."

"Not to worry, we'll take care of these," I said, waving the
envelopes to her.

"Thank you." Trudi Bauer took her leave with a warm smile.
"Please, Mr. Atkins . . ." She let her visitor inside the apartment
and closed the door.

"She seems nice," I said, taking her letters and glancing at the
addressees. One was for the electric bill, to Con Edison. The other
was addressed to a woman in Colorado. Beatrice Hirsh. A friend
or relative perhaps?

"She is nice," Emma said. "Now you said you would take me
for ice cream, Daddy."

"You mean *eis* cream, of course," I said in my best German
accent, and my daughter giggled.

6

Over the next few visits, I ran into Trudi Bauer again a couple of times.

Once when Emma was practicing cursive and I was reading the papers she brought over a cinnamon roll cake. *Zimfladden,* she called it. She was surprised to find me there, but seemed happy to find Mrs. Shearer; they seemed to know each other well.

And I met her husband too. Willi Bauer. He was a jovial man, dapper in a vest with a pocket chain attached to his watch. Plump and seemingly easygoing in demeanor, his thinning white hair combed across his scalp, he also looked like he sampled a bit too much of his wife's rich desserts.

"Uncle Willi," Emma called him, of course, and his ruddy face lit up when she got up from the table to give him a hug.

"My wife informs me Emma has an expert in Swiss languages in the family now," he said to me.

"Not at all," I replied. "I'm afraid I reached the limit of my expertise in our first conversation."

"No, no, modesty is not becoming, young man, and any student of history is a friend of ours," he said. "I dabble at it myself. In any case, I'm sure Emma is over the moon to have you around again."

"I think so," I said, with a glance to her. "I know I feel that way."

"I am." Emma nodded brightly.

"Well, I'm aware you have had a difficult path of it lately," Willi said, with a glance to his watch. "But you've come through. My goodness, look at the time. I'm afraid I must go. An appointment. It would be my pleasure to discuss areas of your studies should you ever wish to share them."

"Very kind of you, Herr Bauer," I said.

"Please, *Mister*. We've been here for many years. And anyway, just Willi would be perfectly fine. Everyone knows me as that. We are no longer back at home."

"Willi, then," I said, extending my hand.

A few minutes later, as Emma and I were leaving, for the second time we caught a visitor knocking at their door. This one heavyset, portly, in a gray tweed suit and homburg, seemingly nervous to be surprised there. He quickly averted his eyes and barely muttered as we said hello to him and continued down the stairs.

Above us, the Bauers' door opened. "Herr Bitner . . . ," Willi Bauer said, letting the man in.

"All these customers," I said to Emma when we got outside. "Do you know what Uncle Willi and Aunt Trudi do for work?"

"Mother says they sell beer."

"Beer? You mean, like in a bar?" There were, in fact, dozens of German bars all around Yorkville.

"I don't know," Emma said. "I don't drink beer. Last one to the park is a rotten egg." She skipped ahead of me.

"Wait a minute, Emma." I ran and caught up to her. "Take my hand." Cars and trucks darted in and out on Third Avenue. It was no place for a child.

"Oh. Daddy, I'm six years old. I know how to wait for the light and cross the street."

That was the way it went for the first couple of weeks. I was pleased Emma looked at me as her father again. And thankful I could make it happen under Mrs. Shearer's watchful and seemingly suspicious eyes. As if I was not to be trusted. And who always took the chance to remind me around a quarter of six that it was time to be getting on. True to Liz's request, I never stayed around to run into her.

"Please, have her back in thirty minutes," Mrs. Shearer would say, always tapping her watch as we went out for a treat or to the park. "Mrs. Mossman wanted me to have her washed and changed before dinner."

"By all means, Miss Shearer," I would reply, purposely teasing her.

"Mrs.," she would say back crossly.

Which made me smile inside.

After another week, I couldn't stay in my car another night so I went to the cheapest clean motel I could find, the Lido Lodge, not far from the beach, in the Rockaways. I swallowed my pride and took a job night to night washing dishes at an Automat just to earn the five-dollar nightly rate. It was clear, no one needed an ex-drunk teaching their kids, especially one who had been held responsible for someone's death and spent time in jail. Jobs were still hard to find; the papers said the unemployment rate still hovered around 14 percent. The only thing that kept me going was my twice-a-week visits with Emma.

One night, to relieve the boredom of being alone, I went to the movies to see Gary Cooper star in *Sergeant York*. The film started with a newsreel, *The March of Time*. It was how most of us saw the war at that time. By that time Hitler's armies occupied everywhere from Scandinavia to North Africa, and his Luftwaffe rained a nightly hell on London. It seemed only a matter of time before the Brits would be forced to give in and sue for peace.

This particular news report was by the famous Edward R. Murrow and showed the relentless nightly pounding of London: bombs exploding, disturbing images of caved-in buildings, and the dead and wounded being carted out on stretchers. And Parliament, with speeches by Winston Churchill, who was trying to hold the flagging spirit of his country together; and an animated speech by a defiant Adolf Hitler, addressing what was said to be a half million Germans about the "special destiny" of the German people and the need for more room to expand. *Lebensraum*, it was called, living space, the way in which the dictator justified his military expansion.

And right now it looked as if no one could stop him, as— though we continued to supply goods and arms to Britain via the high seas—FDR also continued to bow to Congress and waffle on the sideline.

After the film, hungry and lonely, I went to my local Horn & Hardart cafeteria and had a sandwich for dinner.

Lebensraum. I laughed to myself—I needed my own elbow room. My own living space. I couldn't continue this way anymore. I was almost ready to beg Liz or Uncle Eddie—please, let me just flop on your couch. Only for a night or two.

After I ate, I asked the restaurant manager if I could put an ad up on the window, *'36 Buick Roadster For Sale. Very low mileage.*

Need to sell now. I went back to my car. That night, it was in a parking lot behind a closed rug store on Queens Boulevard. The cops had twice found me sleeping in Silver Point Park in Rockaway and told me next time they'd arrest me for vagrancy. It was September now. It was starting to get colder at night. There were still people living in makeshift cardboard homes on the streets; others—loan sharks, booze peddlers, numbers pushers—huddled on corners, preying on anyone who had a dime. I almost felt desperate enough to want to find a way in to that sort of life. I had no idea how I would find real work. The result of the last two years seemed insurmountable. If I wasn't overage I would have gladly walked into an armed service recruitment office and signed myself up. Just to have a bunk under me at night. I once had a dream how my life would go. I'd be teaching somewhere, in some bucolic college in New England. Married. With a beautiful kid or two. A book with my name on the cover. My twin brother would still be alive, practicing medicine. And that punch I'd thrown would never have happened.

"If you're there . . . ," I said with a laugh, summoning my old nemesis on my shoulder who I hadn't heard from in almost two years. "I'm willing to listen to any ideas if you have any."

Fortunately, he didn't answer. I'd banished him long ago back in prison.

But little did I know I'd be hearing from him again tomorrow.

7

It was my Thursday with Emma and we were sitting around the kitchen table working on a jigsaw puzzle I had brought with me. A Swiss mountain scene in the Alps with a large Saint Bernard dog, since Emma suddenly seemed in love with all things Swiss.

Mrs. Shearer stayed in the other room, putting away her newly ironed clothes.

"Aunt Trudi says the Saint Bernard is the national animal of Switzerland. 'Cause they always save people in the mountains. And they always come with a cask of schnapps around their necks."

"I thought it was cognac," I said.

Emma looked at me quizzically.

"It's a liquor. It burns going down so it's supposed to bring people back to life."

"She called it schnapps," she said, and placed a piece in the puzzle. "Look, Daddy, it fits."

"Very good! So have you learned any more German words?" I asked her.

"A few. Let's see. *Blume*," she said. "It means flower. And *Himmel*. That means sky."

"Sky, huh? Look at this. . . ." I fit a large blue-and-white squiggle myself right into where the snowcapped mountain met the blue sky. *"Voilà!"*

"Very good, Daddy. Oh, and *lebens* . . . Lebens to Betsy it sounds like. I like that word."

"Lebens . . . ?" I said. It sounded familiar. "You mean 'heavens to Betsy'?"

"No, lebens. *Lebens-room*. Lebens-*roof* . . ." She tried to squeeze in a puzzle piece around the green meadow, but it wasn't fitting. "Daddy, this is hard."

"It is hard, honey. I agree. So, listen, lebens . . . ?" I asked her again. She had said *room* or *roof*? "You don't mean lebens-*raum*, do you?" Where would she come across such a term as this? I figured there wasn't a chance in the world that this was right.

"Yes, that's it!" Emma said brightly. "Lebens*raum*."

I stared at her. That was the word I'd heard the other night on the newsreel. *Lebensraum*. Living space. Uttered by Adolf Hitler. It had sent a half million Germans into a frenzy of joy.

She continued to try to fit pieces into the puzzle without answering.

"Honey, listen to me a second." I held back her arm to get her attention. "Where would you hear such a word? *Lebensraum*."

"From Uncle Willi," she said. "Where else? I heard him say it."

"Willi?" I put down the puzzle piece I was trying to find a home for. "Heard him say it how, honey?"

"I don't know. . . . He was talking to Aunt Trudi. Daddy, what makes the snow stay on the mountains when it's warm?"

"A lot of it is the altitude. It's cold that high up. Did he tell you what it means?"

"Who?"

"Uncle Willi. About *Lebensraum*. Did he tell you what the word meant?"

She didn't answer. She just continued trying to fit pieces in the puzzle without much luck, repeating, "Lebens-room, lebens-raum. Lebens to Betsy," in kind of a distracted, singsong voice.

"Emma, listen to me, honey." I took hold of her arm. "Did Uncle Willi tell you what it means?"

"He told Aunt Trudi." She put in a piece neatly and looked up with a grin of satisfaction.

"And what did he say?" I said.

"He said it was 'the future.'"

"The future." My heart stumbled to a stop. Mrs. Shearer came back in and seemed to hover near the kitchen, tidying up. And I didn't want to involve her. I thought back to the newsreel speech I had watched the other day. A half million Germans cheering wildly. Hitler pounding his fist. *Lebensraum*. As soon as she left I went back to Emma. "I just want to be clear, honey. Lebens-*raum*? You're sure of that?"

"Yes, Daddy, I'm sure. Why, is it a bad word?" She looked up at me.

"No, of course it's not a bad word," I said, with a glance to Mrs. Shearer. "But let's not use it. Someone might get the wrong meaning."

"All right," she said. She tried a piece in the Saint Bernard's face and it fit perfectly. "Look, it fits!"

As I was leaving later that day, I knocked on the door of the Bauers' apartment across the hall. Willi Bauer came to the door. He was dressed in a vest and tie with his pocket chain showing. A pipe in hand. His ruddy face lit up in a wide smile. "Why, Mr. Mossman! How good to see you. Please, we were just having some coffee. Come in, come in." I heard classical music in the background.

"Thanks. I can't stay," I said.

Trudi Bauer stuck her head out from the kitchen, wearing an apron. "Good afternoon, Mr. Mossman, what a nice surprise. We were just about to have an afternoon coffee."

"Call me Charlie, please," I said.

"All right, Charlie. But please, come in."

I stepped inside the apartment. Their place was considerably larger than Liz's. The living room was spacious, with a window looking out over the street; it was decorated with antiques, a navy embroidered couch and love seat, and a brass-filigreed coffee table. There was an arrangement of silver-framed photos on a front table and some oils, mostly landscapes, on the walls. A large phonograph sat on a side table; it sounded like Mozart playing. Willi went over and lifted the needle. The smell of pipe tobacco wafted in the air.

"Mozart's *Jupiter*. One of our favorites. Come . . ." He pointed to the love seat. "Please sit."

"I'm sorry to bother you," I said, taking a seat. "I'm just curious about a word I heard Emma use today. Something in German."

"Of course," he said curiously. He put his pipe down. "I hope you don't mind us teaching her a bit. And what is that?"

"*Lebensraum.*"

"*Lebensraum?*" Willi's face turned serious. "Are you certain that was it?"

"Yes. I asked her specifically. She repeated it several times. She even made it into a little song. Lebens to Betsy."

"*Lebensraum.* Not a phrase I would ever use," he said, somberly shaking his head.

"I only heard it myself for the first time the other day," I said, "in a newsreel at the Orpheum. In a speech given by Hitler."

"Who else, of course." He nodded with a frown. Trudi Bauer stepped out of the kitchen, wiping her hands on a towel. "That man . . . He's giving everyone with a German heritage a bad name."

"Where would a child hear such a thing?" Trudi said, taking a seat next to her husband.

"Actually," I said, looking at Willi, "she said she heard it from you."

"*From me?*" Willi Bauer's eyes grew twice their size. He looked as shocked and dismayed as I had. "Impossible."

"Yes. In fact, she said you called it 'the future.'"

"The future! *Mein Gott.* Not a future I would ever be a part of. She must have been mistaken." He looked at Trudi, trying to put it together. "*Liebsnatur,* perhaps—a similar-sounding word. The love of nature, or something like that we may have said. I recall you were reading her a poem by Goethe, weren't you, darling? About the linden trees."

"Yes, yes," Trudi said. "I recall now. So many German words, they are all long and sound alike. For her to have heard Willi say such a thing . . . The future . . . Ach, we would never say anything like that around Emma. She's like a part of the family to us."

"Maybe you're right," I said, outwardly giving in. But inwardly, I wasn't as sure. *Liebsnatur* . . . That wasn't even close to what Emma had said. *Lebens-room, lebens-roof,* she had playfully sung. Still . . .

I said, "Who knows what a six-year-old picks up? And where?

Anyway, I'm sorry to have bothered you with this." I stood up. "But you can imagine, if such a word was heard at school and interpreted the wrong way. With all that's going on."

"Yes, yes, of course," Willi Bauer said, standing as well. "We understand perfectly. Surely not any future we would want any part of, right, dear?" He placed his hand on his wife's shoulder. "Of that you can be sure."

8

Over the next month, there were many things that kept bringing my mind back to Willi and Trudi Bauer. After hearing their feeble explanation on *Lebensraum*, how awkward it was, and how nervous they seemed, I found myself focused on little else.

First, there were the visitors, all of whom seemed so uncomfortable to be discovered there on the landing outside the Bauers' apartment. Who always seemed to avert their eyes whenever Emma and I stepped out. In the following weeks, we encountered two more of them. "Customers," Trudi Bauer had sighed wearily, "they come at all hours." They both looked so awkward and fidgety and unhappy to be discovered there. They didn't have the look of customers to me.

Then, there was Emma's use of the word I'd heard. *Lebensraum.* And the Bauers' nervous and uncomfortable explanation for what it was Emma must have surely meant. It wasn't just the word, but Emma picking up that they had called it "the future." *Not any future we would want any part of,* they were quick to defend themselves.

But where else would that have come from? I even took the opportunity to ask Emma about it again, when Mrs. Shearer had stepped
out to do some cleaning. "Are you sure that word was *Lebensraum,*
honey, and not something else?"

"Yes, Daddy, you already asked me," she said. "*Lebensraum.*
But don't worry, I haven't used it again."

"That's good, peach. That's good."

I even questioned the building's maintenance man, a large,
hulking lug named Curtis, from Minnesota or South Dakota or
somewhere, who lived in the basement apartment, as he was outside having a cigarette on the street. I had bumped into him once
or twice, and the conversation had never gone further than the
Yanks or the weather. He never looked very happy in his job. At
some point, I took a risk and asked him about Willi and Trudi.
How nice they were? How long they'd lived in the building?

"For as long as I've been here," he said. He had a kind of a
"home-country" Scandinavian accent I couldn't place. "All I know
is that they're good, decent people. Always treat me well. Nothing
to spend your time on. Now if you'll excuse me, I have this drain
to fix," he said, pointing to an outside runner that had backed up.
"Happens every fall."

"Sure." I thanked him. He seemed like a pretty square guy.

And then there was the time the following week when I was
sitting in the Old Heidelberg again on Third Avenue having a coffee. I'd just left Emma for the night, and was at a table at the outside café, the weather being unseasonably warm, paging through
the afternoon *Sun* (reading of the sinking of the American destroyer the *Kearny* in the North Atlantic by a German U-boat,
many calling it an act of war), yet a part of me was keeping an
eye on the street for Liz, in the silly hope I might catch a glimpse

of her as she came home. I'd noticed the bags from the A&P where she shopped for groceries, just down the street. Some good things had happened for me and I wanted to tell her. I'd found work grading the occasional paper for Otto Brickman. Really, all I wanted to tell her was how great I thought Emma was, and to be back in her life.

Next to the Old Heidelberg was another café called The Purple Tulip, with an outdoor café as well. Before I went away, the place was one of those spots that hosted local meetings of the German American Bund and had speakers there all the time spouting America First and pro-Nazi propaganda. Now the Nazi flags were gone, of course, but everyone knew it was still a place you could have the right conversation over a beer.

It was going on seven and I hadn't seen any sign of Liz. I was just about to get up and leave—I thought maybe I'd catch a show at the Orpheum down on Eighty-sixth—when I suddenly spotted her across the street in her beige coat, heading home. My heart springing to life, I jumped up, and for a moment, thought I would rush over and intercept her. I reached in my pocket and threw a few bucks on the table.

But then she went up to a man who was waiting on the corner. A nice-looking man in a brown suit and hat. They kissed on the cheek. *There's someone I occasionally see,* she had said. *He works for an advertising company.* Suddenly I realized how foolish it might seem, having to explain who I was. Or maybe she already had, and it wasn't so complimentary. So I just stood there. He took her arm and they headed downtown on Third Avenue and I sat back down in disappointment.

My gaze drifted over to the café next door, and it seemed to fall, like a heavy weight drawn by gravity, on the face of someone sitting barely ten feet away, in a brown pin-striped suit, legs crossed, a cigarette in an ashtray.

At first, of course, I had no idea who he was. Casually sipping his coffee. His eyes lifted and for an instant we locked on each other, two people I was sure who had no idea who the other was. Like happens to anyone a thousand times in the city.

Until suddenly through the fog it dawned on me precisely where I'd seen him before.

And this time my heart came to a stop.

It was the first man I had seen on Emma's landing. At the Bauers' apartment door. When we were heading out for ice cream and I had taken Trudi Bauer's letters from her to mail. His long, gaunt face and deep-set eyes and the mole on his chin brought it all back for me. *A customer,* she had called him. He had tipped his hat to Emma and me. And here he was at The Purple Tulip, a place popular with the pro-Nazi crowd, not even a week after the Bauers had had to explain away their use of a word associated with the Nazi cause. A tremor ran down my spine. He glanced my way one more time. This time I averted my eyes. It was simply too much of a coincidence to believe. I had no idea if he had recognized me. If he was on his way to the Bauers'? Or if he somehow lived in the neighborhood. No, *My meeting ended early,* I recalled him saying. But I was sure it was him. Though there was no crime in it, of course. Any of it. It was a public place, the same as any restaurant on the street, and normally it wouldn't have aroused a second thought in me, except for how the Bauers had been occupying my mind lately.

I averted my eyes back to my paper.

Did he recognize me?

A minute or two later it became moot, as the man stood up,

tossed a bill or two on the table, took hold of his raincoat, and made his way out of the café, never even looking my way. At a lull in the traffic he crossed the street mid-block and turned down Eighty-eighth. Toward where the Bauers lived. Where Liz and Emma lived.

My heart continued to pound until he finally turned the corner and disappeared.

I felt no more nervous than if I'd discovered a Nazi spy.

9

The next time I came to visit Emma I stayed on until after six. Ironing, Mrs. Shearer subtly reminded me of the time. "Five thirty, Mr. Mossman," she announced, looking at the clock. Then, a quarter to six. Then not so subtly: "Mr. Mossman, don't you think it's time you got along your way? Mrs. Mossman will be home shortly."

"I'm aware of the time, Mrs. Shearer."

Emma seemed happy to have the extra time with me to read through a *Ginger* comic book I had bought her, about a buxom teenage girl who batted her eyes at every boy in school and had quickly become America's high-school sweetheart.

Around six twenty, I heard Liz's key in the door.

She stopped in the entrance, both smiling slightly and slightly cross, surprised to see me there. I could read on her face the exhausted demeanor of someone at the end of a long day. But she quickly lightened at the sight of Emma and me paging through the adventures of the country's most flirtatious teenager.

"Charlie, she's six," she said in a mildly rebuking way, putting the groceries down. "I didn't see that on her first-grade reading list."

I said, "You know, I was told someone asked Ginger, 'So what do you consider to be the most outstanding development in recent years in history?'" I held up the cover, showing Ginger mooning over a boy at her desk. "'The history teacher,' she said." Then, the moment the words got out of my mouth I realized how insensitive it had sounded, given Marymount and Natalie. "Sorry."

"Well, I'm so glad that's what you've got my daughter reading," Liz said, seeming not to take offense. "I didn't expect to see you, Charlie." Instead of upset, her eyes actually appeared pleasantly surprised.

"Actually, there was something I wanted to talk to you about . . . ," I said.

"Good evening, Mrs. Shearer. Has Emma had dinner?"

"She has, ma'am. I tried to tell Mr. Mossman it was time to get her in her pj's," she said, putting the groceries away. "And, that the choice of reading was not altogether appropriate."

"Don't worry about it," Liz said, taking off her coat. "My husband's never been particularly appropriate."

I wasn't sure she took it as a joke. "Well, I'll be going then if it's okay with you," Mrs. Shearer announced. "I'm late as it is for my bus." She slowly put on her coat, taking her time, but I waited in awkward silence while she tidily put her things in her purse, went through with Liz a list of things that were needed from the market, and finally said goodbye. "I'll see you tomorrow then." I waited until I heard her shoes heading down the staircase before I said anything else.

"That woman barely trusts me with five minutes with my daughter," I finally said, shaking my head.

"I admit, she does feel a bit proprietary toward Emma. She's had her to herself these past two years. Emma, darling, would you go get into your pajamas for me?"

"Yes, Mommy. Look how Daddy helped me with my writing." She showed Liz the lined composition book. "You know how I always have trouble with my *G*s."

"I was always a whiz at *G*s," I said. "Goya. Galileo. Gregory IX . . ."

"Gregory IX? Who's that?"

"Famous pope. Lived around 1230 AD. Responsible for decreeing the Inquisition."

"Lovely, Charlie. A legacy to be proud of. I might have said Betty Grable myself," Liz countered. "Anyway, good work, sweetheart." She draped a hand against Emma's cheek. "We'll go over it later. Right now, just get yourself together."

"Okay, Mommy."

Emma left and I waited till I heard her open her chest inside to say, "Basically I just wanted to tell you how great Emma is, Liz."

"She is, isn't she? Thank you. I'd offer you coffee, but I'm not sure it's best for Emma to get the wrong idea."

"The wrong idea?"

Liz draped her coat across a chair and put down her purse. "Look, I talked to my lawyer, Charlie. Rollie Gretch."

"Oh." I felt my heart sink. "Another *G*."

"This isn't a surprise, is it?"

"No, it's not a surprise." I shrugged. "I just wanted you to know, Otto Brickman has started paying me to go over some of his papers at Fordham. It's not exactly a full-time position, but he said if it went well, he would talk to someone there. It does give me enough to take a room in a boardinghouse in Brooklyn and get off that couch I told you about."

"That's great, Charlie. That's swell. Really. I'm glad you're getting back on your feet. Look, I didn't mean to be rude. I just don't want Emma to see us together right now and get the wrong idea about things at a sensitive time."

"I get it," I said, and stood up. "I won't stay. Okay if I leave her this?" I dropped the *Ginger* comic on the table.

"I think I can promise it'll be in the trash within ten seconds after you leave." She smiled.

"I figured. But actually, there was something else I wanted to talk to you about, which was why I stayed."

Liz opened the fridge, searching for a plate of chicken Mrs. Shearer had left for her there. "What's that?"

I said, "I've had a couple of unusual chance meetings with the Bauers. I was just wondering what you know about them?"

"Trudi and Willi? What do you mean?"

"I don't know what I mean. I mean, there's something about them that just doesn't add up."

"Add up how, Charlie?" She pulled out the dish. "What I *know* is that they're the nicest people I know. They adore Emma as if she was their own. And she, them. They even found Mrs. Shearer for us, and what would we ever do without her? I'm sure that will forever endear them to you." She laughed. "And when *she* can't make it, they're always willing to step in with Emma till I get home. So what do you mean, 'doesn't add up,' Charlie? Add up how?"

"I don't know. . . . How they say they're Swiss, but they're always reading and talking German to Emma."

"They *are* Swiss. And anyway, is that illegal today?"

"No, it's not illegal. It's just . . . Look, Emma used a German word to me a while back that opened my eyes. '*Lebensraum.*' You know what it means?"

Liz placed the plate of chicken on the counter and took out a pitcher of water. "No, I don't." She shrugged impatiently. "But I'm sure you'll tell me."

"It means 'living space,' Liz. Elbow room. It's how Hitler justified all his military expansion into Czechoslovakia and Poland and beyond. Emma said she overheard Willi and Trudi using it, and when I asked her what it meant, she said, 'the future.'"

"*The future* . . . Willi and Trudi? Now I know you've got it wrong. The Bauers are against the Nazis more than anyone I know. They have family, Trudi said, who have been imprisoned by them."

"I hear you. But then there are these people who go in there from time to time." I lowered my voice so Emma wouldn't hear. "Emma and I have bumped into them on our way out. I'm sure you've seen them."

"No. In fact, I haven't seen them, Charlie. I'm not always around. But now that you mention it, they do have visitors sometimes on the weekend. Is that illegal too?"

"So far, we've seen four different ones. They always seem to hide their faces, like they don't want to be seen here. Trudi Bauer calls them 'customers.' Customers for what, Liz? Then I happened to see one the other day. I was actually looking for you, at Old Heidelberg—you remember, that café near the subway station, I don't know if you go there anymore. . . ." I was about to say how I'd spotted her with someone across the street, but held back. "And I saw one of them. . . ."

"One of whom?" She looked at me, tired and exasperated like she wanted to sit down and eat.

"One of the people I'm talking about. Who we had run into on the landing. He was at The Purple Tulip next door. You remember, The Purple Tulip is a place where the German American Bund types always congregated."

"Charlie, I'm really having trouble figuring all this out. Do you have any idea just how you're sounding?" Liz looked at me.

"I don't care how I'm sounding, Liz. I'm just trying to put a few things together. Do you have any idea how long they've been here? Or what they do? Emma said they sold beer?"

"They've been here for years, as far as I know. Since the late '20s, I think. And Emma's right, they do make beer. Or did, I don't know. They have a brewery of some kind. Old Berliner, I think it was called. On Ninetieth somewhere. Originally, they said they would take Emma over for a visit. I know they sold it to many of the German bars around here. I really don't keep up with them that way."

"*Old Berliner?* I thought they were Swiss."

"You can't be Swiss and make beer, Charlie? Do you just have to make chocolate? Who are you now, Hector Poirot? You're sounding a little silly now. I mean, just what are you suggesting? Trudi and Willi are spies?"

"Don't mock me, Liz. I'm sure you saw that twenty-six of them were arrested not two weeks ago. Right here in New York. So they do exist. We're inching toward war. It's not exactly far-fetched."

"I'm sorry, but it is to me, if you're talking about the Bauers. And we're not at war, Charlie. At least, not yet. Trudi and Willi . . . ? Next you'll say they're recruiting Emma. And what are they using as their secret weapon, strudel?"

She stared up at me and I admit I had to smile at that, and Liz smiled too. Then laughed. The way it all came out, it did sound a bit far-fetched. Even to me.

"Honestly, Charlie, you must be watching all those war movies that are coming out now. You know, *Confessions of a Nazi Spy?*"

"No." I shook my head. "In fact, I haven't."

"Well, it certainly sounds like you have been."

Emma came back out in her squirrel pajamas and we tabled the conversation. "Are you going to be staying for dinner, Daddy?" She looked at Liz. "Please, Mommy."

"Look, honey . . ." Liz didn't know how to answer her.

"I wish I could, peach, but not tonight," I said, chipping in with what I knew Liz would want me to say. "But maybe sometime soon. Or maybe *we* can go out. Just the two of us."

"I would rather it was all of us," she said. "Like before."

"I know, doll. I wish it could be like it was before too." I pinched her on the cheek. "But it can't be. Not right now. I'll see you Thursday, okay?" I took my hat and jacket.

"See you Thursday," she said, nodding with a tinge of disappointment.

"To be continued." I gave Liz a tight smile, and with a one-fingered wave toward my daughter, I was out the door.

Heading down the stairs, thinking on it all again, maybe it did all seem a bit silly. Maybe I was making it up as I went along, piecing together bits and pieces of things that didn't fully fit, like Emma's puzzles. Still, at the same time, I couldn't put it away. Just as I couldn't put away that Liz was now speaking to her lawyer and that any hopes I had of picking up the life we had before were gone. Or at least, they were listing badly.

Still, on the street, my mind kept coming back to the Bauers. To Old Berliner . . . They had been in the beer business. What they had done in the years before.

I stopped back in at the Old Heidelberg café and sought out my waiter, Karl.

He seemed surprised to see me again so quickly. "Did you forget something, Mr. Mossman? I didn't find anything at your table."

"No, I'm just curious about something, Karl. Maybe you can help. Ever hear of a beer called Old Berliner?"

"Old Berliner, why, of course. We served it in this restaurant for years. It was Wilhelm Bauer's beer. He and his wife still eat here occasionally." He pointed eastward. "It was brewed right over there near the river in an old firehouse on Ninetieth Street, near York."

So Emma and Liz were right, I said to myself—the Bauers *were* in the beer business. Maybe the people we kept running into could be merely customers after all. Bar owners. Distributors. Though it occurred to me, why would they be coming to them? At their home. Instead of to the brewery.

Karl tucked two menus under his arm. "Is that all for now?"

"Yes," I said. "Thanks, Karl." Then as I was about to leave: "Just one more thing. . . ."

"Of course. If I can help . . ."

"You used the word 'served.' In the past tense. How come I don't see it on the menu anymore?"

"Well, that's because they don't make it any longer," the white-haired waiter lamented. "The Bauers had to close their doors." He scratched his head. "A year ago, I'm thinking. Maybe more."

"Closed . . . ?" I looked at Karl. "A year? You're sure?"

"Yes, Mr. Mossman. Or more. Why . . . ?"

"No reason. Thanks."

But what I was really thinking was that I was now sure Trudi Bauer had lied about this after all, just like they had about what they'd said to Emma.

They closed their brewery a year ago, Karl had said. *Or more.*

Whoever these people were, I was now sure they likely weren't customers of the brewery at all.

10

September moved into October. America teetered on the precipice of war.

While Britain held on, Germany looked east and pushed deeper into Russia. Tensions were high in the United States as we continued supplying arms to England and Russia through the lend-lease program FDR had worked out, in defiance of the Neutrality Act and a stubbornly resistant Congress. Lindbergh gave a speech that was broadcast across the entire country, begging the United States to remain neutral, blaming Roosevelt, the British, and the Jews for dragging us to the edge of war. In the North Atlantic, German U-boats preyed on American merchant ships ferrying aid to England, including the sinking of another destroyer, the USS *Brent,* where eleven sailors lost their lives, the first casualties of the impending conflict. Every day things seemed to bring us closer to war.

But here, I was starting to slowly put my life back together. I got my old job back, teaching American history at night to aspiring citizens twice a week, and continued to earn a little cash reading term papers for my old boss, Otto Brickman, now at Fordham. I managed to sell my car for four hundred dollars, enough to keep a roof over my head for a while. Sometimes I came twice a week to see Emma, other weeks only once, depending on my schedule.

For the moment, life kept me clear of the Bauers.

But one Wednesday I surprised Emma as an appointment with my parole officer had brought me near the Upper East Side. When I showed up unexpectedly, around our usual time, three thirty, Mrs. Shearer, who was ironing, said rather coolly at the sight of me that Emma was next door.

I hadn't spoken to the Bauers since our little chat about *Lebensraum*.

I knocked on their door. I heard classical music coming from within. In a moment, Trudi Bauer opened up. "Ah, Mr. Mossman!" she exclaimed with a pleased demeanor. "We have a guest, Emma. Look who's here!"

"Daddy!" Emma jumped up from the love seat, ran over to me, and gave me a hug around the waist.

"I'm very sorry to intrude," I said. "Mrs. Shearer said she was here. I was in the neighborhood and couldn't be close by without seeing my little girl."

"Aunt Trudi was just teaching me about music," Emma announced excitedly.

"Schubert," Trudi Bauer confirmed.

"Yes, I hear it. His Ninth, I believe. The Great. In C major," I said.

Trudi's grayish eyes came alive brightly. "Good for you!"

"I only know because—and you may not even know this," I said to Emma, "but your mother took a course or two on Schubert back at Columbia before we . . ." I caught myself mid-sentence, knowing where continuing would have taken us, a place I didn't want it to go. "She was actually writing her doctorial thesis on Chopin when we met. In musicology."

"Chopin? Is that so?" Trudi Bauer said, impressed. "I had no idea."

"I guess she doesn't talk about it much now. But ask her," I said. "I'm sure she'd love to bring it out for you."

"I was just taking Emma through the different movements of a symphony or concerto. How slow is called andante, right?" Trudi waved her arm slowly. "And fast, the allegro vivace, and the final movement, the finale, the merging or coda of all the themes. I think it's all a bit over her head, I'm afraid."

"I just like the music," Emma said. "Especially the fast parts. It's pretty."

"It is indeed pretty," I said. "And did you know that Schubert was discovered and actually tutored by the very same Antonio Salieri who taught Mozart."

"And who was thought to have murdered the maestro," Trudi chipped in herself.

"The same." I nodded. "And, that the Ninth is considered Schubert's masterpiece of symphonic form. That's why it's called The Great. Oh, and that he was only five foot one in height. Barely taller than you, peach."

"You are a truly Schubert expert!" Trudi Bauer exclaimed.

"Well, for a semester back then, Liz barely thought of anything else. I was bound to pick some of it up. You were just a little tyke," I said to Emma. I looked around. "Your husband's not at home?"

"Not at this time. He's out on business. But I wonder if I can tempt you with a slice of fruit tart. I just cut a piece for Emma. It would be no trouble."

At first I was set to decline, and say we should probably get along now and out of her hair, but seeing Emma scooping hers up with a messy, red and creamy smile, I reversed course and replied, "If it's no trouble, why not then? No reason to break up the party."

There was a *New York Times* folded on the coffee table and Trudi saw my eyes fix on the headline: "German Tanks Stream Toward Stalingrad."

"That lunatic has now turned his sights on Russia," she commented, shaking her head. "A far better general than he had to learn that same lesson the hard way."

"Yes, and like Napoleon, he obviously believes he'll be in Moscow before winter," I said.

"Well, we'll see," Trudi said, slicing a piece of cake at the kitchen counter. "History proves different, of course."

She handed it to me on a pretty plate, with a filigreed silver fork and a cup of coffee that had been brewing.

I heard you have family back in Germany, I was about to inquire of her, recalling what Liz had said, about the Nazis imprisoning them, when Trudi waved her hand dismissively and opined, "Well, enough of this conversation about war. It's not fitting for a young girl's ears. It's why we Swiss remain neutral in such matters, as we've learned that all war is without its winners, only those who suffer the least casualties. Emma, what do you call this particular movement?"

It was the third movement of the Schubert. Lively and whimsical. I'd heard this piece a dozen times during Liz's and my early life together.

"Al-le . . ." Emma stuttered.

"Allegro. Allegro vivace, in fact!" Trudi said. She smoothed her gray hair back off her ears. "So how do you like the cake, Mr. Mossman?"

"Charlie," I reminded her. In front of me on the coffee table was a large edition of Darwin's *Voyage of the Beagle*. In German, I could see.

"Yes, Charlie. My apologies . . ."

"Anyway, it's delicious, right, peach?" I pointed to the Darwin. "So who has the interest in the natural sciences in the family?" I asked.

"Oh, my husband," Trudi said. "He maintains lots of interests."

"I actually heard you and your husband were brewers," I said, shifting the subject.

"How did you know that?" she inquired.

"Liz told me."

"Oh. Yes. We did have a small brewery on East Ninetieth. We bought it when we came over, back in '28. It was never much of a money-maker however. It was always hard for Willi to go up against the more established local brands. Like Rheingold and Knickerbocker."

"Old Berliner, it was called?"

"Indeed. We had a German brewmaster and we distributed to many of the restaurants in the neighborhood. It was quite the time then. But we had to close the business a while back. At first, it was Prohibition. But now, nothing with such a name could be popular with what's going on now."

She meant the war, of course. Anything German-sounding was no longer in the style. "But you still have customers, I see?"

"Customers . . . ?" Trudi looked at me quizzically.

"You recall we've bumped into a couple on the landing. Emma and I. Once, when we mailed your letters. . . ." I waited for her reaction. "And another time, when we were headed out for ice cream."

"Ah yes, of course. . . ." Trudi Bauer cleared her throat and nodded, as if catching herself in a fib. "Yes. They are customers. Willi's in a different business now. We are trying to rent out the building. Now, Emma," she quickly changed subjects, "I said I would show you a picture of Willi and me at the Zurich zoo when we were first married? Would you like to see it? I have it in the bedroom."

"Yes, Aunt Trudi." Emma seemed excited.

"And then I must begin making dinner for Willi. He'll be home soon. And I'm sure Emma would like to spend a little time with her father on his surprise visit, and not me. Come, child."

She took Emma's hand and led her inside their bedroom.

"I'll clear," I called out, reaching for Emma's plate. "The cake was delicious."

"No, no, don't bother," Trudi said from the bedroom. "That's for me to do."

"No bother at all," I said.

Ignoring her wish, I stacked Emma's plate and silverware on mine and took them into the kitchen. I was thinking maybe I'd been rash after all in what I'd thought of the Bauers. Looking around—the cake, the old photographs, the completely orderly decorum—it seemed they could not possibly live more ordinary lives.

"The trash is where?" I called, looking under the sink for the bin.

"Please, just leave them on the counter. I insist," Trudi said again, hearing me fumbling around.

"Found it!" I said. I started scraping the crumbs into the wastebasket when suddenly something caught my eye.

Facing up at me were several strips of paper. Torn strips of paper. Lined writing table paper ripped into half-inch strips. But that wasn't what caught my attention. It was that the strips had not only been shredded, but seemingly burned as well, from one side to the other as if lit by a match. And what I was looking at were the charred embers curled up in the trash.

I noticed that one of the shreds had not completely burned.

Part of it was still a curled-up fragment with writing on it. Numbers, I could read. Organized into what seemed like groups of three:

128 3 7. 14 12 3. 0300.

I leaned in closer and my heart stopped.

It was as if I was looking at some kind of code.

I glanced to the bedroom, about to reach into the trash and pick up the unburned fragment—why would they be set afire in the first place?—when Trudi suddenly came back in. "Don't! Please!" she said peremptorily, catching me over the trash.

At first, she seemed to lose all color. A grayish pall took over her face. Then, just as quickly, she regained herself and merely smiled. "I simply didn't want you to go to any trouble, Charles, that's all. That's for me to clean up. Please, be with your daughter."

"It's no trouble at all," I said.

But inside, my heart had begun to pound like the drums at the end of the fourth movement she'd just been talking about. As if we had both stumbled on something important. For a second, neither of us spoke or acknowledged a thing, perhaps not sure exactly how much the other had seen. Finally, I just placed the two plates in the sink. "It was delicious," I said. "There you go."

"Daddy, Aunt Trudi and Uncle Willi have a picture of them in front of the lions in a zoo," Emma said, coming out of the bedroom holding a frame.

"One of the very finest in Europe," Trudi said. "Emma, darling, it's been wonderful spending time with you today. Please give my best to your mother."

"All right."

I closed the cabinet under the sink and said goodbye, took my daughter's hand and led her back across the landing to Liz's place, but by the time we stepped inside, I had no doubt Trudi Bauer had already reopened it and stood over the bin, staring at the charred, curled-up remains of what had been written there that was meant to be destroyed, wondering just what I had seen.

11

"You think he saw this?" Willi Bauer inspected the charred strips of paper Trudi had taken from the trash and shown him on his return.

On the part that was not fully burned, the scheme of numbers ending in 12 3. 0300 were clearly visible.

"I don't know." Trudi looked back at him. "He was asking so many questions. About the brewery. About the people who have come by. I got nervous once when they ran into Herr Atkins on the landing and I told him he was a customer. But he also knows we closed the business a year ago."

"Yes, he's a nosy sort." Willi nodded, tugging on his pipe. "That *Lebensraum* thing. From now on, we must be far more watchful. But not to worry, darling." He affectionately squeezed her arm. "He's a nobody. Just a drunk with a serious conviction on his record. He barely has a roof over his head. Who would he even turn to?"

"Maybe, but he's smart, Willi. And no one's fool. Tomorrow, our friend Kubler is scheduled to come by in the afternoon."

"No matter, it's not Charlie's day to visit, if I recall. He comes Mondays and Thursdays."

"Yes, but maybe our customers should no longer come around the house. Perhaps we need to find a new place to meet, Willi. The park perhaps? Near the concertina."

"You might be right, darling," Willi said. He laid the half-burnt strip of paper in an ashtray. "And maybe we should move this, as well. . . ." He patted the Darwin book. "Out of sight. Just to be sure. In any event, we must conduct our business with a shade more secrecy, I'm afraid. Now is not the time for any mistakes."

"No, it's not," Trudi agreed.

Willi took out a match and struck it, then dropped it into the ashtray and watched the remaining part of the strip that had not been burned curl and turn to ash, the damning set of numbers along with it. "See, my dear," he smiled and brushed his hands clean, "all gone."

"I'm sorry if I didn't handle things perfectly," Trudi said, taking a seat next to him. "It won't happen again."

"Now, now . . ." He squeezed her hand. "It all works out. You'll see."

She looked straight ahead in a fretful way, nodding, as if to say, *Yes, it always does.* "Would you care for a schnapps before dinner?" She smiled back at him. "I've made your favorite. Rosti. With dumplings. It will be ready at seven."

"Yes, a schnapps would be just the thing," Willi said, smoothing his white mustache.

"And what would you like to listen to?" Trudi asked, on her way to the bar. "Brahms, perhaps. It always helps you relax."

"Yes, Brahms's Second would be perfect, darling." He sat back and refilled his pipe as Trudi went over and removed the recording from its sleeve.

"And don't you worry too much about this." Willi stoked the gray ash around with the bowl of his pipe. "If our friend becomes too big of a nuisance, we have the ways to deal with him."

"Yes, I know, Willi." Trudi nodded.

"And the good news is, my dear," Willi smiled, "I only know of one person in the world who would even miss him."

12

"It clearly looked like a kind of code," I said to Sam Goldrich, who'd been the defense attorney at my trial, and was the only person I could think of to go to on such a delicate matter.

He listened attentively to how I described it from across his desk.

"There were numbers. Organized in groups of threes." I pushed a piece of paper across to him. "As soon as I left I wrote them down. The rest was burned beyond recognition."

"A code, you say . . . ?" Sam inspected the paper with a skeptical frown. The lawyer was the son of a family friend and had done an excellent job of playing upon the shift in public opinion against Germany in getting my sentence reduced. "Don't you think you're getting your oars ahead of you just a bit on this, Charlie?"

"You wouldn't say that if you saw the look Trudi gave me when she caught me staring at it," I said. "She turned white as a ghost."

"Maybe she thought you were throwing out the rest of her fruitcake," he said, suppressing a grin.

"Very funny," I scoffed. "Anyway, that's what Liz thinks too. That I've been seeing too many war propaganda films."

"And have you?"

"Unless you call *Sergeant York* a propaganda film." I looked at him. "No."

"All right then. Let's go through it again. There are a couple of unusual visitors you've bumped into on Liz's landing or spotted having a coffee at a restaurant where pro-Nazi agitators have been known to congregate. Then there's this particular German word that this elderly couple who lives next door supposedly taught your daughter."

"*Lebensraum,*" I repeated for him. "And it's not just a word, Sam. It's a core Nazi belief. You might recall, it was their basis for annexing the Sudetenland and invading Poland back in '39."

"Yes, I do know that, Charles. But to be fair, half the neighborhood speaks German up in that part of town, do they not?"

"The Bauers claim to be Swiss," I corrected him. "Or so they say."

"Yes, Swiss. Of course. Though what's the most common language in Switzerland, if I'm not mistaken . . . ? Anyway, what else . . . ? Oh, yes, these burnt strips of paper you say you found in their trash bin. When you were throwing out the fruitcake."

"You're making it all sound so trivial, Sam," I said with an edge of frustration.

"Okay, sorry, with numbers on them then. These numbers. That you're interpreting as a kind of code. But just as easily, and in fact far more likely, could simply be a date. Or a telephone number. Or the number of a receipt for a pair of shoes Mrs. Bauer purchased."

"These are no telephone numbers, Sam. And tell me if they resemble any receipt. And why would they be torn up into tiny strips," I asked, "and then set on fire? All but this one fragment. Unless they were trying to hide something."

"Maybe because the wife didn't want her husband to find out?" he surmised.

"About what?" I asked.

"About the shoes. All very nefarious." Sam's eyes twinkled. "Who knows?"

"You're making me sound like a fool, Sam. Like I'm inventing the whole thing. I assure you I'm not. You know I'm not the most believable person in the city right now. I didn't have anyone else to go to."

"I know that, Charlie. I'm sorry. And I trust you're not making it up. But it is possible you are attaching some unjustifiable importance to all these events. That's possible, isn't it?"

"It's possible. But putting it all together, it all adds up."

"To what? What exactly are you saying, Charlie? That these people are spies?"

"I don't know what I'm saying, Sam." I pushed myself back in my chair.

His secretary stepped in, saying, "Excuse me, Mr. Goldrich . . ." and put a message on his desk. He glanced at it a second, then nodded soberly at her. "Just give me a minute," he said.

I said, "The government itself is concerned about the existence of some kind of fifth column at work here." The term had originated in Spain, during the civil war. A Nationalist general announced that five separate columns were advancing on Madrid.

One from the south, one from the north, another from the southwest, and a fourth from the northeast. A fifth column, he said, made up of foreign agents and domestic traitors, who employed espionage, was ready to erupt from within the capital itself. People were now concerned that a German "fifth column" could happen here.

"You saw the headlines last month, Sam. Twenty-six of them, operating right here in New York. Ordinary citizens," I said. "Engineers, accountants, even attorneys. And look what they were on to apparently—some supersecret bomb site no one even knew existed. But they knew."

"Yes, and the FBI was all over them, weren't they?" Sam countered. "They didn't need some out-of-work history instructor drawing pictures with his daughter to root them out."

"I don't know how they got onto them, Sam. Maybe at some point it was just someone attaching an 'unjustifiable importance' to something he saw that didn't seem kosher."

My lawyer exhaled a breath and put up his palms, as if granting me the point. Then he said, "Your brother died in Spain, right, Charlie?"

I stared. "What does that have to do with anything?"

"I'm just saying . . . He was fighting the Nationalists, no?"

"Sam, this isn't some suppressed attempt to come to terms with Ben's death," I said, not liking the inference I was drawing. "I'm presenting you facts. This is real."

"More like suppositions," the lawyer said. "And I'm not saying that's what it is—about Ben. Look . . ." He pushed back his wire-rim glasses. "This isn't exactly my expertise. If they sued you for slander, or beat you up on the street—Christ, bad example, sorry"—he put up his palms in apology—"then I'd know exactly what to tell you to do. With this, I suppose you could go to the police. Or the FBI. But I'm pretty sure the police would tell you that half the people in Yorkville are seeing Nazi spies across the hall these days. And let me remind you that as of now we're not at war with anyone. It's not a crime, congregating with Nazis. Of course, with what happened in the North Atlantic a couple of weeks ago . . ." The *Kearny,* a destroyer, was sunk by a German U-boat, while guarding an Allied convoy, with fourteen sailors lost. The first U.S. casualties with Germany. "We may soon well be."

"So, in your non-expertise, Sam"—I exhaled in frustration— "what would you have me do?"

"What would I have you do . . . ? I'd have you do nothing, Charlie. Mind your own business. As you said, you don't exactly have the kind of résumé that would be an asset in court. Just work on getting yourself back into society's good graces. That would be my professional advice."

I snorted an annoyed blast out my nose.

"Now as a matter of domestic security . . ." He shrugged. "My gut is that you would need a bit more tangible evidence to interest someone in what you have. Not that I want you to go around dig-ging for it, mind you. Leave that up to the professionals. Please. And not a good thing at all these days for a Jew," he wagged his finger at me, "to be going around ratting on their neighbors, if you know what I mean. It only makes it seem as if we're trying to gin up a war, to protect our own interests with what's happening in Europe. Not the country's interest. You heard Lindbergh's speech last month. Even though as a member of the tribe, and as someone who hates these Nazi bastards as much as anyone, I'd be the first to stand up and cheer if we did. It's going to happen, Charlie. Sooner or later. We all know that. Then maybe some of the things you're alleging might actually get someone's attention.

"But now, if you don't mind, since I'm not charging you a dime for this conversation, I'll have to take this . . . ," he said, holding up the message. "Wife shot her husband who was cheating on him. Precisely my stock-in-trade."

"Well, I may need you on something else," I said, standing up and taking hold of my hat. "Closer to your usual business. Liz is going to seek a divorce."

"Oh. I'm sorry to hear that," the lawyer said. "Though it's not completely out of the blue, is it? Sorry for your little girl though. Keep me posted and I'll get you with the right people. They'll fleece you dry though. And Charlie . . ."

I turned at the door.

"Please stay out of this espionage thing. You hear me? Either you're right and they're truly bad sorts, or you're wrong, and they're the nicest people in the world. Either way, you'll only get yourself in trouble. Or worse—God forbid—if you catch my meaning. If they're engaged in the kind of business you're thinking they are. Whichever way, it doesn't bode well for you. You understand?"

"I understand." I nodded, opening his office door. "And I'll be in touch on that other thing. With Liz. Thanks."

13

My lawyer's words rang clear. *Let the professionals handle it. You need more tangible evidence.* All I had were pieces of a puzzle that didn't fully fit together. Threads that led nowhere. *I bet half the people in Yorkville are seeing Nazi spies across the hall these days. . . .*

His other statement hit me square in the face as well. *Your brother died in Spain, right . . . ?* From an act of sabotage committed by a Nationalist agent. Part of the fifth column resistance there. A stretcher carrier, a member of the medical personnel in Ben's own unit. The blast brought down half the lobby, which was being used as a makeshift hospital. For a day or two, I sat around and tried to assess if what Sam said carried any truth. Was that why I reacted so aggressively in the bar? That, and four Rob Roys? On our birthday. Because of Ben? Was it why I felt so driven to find something on the Bauers? To prove they weren't who they said they were. Was it all no more than just a deeply buried attempt to resolve the guilt I felt over my brother's death?

No. I was sure it wasn't that. It was that I was certain the

Bauers simply weren't who they said they were. And that they were hiding behind some veneer, as clean and polished as the Biedermeier table in their front parlor. I knew it and no one else seemed to. No more.

My next visit with Emma, I stayed around as long as I could before Liz came home. The Bauers actually stopped in to drop off some crumb cake to Emma—and to Mrs. Shearer as well, who they clearly seemed to like—another characteristic I put on the ledger against them—and mentioned they had an engagement later that night.

So after I left that night, just before six, I remained in the shadow of the stairway of a brownstone across the street. *Tangible evidence,* I said to myself. *There has to be something.* I felt foolish, hiding there in the darkness. Not even knowing what I was looking for. Slinking back into the shadows whenever someone walked by. I was just curious to see where they went or who they met with.

After about twenty minutes, Liz got home, carrying a bag of groceries, and I huddled deeper into the cover of the stairway so she wouldn't see me. She'd be furious. *We've been all over this, Charlie.* No telling how she'd react. Shortly after, I also saw Curtis, the janitor, come out, still in his work clothes but with a plaid wool jacket over him, to smoke a cigarette in the crisp night air. He once told me he had a daughter himself. I asked him where. "Here?" I inquired. I knew nothing about him. He clearly lived alone in the basement. He just shrugged and said, "No. Back home," without volunteering any more information. It was clearly something he didn't care to talk about. That was about the deepest conversation I ever had with him.

Around fifteen minutes later, at six forty-five, the front door of the brownstone opened and Willi and Trudi Bauer stepped out.

They came down the stairs, he in a tweed Alpine cap over his jacket, a vest and tie, and a walking cane; Trudi in a dark dress and wide-brimmed hat. They turned east on Ninetieth toward Third Avenue. I waited until they'd gone about twenty yards down the street, then decided to set off after them. I knew it was wrong; Liz would be fuming at me if she found out. She would probably ban me from coming to visit. But, I thought, if I stayed back from them at a reasonable distance, what harm could there be?

They walked, arm in arm, at a leisurely pace, to the corner, and then turned north. Third Avenue was busy with cars and trucks zooming by and the sidewalks were lined with German beer halls and cafés and banners. An open delivery truck was parked in front of Shein's Market on Ninety-first.

I have to admit I felt a little foolish, following them, scared they would suddenly turn around and recognize me. I had no training in this. I was no FBI agent. My lawyer had made that clear. I wasn't even the most patriotic of people. I just felt like I had stumbled onto something no one else could see, and if I was right, something very bad could result from it. And the government should know. It was a puzzle to be solved.

They continued north a block or two, pushing against the crowd. I kept a good distance behind. On Ninety-third they stopped at the corner and appeared set to cross. The light was against them. Willi Bauer casually glanced back around.

I ducked under a canopy of a store that sold candies, behind a woman filling a bag of dried fruit. Otherwise, his gaze would have gone directly through me. In any case, he didn't seem to notice me there, but looked back, pointing to something ahead, drawing his wife's attention across the street.

When the light turned green, they crossed.

Part of me said to myself I should just give this up and go home now. That was the voice of reason on my shoulder, the one that always made sense. That all I was doing was trying to man-ufacture facts to fit the conclusions I had already drawn, and any student of history would tell you that was an invalid thesis. A pat-tern had to be determined from facts, events. I was bad at doing puzzles, and none of these pieces were really fitting together, other than my own stubbornness to be right, maybe. But this was not some board game I was playing with Emma. If they turned again and saw me, what would I say? I'd never be able to show my face at the apartment again.

On my other shoulder, my other voice, the one that always dared me and generally steered me in the wrong direction, had another opinion completely.

I waited for the light to go to yellow and then hurried across after them, mid-block. The avenue was lined with German beer halls, their bars overflowing. Shouts of merriment and music from the home country could be heard coming from any one of them. Germans were nothing, I thought, if not loud drinkers. There were lots of other restaurants too, even Zurich, a well-known Swiss one. Or The Purple Tulip, where I had seen the Bauers' "customer." Willi had even mentioned it once. Maybe that's where they were headed now. I wove through the crowd, staying about twenty yards behind them, as they walked leisurely, arm in arm.

Then they stopped. Taking Trudi's arm, Willi led her into one of the beer halls.

Marienplatz, the awning read.

I knew that the Marienplatz was the central square in Munich, Germany.

I angled my hat down over my face and stopped on the sidewalk outside. I'd never been in the place before. A boisterous crowd was gathered at the bar. Mostly young men engaged in animated conversation. The politics of the day were never far away from a beer. The Bund might have been driven inside, with all that was happening in Europe that made it unpopular, but that didn't mean it was driven out. Behind the bar, amid pictures of Chancellor Hindenburg and other prominent German figures, I saw one of Adolf Hitler.

Inside, a heavyset, dark-haired man in a black jacket came up to the Bauers, welcoming them as if they were expected. He was someone in charge, it seemed. Maybe the owner. He put his hand on Willi's back and patted him familiarly and gave Trudi a respectful kiss on both cheeks. Then he snapped his fingers to the bar for drinks, like the Bauers were important guests.

VIPs.

And why not? I thought. Hadn't they been in the beer business for years? They likely supplied many of these places up and down the avenue. And hadn't they also lived in the neighborhood? Who knows how many times they may have dined there? So nothing unusual here. Nothing to justify how I had followed them, Sam Goldrich would surely say.

I observed all this from the street, feeling a wave of foolishness and stupidity about the whole thing now, thinking I should just call it a night and get on home.

Probably every other person in Yorkville, I heard my lawyer say.

Then, after the briefest toast, I saw the man in the black jacket motion the Bauers to follow him to the rear of the restaurant. Making way a path for them through the congested bar crowd.

I stepped inside.

There, I was confronted by a raucous throng of drinkers,

conversing mostly in German. I edged my way through to the back, concealed in the crowd. Beer flowed handily. German music played; an accordion player jumped up on the bar. At every pause in the song the crowd would chime in as one, thrusting their mugs into the air. I wasn't sure what they were saying at first, but then even with my limited German it came clear. *"Schicksal. Schicksal. Schicksal uber alles,"* they were chanting.

Destiny, they sang three times. *Above all.*

The Bauers and their host went past the bar and a row of wooden booths, heading toward what appeared to be a back room. I craned my head through the crowd, uttering, "Excuse me," and "Sorry," to anyone I bumped into as I jostled by, beer spilling on my jacket. "Hey, watch yourself," someone said, annoyed.

"Sorry."

From this vantage point I could see the door to the back room opened. Through the jostling throng, I made out a long table inside, with several people around it. All men. It clearly looked as if there was business being discussed in there—just maybe not the beer business.

As the Bauers stepped in, the people around the table all stood up. And as the door opened wider—me craning my head through the jostling crowd—I saw something else that made my heart come to a sudden stop.

On the wall behind the table was a red-and-white flag with the Nazi swastika on it.

"Liebsnatur," I muttered to myself, mouthing the word as if it had a bitter taste to it. I recalled how the Bauers had attempted to explain away the word Emma had heard them use.

Liebsnatur, my ass.

The Bauers were Nazis. I saw it now with my own eyes. There among the chanting German crowd. Under the Nazi symbol. There was no denying it now.

The man in the black jacket motioned Trudi and Willi inside. Standing, the people around the table stuck out their arms stiffly and gave the Nazi salute.

Through the doorway, Willi and Trudi extended their arms in return.

Then Willi turned at the door. His gaze swept back across the outside room, not merely on the crowd, which was now singing *"Die Wacht am Rhein"* in unison. Maybe a last note of caution to make sure no one was watching them.

And it seemed to land, through the throng of raucous drinkers celebrating their homeland, almost as if he knew precisely where to look, directly on me.

There seemed to be the slightest smile on his face. As if he was saying, *I see you now, Charlie. So now you know.*

Now you know, and there's nothing you can even do about it.

Then, with a bloom of satisfaction on his appley cheeks, he shut the door.

14

More than ever, I was sure I had stumbled onto something.

"Unjustifiable importance" or not, I now knew that everything about the Bauers was utterly false, completely at odds with the public persona they maintained: that of kindly Swiss grandparents, dimpled cheeks and white hair, with all that pretended disgust they showed for the madman who had taken over their homeland. Who had put Europe in turmoil.

Not any future we would want any part of, he had said.

It made the bile rise up in my gut.

For days, I kept reliving the sight of Willi Bauer shutting the door on a room full of *Sieg Heil*-ing compatriots under a Nazi banner. And what to do about it? Who to tell?

It was still no crime.

Whether he had seen me or not—and as I went back over the events, I could only come to the conclusion that he had not—there was something about them I now knew was a complete lie, and went far deeper than just their politics and the beliefs that they put in so much effort to hide.

I had to believe that they were engaged in something that I could not quite determine, but feared was set in motion already. The steady flow of strangers who came to their door; the shreds of some kind of code I felt for certain I had found half-destroyed in their trash; and whatever it was that was being discussed in that back room at the Marienplatz restaurant behind closed doors. That it was both secretive and conspiratorial and most likely a threat. Something the police or the FBI would want to know.

Something dangerous.

I'd already taken my original suspicions to my lawyer, Sam Goldrich. A prominent Jew with connections. I imagined myself calling him up again now, describing what I'd seen at the beer hall last night—*You wanted more tangible evidence, well, here it is!* The Nazi greeting. The brazen swastika on the wall behind them.

I told you, sympathizing with the Germans is not a crime, Charlie, I was sure he'd reply. *Look at Lindbergh. He got a fucking medal from them.*

But then he would lean forward and say with all lawyerly seriousness: *But secretly following them is.*

And so is plotting with them, Sam, I would counter. *Come on, you have to know in your heart, something's going on.*

Still, I was a nobody. Someone recently released from prison, with a felony conviction around my neck. And a boy's life on my conscience. And as Sam said, not exactly the best person to be pointing a finger at the Bauers, who were respected businesspeople, and by all accounts, established and well-liked members of the community. Immigrants, yes, but who had been here since the late '20s. Who everyone seemed to have a good word for. And as my lawyer had reminded me, congregating with Nazis, even if they had gone to such lengths to cover it up, wasn't illegal. There were still pro-German rallies and speeches going on publicly. Lindbergh had given a talk that every radio station in the country covered only last month, and even though there was great public outcry against it, no one had arrested *him*! Indeed, half of Congress was still pushing back against FDR's call to support the Brits and get us into the war.

But if there was truly something going on with the Bauers, something more than met the eye, it was stuff the government should know about. And I realized that the person closest to this, who it was my duty to protect, was Emma. If they were subversives, it was illegal and dangerous work. What if she was over there and something happened? What if they were even using her in some way, or Liz? As a cover. What then?

So that Saturday, I went back up to Liz's apartment, even though it wasn't my day to visit. I knocked and found her alone in the apartment in a pair of slacks and a plaid flannel shirt knotted at the waist. A scarf tied in her hair.

"Charlie, I wasn't expecting you," she said. "Emma's with her friend Charlotte."

"That's okay," I said. "Got a minute? I'm actually here to talk to you."

"Me? All right." She seemed surprised at that. "Come on in." She ran her forearm across her brow. "I was just tidying up a bit. The place is such a mess." She had the sheets rolled into a ball and a load of wash in a basket. I used to help her with all that when we were a couple. Indeed, I was a champion folder. She used to say that no one could fold a set of sheets like me.

"Don't worry." I stepped in. "I won't stay long."

"That's okay. In truth," she smiled contritely, "I was looking for any excuse I could find to push all this off. Sit down."

I did, and for a while, the conversation stayed on Emma. How much my life had changed with her in it again. How much I admired the way Liz was raising her. And I told her how I was slowly getting myself back on my feet. "That's great, Charlie, great." Her eyes appeared soft and nonjudgmental. She seemed genuinely happy for me.

Then I got to the real reason I was there.

"I know this won't go over big, Liz." I cleared my throat. "But I'd really like it if Emma no longer had anything to do with the Bauers."

"Trudi and Willi?" She looked at me, kind of shocked. "Why?"

"Look, I know how you feel about them, Liz—you've made that clear. But they're simply not who they say they are. Or who they want you to believe they are." I told her about the strips of charred numbers I had found in their kitchen trash, and then following them to the beer hall and what I saw take place in the back room there. The Nazi salute and the banner with the swastika on it.

"You actually tailed them?" She looked at me, aghast. "Willi and Trudi?"

"I did," I sighed with a guilty shrug. "What can I say? But that's not the point. Look, I know Emma's fond of them and maybe they're legitimately fond of her too. Maybe that's the only part of them that *is* real. But as for the rest, they're not being honest with you, Liz. All this stuff about Heidi and Swiss chocolate and the desserts she prepares. They're Nazi sympathizers. Maybe even more. I'm starting to doubt if they're even Swiss at all. Doesn't that concern you?"

"What do you mean by 'maybe even more,' Charlie?"

I looked at her directly. "There's a war going on, Liz. You know exactly what I mean."

It took a second for her to fully see where I was heading. Though in truth, I didn't even know what I was suggesting. Collaborators? Conspirators? Provocateurs? Everything was just a puzzle piece right now.

"You're suggesting they're *spies* . . . ?" she said, her eyes locked on me. Then she laughed. "Well, that's absurd. And even if there was even a kernel of truth to it," she shook her head, "is it suddenly a crime to be a Nazi sympathizer? This neighborhood is full of them. Look at Lindbergh, our biggest hero, for God's sake. He just made a speech in Des Moines supporting them. And he's the second-most-popular person in the country, after the president. There are even U.S. senators who openly defend them on the Senate floor."

"I know. I know all that. I do. But I also I know you're aware exactly what's happening over there, Liz. And it's not all just the war. Jews are being relocated throughout Europe. Their businesses are being taken away. God knows what's happening to them wherever they go."

"For someone who barely took Emma to temple, I never knew you were so concerned," she said, trying to wound me with an old complaint of hers, my lack of Jewish commitment, and it carried a sharp edge to it. "If it wasn't for me she wouldn't even know she was a Jew."

"You're right, Liz. I don't want to fight about that. All I'm saying is, you really don't know anything about these people. They don't add up."

"Other than they've been like family to us. At a time when

I really needed it, Charlie. A time, must I remind you, when you couldn't be. That adds up. So is that part of their cover? Do I have to know any more?"

"Maybe you'd want to know why they've pretended to hate the Nazis so fervently when they're in a back room of a Nazi beer hall *Sieg Heil*-ing with a roomful of them? Would that concern you?"

"Charlie, they've been here for years. They were in the beer business, for God's sake. They may even be American citizens for all I know. They didn't just parachute in here and set up operations."

"Those agents who were arrested last month, some of them were purchasing agents and engineers. They didn't just parachute in here either. I'm just asking you, Liz, keep Emma away. For now. At least until we learn more. If they are what I think, it could be dangerous for her."

"Now you're telling me how to watch out for my own child?" With that, she got up and went over to the window, letting off steam, and lit a Parliament. "And just how *are* we going to learn more, Charlie? With more of your ridiculous subterfuge? Are you going to set up a permanent stakeout on them? I'm sorry, but I won't tell Emma not to see them. It would break her heart. And how would I even go about explaining it?" She blew out a stream of smoke. "That my soon-to-be ex-husband has been playing J. Edgar Hoover and thinks they might be foreign agents? That he followed them to a Nazi hangout and doesn't like who they keep as friends?"

"We may not be at war yet, but we may be soon, Liz. Then what about their friends?"

She took an angry drag. "So if you're such a fucking patriot, Charlie, sign up with the RAF, and go fight over there, like—"

She caught herself. We both knew what she was about to say. *Like your brother, Ben.* That was clear. And we both knew that it stung. She pressed her lips together with guilt on her face and blew out a stream of smoke from her nose, and came back over and sat down next to me again. She put her hand on my arm. "I didn't mean that, Charlie. Of course I know there's a war going on. And of course I don't like what these people stand for, and what they're doing over there. To Jews and to Britain. Contrary to what you think, I don't put my head in the sand. But I'm sorry, I trust the Bauers and I won't tell Emma she can't see them. Whatever their political views, and why ever they feel they have to hide them, to us, Willi and Trudi are the nicest couple in the world."

I nodded—more just from weariness of the argument than from any agreement. "You know, the nicest people in the world put that madman in power over there. And half of them probably read Schiller and Heine. And make delicious strudel. The nicest people in the world all probably look the other way while their Jewish neighbors and friends are being shipped out to work camps somewhere. Could you really be their friends, Liz," I looked at her in earnestness, "if you knew for sure they felt that way?"

"Really, Charlie . . ." She tapped her cigarette in an ashtray on the kitchen table. "I think you're blowing this whole thing way out of proportion. I just can't do it. Honestly, I wouldn't even know what to say to them without any proof. In a million years, I don't think they would ever put Emma in any danger."

I shrugged, feeling I had to give up. "All right. On that, maybe you're right."

"And I want you to stop this, Charlie. All these innuendos. And if you can't, then please stop coming up here for a while. You're starting to act like the Old Charlie again. With all these things . . . And I don't like it. You haven't been drinking, have you?"

"Not even a beer, Liz." I looked at her. "You know that's a condition of seeing Emma."

"Well, that's good. It really is. But I'm sorry, I trust them. I do."

"What you're saying is," I said with a resigned smile, "you trust them more than you trust me."

"I guess what I am saying is, they've given me a whole lot more reason to, Charlie, if you know what I mean. Now, look, if you'll excuse me, I've got to get on to tidying up this place."

"Okay." I got up. "If you like I could stay and help?"

"Really . . . ?" She looked at me dubiously. "Thanks though." She picked up the laundry bin again and shook her head. "Willi and Trudi as spies . . ." She gave me an amused chortle. "Please . . . You know that British film director Hitchcock would surely have some fun with that."

15

For a couple of weeks nothing much happened. October crawled into November. I taught my classes, saw Emma on Mondays and Thursdays, and minded my own business.

But in the world, FDR pushed hard against the isolationists in Congress to finally put an end to the Neutrality Act. The destroyer *Reuben James* was sunk by German U-boats off the coast of Iceland with 115 of its crew, and everyone thought, This could be it. Roosevelt had no choice but to declare war. But no. After a week or so, I asked Emma if she had seen Uncle Willi and Aunt Trudi, and she said she had been to their place just the other day. They had brought her some new slides for her View-Master.

"Oh," I said, "I could have brought you more, honey."

"No, they wanted to do it, Daddy. We talked about famous rivers."

"Rivers?"

"Yes, they wanted to show me pictures of the Rhine."

The Rhine runs through both Germany and Switzerland, Charlie,
I reminded myself.

"Okay, good, honey."

Then that Thursday I happened to bump into Willi leaving
the brownstone as I arrived. It was the first time I had actually
seen him since the night I'd followed him to Marienplatz. If he
had spotted me there, he surely showed no sign of it, tipping his
hat to me on the stairs, commenting that he had just seen Emma
the other day and how pretty she looked. Reminding me that they
would have to have me over sometime soon, to discuss, as he put it
with a genial smile, "all things historical."

I said yes, we would have to do that sometime soon, holding
back the urge to confront him on what I'd witnessed at the beer
hall.

"Enjoy your visit," he said cheerily, with a nod of his cane.
Then he headed down the block toward Third, never looking back.

That day, I helped Emma with her schoolwork. Mrs. Shearer
excused herself and went down to the basement to do some laundry. From the kitchen table, over a multiplication table, I heard the
sound of the door opening across the hall. At first, I thought maybe
it was another of those so-called customers again; I hadn't seen one
in a while. Emma was telling me about something at school. How
one of her friends made a big mess finger painting and got it over
a bunch of her classmates and— I held up my hand for her to be
quiet. "Hold it a second, honey."

"What, Daddy?"

Instead of someone coming up the stairs, I heard the sound
of Trudi Bauer going down, engaged in conversation with Mrs.
Bainbridge, the landlady, who I'd heard her converse with from
time to time. Excusing myself, I went to the door and peeked out

onto the landing. Trudi was all the way down on the first floor. I thought I heard some kind of delivery taking place.

Across the landing I noticed her door was slightly ajar. She had not locked it, clearly intending to be back up quickly.

Downstairs, I heard the outside door open and she and Mrs. Bainbridge engaged in conversation.

Sometimes they could go on and on for a while.

I stared at the cracked-open door just a few feet in front of me. I don't know what finally gave me the courage—or the foolishness. *Tangible evidence*—that was what was ringing in my mind. Some kind of confirmation to my suspicions. *So how will you learn more?* I knew that Willi was out. I'd seen him leave.

The opportunity was just staring me in the face.

If there was ever a time to peek into the Bauers' lives, Charlie, I stood there, staring, *this is it now.*

"Emma, just keep at what you're doing for a short while, honey," I told her. "I'll be right back."

"Where are you going, Daddy?" She looked up.

"I left something downstairs" was the best I could come up with.

"Okay, Daddy," she said, leaning over her writing tablet, doing numbers.

I stepped outside, keeping Liz's door slightly ajar. My heart beat insistently. I felt certain, if Trudi came back up, I'd hear her approach on the stairs long before the third floor and I could get back in. The house was so old and creaky you could hear someone two floors below you with plenty of time to run back.

And often, her conversations with Mrs. Bainbridge could go on for minutes.

My heart picking up a beat, I stole across the landing and

edged her door open wider. I thought this was surely the craziest thing I'd ever done. Or the dumbest. Well, the second dumbest, I reminded myself, thinking back to the bar that night. I placed a stool I found inside to block the door from closing behind me and to be able to better hear downstairs. I was certain, once Trudi began her way back up, I'd have adequate warning. I'd probably even feel it on the floorboards. The hairs on my arms stood on edge.

I crept inside.

Their apartment was exactly how I'd seen it the last time I was in there. I was hit by the familiar smell of pipe tobacco. The place was clean, tidy, orderly. The same photographs in silver frames arranged on a round wood table, all brightly polished. The Tiffany-style lamps, emitting a soft glow. The love seat, fresh and plump, without a single wrinkle on it—embroidered pillows puffed out and neatly arranged. Covering the floor were dark, hand-loomed rugs.

Quickly, I went over and skimmed through a pile of record jackets next to the phonograph: Brahms, Beethoven, Berlioz, Liszt, even Benny Goodman and Cab Calloway. They obviously liked jazz.

Looking around, it seemed as ordinary as any apartment in the city.

No sign of her from downstairs.

Only one thing seemed to strike me as different from the last time I was in there—the sense that something was missing. I looked around, trying to determine exactly what that was, and finally, it hit me.

The book of Darwin's journeys that had been on the coffee table was no longer there.

Instead, there was an art book on the French Impressionists.

Why would the book be missing? I noticed a stack of large books on a shelf and went over and checked, but didn't see it there either.

Not exactly a crime, I thought, or proof of anything diabolical.

I took a scan around. I didn't know what I was even looking for: a large Nazi banner hung on the wall? Photographs of Hitler and Göring shaking the Bauers' hands; ones that they took down the second company would come in? Just something, I told myself. Anything. I'd know it when I saw it.

In any case, I saw nothing at all.

I went back to the front door and stuck out my ear. I could still hear the occasional sound of Trudi and Mrs. Bainbridge conversing downstairs. Maybe she had even invited her in for tea.

Feeling like I still had time, I went in and took a peek around the bedroom. I'd never been in there before, of course. My heart beat against my ribs. *Just find something, anything,* I exhorted myself. *There has to be something here, Charlie. Find it.* I knew the Bauers weren't who they said they were, yet as I scanned the room, there was nothing, not a single sign anywhere, to back up my suspicions. I opened their bedroom closet and peeked inside. On one side were his belongings, suits arranged in neat rows. On the other side, dresses and skirts. Earrings and necklaces in little boxes on the shelf. I took care not to disturb a thing or give any sign that someone had been here. Quickening my pace, I went over to their night tables. A stack of books. A leather-bound book of poems. Rilke. A copy of Thomas Mann. *Buddenbrooks.* In German.

Nothing at all.

In haste now, I went over to the dresser and rummaged through the drawers. Just clothes. I started to feel completely foolish when I stopped to think what I was doing. On the top of the dresser, in a glass bowl, there was some loose change and an old brass key.

I'd been in there for three minutes now. I'd better get out of there, I thought. I was already pressing my luck.

Disappointed, I headed back to the front hall, careful not to make noise on the floorboards. Before heading out, I looked around one last time to see if I was missing something. I'd found nothing. Not a thing to support my belief that anything untoward was going on. And maybe that's all that it was, I was starting to think: their beliefs. Maybe the Bauers were simply too ashamed to admit they admired the Nazi regime and had made up stories to mask their convictions. Maybe I had, as Liz had said, just wanted to find something on them and blown the whole thing out of proportion.

I looked at my watch. Five minutes now. Trudi might be heading back up any second. And what if she came back up and caught me here. What then? Then I'd never live it down with Liz. This whole thing had just been an exercise in futility. Maybe I had to give up this silly wild-goose chase once and for all.

As I put the stool back where I had found it and was about to exit, I noticed the hall closet near the front door. I figured, what the hell, I'd already gone this far. She wasn't coming up yet. I still had time. I went over and opened the closet doors. Inside were coats, boots, galoshes neatly arranged on the floor. Umbrellas hung over the rail. Nothing out of the ordinary again.

You'd better get out of here, Charlie.

In the corner I noticed an old black steamer trunk, like from a shipping line. With a hand-painted number seven on the side and a large, locked clasp. Blankets and linens were folded neatly on top of it. I listened for her coming back up the stairs, but still didn't hear anyone coming.

So what the hell . . .

I kneeled down and transferred the linens onto the floor. Then I tugged at the trunk's clasp—locked. I tried to see if there was any way I could lift the top at all, but no . . . It was locked tight.

The clasp and the hinges were kind of a burnished brass— antique.

Then something flashed inside me. Brass.

I ran back into the bedroom and found the old key I had spotted in the bowl on the dresser. It was a long shot, I knew, but it was brass and old and seemed to match the trunk's clasps. It looked like it might possibly work. I squeezed it in the keyhole and turned it, and to my delight, the lock opened cleanly. I flicked open the clasps, lifted the top, and peered inside. It had a musty, mildewy smell, just more linens and clothes—a blanket and a duvet cover. Not exactly the bonanza I was hoping for. I pulled a pile of folded sweaters off the top.

My eyes went wide in shock.

I was staring at the missing book by Darwin.

"Sonovabitch," I said.

The Voyage of the Beagle. The large tome in German that was on the coffee table my last time here. In the trunk. What was it possibly doing locked away in here? I picked the book up and flipped through the pages. Several of the page numbers had been circled in pen. And many individual words throughout had been circled or underlined as well, seemingly at random. The text was all in German, and while I spoke a bit, I didn't grasp what many of the words meant. But why had it been hidden away in here? Under lock and key. I just kept flipping through the pages. I knew I was onto something.

Why, Charlie?

I just kept staring.

Then I suddenly flashed back to the charred strips of paper I seen in the trash that day.

Numbers.

Though it had been a month, they were still fresh in my head—I'd memorized them—as if I'd seen them yesterday:

128 3 7. 14 12 3. 0300.

It had to be some kind of code.

I wished I could take the damn thing and try to figure it out. Someone should. Why had they locked it away in here? But then an idea hit me completely out of the blue.

I flipped to the page of the first number—128. Continuing, I counted down the lines to the line corresponding with the second number—3, then on a whim, over seven words—the third number—and came upon a word that indeed had been circled.

December.

It was the same in German. December. I sounded out the German words: "We skirted around into the harbor on the third of December. . . ."

Quickly, I flipped to page 14, the first of the second set of numbers I'd seen in the trash. In the same manner, I scrolled my finger down to the twelfth line and then across to the third word.

It too was circled. This time it was the word "*sechs,*" which I knew enough German to know was the number six. I read: "Six of us got in the launch . . ."

I put them together. December 6.

The last number was 0300. Could that be three A.M.?

December 6, 0300.

It could just be.

It damn well could be a code I'd fallen onto. And Darwin's *Voyage of the Beagle* was the key.

Suddenly I heard Trudi's voice, calling from below. "Yes, there's a Humphrey Bogart film at the Orpheum, Millie. We should go. Shall I ask Willi?"

It sounded as if she was at the bottom of the stairs.

Hurriedly, I put the Darwin back in the trunk. But as I did, I felt something hard and resistant beneath the padding. Metal. I had to get out of there. I didn't have much time. But consumed now, I folded back the blankets and sweaters to see what was underneath.

Again, my breath was stolen away.

It was a radio transmitter. I mean, I'd never seen one before—maybe in some Hitchcock film—but it was a dark gray box with some kind of a frequency gauge and knob, an antenna and headset. A transmitter.

That's all it could be.

And next to it, wrapped in a blue towel, I felt a gun.

A gun and a transmitter. The perfect Swiss couple.

What more proof did I need?

Suddenly the floorboards creaked and someone came up behind me. "What is that?" I heard. My heart climbed in my throat. I spun around, and to my relief, saw my daughter there, staring at me. She couldn't see exactly what was in the trunk, but just as bad, maybe worse, was that she had found me there—in the Bauers' apartment, rummaging through their closet. She may be only six, but she was in their company all the time. She could easily divulge this.

"Nothing, honey," I said, covering the gun and transmitter. "Just a phonograph. A toy."

"Uncle Willi and Aunt Trudi wouldn't be happy to see you do that, would they, Daddy?"

No, I suppose they wouldn't, my look back said. "Let's not say anything about this, peach," I said. "Okay? How about we let it be our little secret."

Her gaze drifted past me to the open trunk. "Okay."

Suddenly, from outside, I heard the thump of footsteps coming up the staircase. Trudi heading back up. *No way she can find us here.*

Quickly, I stuffed the linens back on top of the transmitter and lay the Darwin back on top, covering it like I had found it, and closed the trunk, quickly locking the clasps. I picked up the pile of bedding from the carpet and placed it neatly back on top.

We had to get out of there now.

"Come on, honey, *shhh,*" I said, and put my finger to my lips. I put the key back in the lock and twisted it closed. "Let's go."

By then, Trudi had already made her way up to the first floor. I leaped up and took hold of Emma's hand, and we headed to the door. Suddenly I looked down and realized I still had the trunk key in my hand. *My God . . .*

They'd know someone was in there.

I shot a glance to the bedroom and didn't think there was any way I could make it back there and put it back into the bowl on the dresser without her coming in and finding us there. But if I didn't, it was a sure thing they'd know someone had been inside.

Even worse, seen things.

Emma looked up at me and saw the whitened terror on my face. "Daddy, what's wrong?"

"Just stay there, honey."

I hurried back into the bedroom, not caring about noise now, and tossed the key in the bowl. But in my haste, it ringed around the edge of the bowl and instead of tumbling in, fell out.

It sat in plain sight on the dresser for anyone to see.

For an instant I just stared at it in horror. Paralyzed. But by that time I was already a step toward the door again and realized I'd never make it out if I went back for it now.

There was no choice but to get out of there. *Now*.

Feverishly, I ratcheted through whatever excuses I could think of in that instant—about Emma noticing the door was unlatched or hoping Aunt Trudi had some cake in there for her. Praying she would back me up and wouldn't give me away. I ran back out and took her by the hand, whispering frantically, "Let's go, honey." We slipped out to the landing through the front door. I was half expecting Trudi Bauer to be staring up at us from the bottom of the third-floor stairway, and I'd have to stumble guiltily through that excuse about Emma, and pray she wouldn't see right through me.

Instead, miraculously, she was at the bend at the foot of the staircase between the second and third floors, just about to turn up and catch us there.

I froze, caught in mid-breath.

Suddenly someone called out to her from behind. "Mrs. Bauer . . ."

It was Mrs. Shearer, coming up with the laundry.

To my elation, Trudi turned and looked behind her. "Ah, Mrs. Shearer, good afternoon."

I don't think she ever caught a glimpse of us slipping out of her apartment, only ten feet above her. But a moment later she and

Mrs. Shearer came up the stairs together and stared at Emma and me, standing there.

"Trudi." I nodded. I'm sure my voice cracked. "Mrs. Shearer. Emma and I were just heading out for a walk." I squeezed my daughter's hand, praying she wouldn't give me away.

Trudi's eyes seemed to drift from us to her open door. Had I left it cracked just a little farther open than when she had left? There was no more of the cheerful good nature in her demeanor as when we'd first met. Before I'd found that shredded message in her kitchen. What was clear now in her gaze was that she trusted me no more than I did her. Which was zero.

"Without your jackets?" Mrs. Shearer said, with kind of a curious expression. "It's almost November. A child could get her a whiff of cold, Mr. Mossman."

"Yes, sorry," I said, with a chagrined shrug. Inside, my heart careened back and forth against my ribs. "I forgot. Stupid of me. C'mon, Emma. . . ." I took her back inside 3A.

Before Mrs. Shearer even came back in I let out a deep, relieved breath, my heart pounding out of control and my body encased in sweat, my back pressed against the door.

"Are you all right, Daddy?"

All I could picture were Trudi's eyes going from me to Emma to her own slightly open front door, and the key to the Bauers' trunk sitting visibly on the dresser, no longer in the bowl, which she would see in a second and wonder, looking around the apartment with a rising beat in her heart, *Were they in here?*

"Yes, honey, everything's fine."

16

"Willi, come quickly!" Trudi Bauer said with alarm not two hours later as he stepped back into the apartment.

He put down his cane and took off his scarf and coat. He saw the peremptoriness that had come over his wife's pallid face. "What's happened, dear?"

"In here." She drew him into the bedroom.

She stood over their dresser and pointed to the glass bowl on top, and to the brass key lying next to it.

The trunk key.

"Did you happen to place that there?" she asked.

Willi looked at her and shrugged. "No."

"You didn't happen to go inside the trunk when I went out to the market earlier?"

"I haven't been in there since the last time we opened it the other day. What are you saying?"

"I'm saying that when I tidied up the room this morning, the key was where we always keep it. In the bowl. Not on the dresser."

As he began to absorb the importance of what she was telling him, the lines around Willi Bauer's eyes deepened. "You're certain of this, Trudi?"

"As certain as I am of my own name. Look, the counter is perfectly dusted. I cleaned it earlier. I would have noticed it here. And anyway, that is where we always keep it. It's not a thing to be uncertain of."

"No, it's not." Willi nodded, knotting his brow with concern and scratching his white mustache. "You're saying someone was in here?"

"This afternoon I left the door open a crack when I went downstairs to talk to Mrs. Bainbridge for a short while. I didn't have my door key handy. I was only gone a few minutes. And when I came back up, Emma and her father were standing right outside our door."

"If I'm not mistaken, it is their door too," Willi said.

"Yes, but you would had to have seen them. He was rigid as a board. It was like we came upon them completely unexpectedly and caught him in the act of something."

"We?"

"Mrs. Shearer and I. She was doing laundry downstairs. You would had to have seen his reaction. He muttered something about them going outside, but neither of them were wearing their coats. You were out. You know how chilly it was today. Would you take a child out in the cold in a flimsy dress? If I didn't know better I would have thought they were coming from *our* apartment."

"Our apartment?" Willi's eyes widened.

"Yes. And then I found *this* on the dresser." She held up the key. "This is not good, Willi."

"No, it is not good at all." He sat on the bed. "Is anything missing?" he asked. "Have you checked?"

"Of course. I went through the trunk as soon as I came home. Everything is there. Completely undisturbed. But I'm still worried. He's been snooping around since I caught him over those shredded messages in the trash."

Willi rested himself on the edge of the bed. He put his thumb and forefinger to his forehead in thought. Then nodded pensively. "This man is becoming far too much of a nuisance."

"A pest is a nuisance, Willi. This Mossman has become a threat. And threats . . ." She looked at him with a steeled determination in her eyes. "Must be dealt with."

"Please, Trudi . . . let's not get ahead of ourselves on this. He's a nobody. A nobody with a fancy degree and a felony conviction around his neck. Who would possibly believe a word he has to say on anything? He barely has a roof over his head."

"Still, he is no one's fool, Willi. You are underestimating this. And he saw the shredded messages last month. Who knows what he's put together. Now this . . . There's too much at stake, Willi. We have to find out what he knows."

Willi looked up at her. "That's a big step, Trudi. But yes, I agree."

"You are always slow to take the difficult steps, Willi. This must be done."

Willi exhaled a breath from his nose and nodded. For a moment he seemed lost in thought. "He and his wife have no hope of reconciling, do they?"

Trudi shook her head. "From what she tells me, no."

"Then there is a way. Still, in the meantime there is also a way we can be sure if he was in here or not."

Trudi looked at him.

"You said he was with Emma, didn't you?"

"Yes, but Willi, he's her father. Who knows where her loyalties lie now?"

"Her loyalties are with us. Do not doubt it. Our darling Emma will always talk to her Aunt Trudi and Uncle Willi," Willi said with a knowing smile. "Especially when there is a big slice of apple cake to entice her with, my dear."

"Yes, we must do whatever it takes, my husband, I agree. There is far too much at stake now for us not to be sure."

"Do not worry yourself." He patted her shoulders. "I have a way."

17

I made Emma promise that what she saw at the Bauers' would stay between us. That I was merely looking for my hat, which I thought I'd mistakenly left there, but that Willi and Trudi—or even Mommy, I told her—might get the wrong idea if they ever thought we had gone inside. I hated to manipulate her in that way, my own daughter, but what other choice did I have? The Bauers couldn't know we were in there. Or Liz, for that matter. There was so much at stake. I couldn't let what I'd seen come out to them.

And Emma promised she would keep this our little secret. Even if they tried to ask her about it. Even over a bowl of *schoggibirnen*.

But now what to do about what I saw?

I was sure it was a radio transmitter I had seen in the Bauers' closet. The meeting in the back room at Marienplatz might have been something one could overlook; seeing the burnt strips of paper with a lot of numbers was something I could never fully prove— and in any case, that evidence was long gone; and the jumble of

circled and underlined words in a book could be just random jot-
tings without those shredded numbers— nothing in and of itself.

But a transmitter! Hidden at the bottom of a steamer trunk
in their home. On top of everything. That was something the authorities would surely want to know about. Especially with all that
was going on in the world between the United States and Germany
as our countries lurched toward certain war. That was damning!
I didn't know the law, but I was sure having such a thing in one's
possession had to be illegal. Certainly the kind of thing people who
focused on such matters would want to know about.

But just who did I take this to?

My lawyer had already told me to stay clear of it. That this
wasn't his expertise. And I was pretty certain, the precise way
I'd come upon it, sneaking into their apartment, if not actually
breaking into it—well, certainly breaking into the steamer trunk—
wouldn't sit well with Sam at all. *You don't exactly have the perfect résumé to be pointing the finger at people,* about Nazis, he had
pointed out to me.

Still, this had to be something the police would want to be
aware of.

Or the FBI.

And I also knew it would kill Emma to lose her "auntie and
uncle," and that she might well not understand why—how could
a six-year-old possibly understand how people so apparently loving
could be trying to do harm. And even though I knew any investigation of them would inevitably be traced back to me—no matter
how diligently I pushed to keep myself out of it—and Emma might
well hold it against me, as might Liz—there was still a greater duty
here that had to be done. Far, far greater than the mere satisfaction I felt at being proven right about the Bauers. Spies were spies.

One's duty to country had to come first, didn't it? To a cause. What would Ben do, I asked myself? I didn't even have to answer. Whether the Bauers truly loved my little girl; whether they made the greatest strudel, or had found them Mrs. Shearer, and had been the best of friends and support to Liz when she needed someone at a trying time in her life, when I, her husband, had failed her, I spent the night going over and over what was the right thing to do. If there even was a right thing. If I could simply just look the other way. And let this go. For the sake of Emma.

Or do what I knew was the right thing. The only thing.

And I came up with only one answer.

The 19th Precinct on East Sixty-seventh Street served the entire Upper East Side, including all of Yorkville. It was a dreary, four-story brownstone building with high, arched windows, and looked like it had been built in the worst gloom of the early 1930s, with a dozen or so police cars angled on the street outside.

I went there the following day, and walked up to the duty officer who sat behind the elevated counter. He pushed aside some papers and looked at me.

"I have a complaint I'd like to register," I said.

"Nature of the complaint?" he replied officiously.

"It's difficult," I started to explain. "My wife has an apartment up on Ninetieth Street between Lex and Third. And I think the people across the hall from her might be German spies."

"Spies?" The balding cop sniffed with an amused roll of the eyes. "Hey, Eddie," he called to a colleague, "we got more spies."

"I'm not a crank," I said to him. "I have a doctorate in European history." Well, almost a doctorate, I meant. "I'm pretty sure what I have would interest the FBI."

The sergeant behind the desk looked at me plainly, seemingly sizing me up. "Name?"

"Mossman," I told him. "Charles."

"Mossman." He wrote it down on a pad and pointed to a bench. "Just wait over there."

He picked up the phone and rang someone, twisted around in his chair so I couldn't hear him, and then after a few seconds put the phone back on the cradle. "See Lieutenant Monahan." He pointed upward. "Third floor."

"Thanks." I walked up the two flights, uniformed cops and plainclothesman coming down past me, and got to a large bullpen of desks set back to back. About half of them were manned, the rest empty. I asked someone sitting near the front for Monahan's desk, and was pointed toward the back and a kind of pudgy, ruddy-faced detective with Brillo-like white hair, wearing a white shirt, loose striped tie, and suspenders.

"Take a seat," he said as I stopped in front of his desk, without getting up or even looking at me. The desk was cluttered. Shelves behind him were stacked with thick, bulging files. "You're . . . ?"

"Mossman," I said. "Charles. I spoke to the officer downstairs. . . ."

"Yes, Mossman," he said. He finished up some kind of report, then looked up finally and pushed his chair back. "All right . . . So you live up in Yorkville."

"My wife lives in Yorkville," I said. "With my daughter. We're separated."

"All right." He took out a new form. "And you live where?" he inquired.

"In Brooklyn. 157 Powers Street. I rent a room there."

"A room . . . So why don't you take this matter to Brooklyn," he shrugged perfunctorily, "if that's where you live?"

"Because what I have to say takes place here," I explained. He didn't even react. Just started writing. *Hey Eddie, more spies.* Did I end up with the most brusque and completely functionary detective in the precinct?

He jotted down my name and address and finally looked up at me, seemingly ready to listen. "All right, Mr. Mossman, you say you have a lead on some German spies. Your dime . . ."

Though I already had the feeling I was about to be pushing a large boulder up a very steep hill, I took him through everything I knew and had put together, starting with the first times I had met Willi and Trudi, and the kinds of visitors that were showing up at their door, *customers,* they called them. . . .

"Hold it a minute," he interrupted me right away. "I thought you said they're German?"

"I think they are German. But they claim to be Swiss. I can't know for sure. They say their family was from Germany, and German is definitely their first language."

"You realize the Swiss are neutral so far," he felt an urge to remind me, "in what's going on over there."

"I understand that," I said. I found my frustration starting to rise. "Can I go on?"

"Be my guest. I was just reminding you of the facts. . . ." He waved me onward. And I continued, describing the word Emma had overheard them using, *Lebensraum,* which I already knew was way over his head, or at least, way beyond his interest.

"Your daughter's six, you said?"

"Yes, six."

"And she's the one who overheard them using this word?" He rounded his eyes. "*Lebens-room?*"

"Lebens-*raum*," I corrected him. "It means elbow room."

"It could mean 'storm the Bastille' for all I care, Mr. Mossman, ain't no crime people speaking German. And to a six-year-old," he added. "So she's the witness?"

"I'm perfectly aware it's no crime," I said. "If you'd let me just go on . . . ?" I told him about the torn, burnt strips I had seen in their kitchen trash, a message of some kind, I was sure. "It could well be a code." But his interest didn't seem to peak any higher. "They seem to adore Emma, and my wife isn't happy with any of this." I shrugged.

"You and your wife fight a lot?" he asked.

"We used to. But what does that have to do with anything? I'm trying to tell you something important."

"And this Swiss couple have taken a liking to your daughter?" he said with plodding gray eyes.

"Yes. I was away for a while. She actually calls them her aunt and uncle. But . . ."

He jotted a note down, then looked back up at me. "You were saying . . ."

"I was telling you about these strips of paper I found. That it was a message, I'm sure. That she didn't want me to see. A bunch of numbers. But in a kind of pattern. Groups of three numbers. Like a code. I even think I might have found the key to the code."

"What makes you think it's not a telephone number or maybe the numbers racket?" he asked.

"Who tears a message into strips and then burns them?"

"Maybe someone who lost. Happens all the time. Truth is,

I can think of a dozen credible explanations. And so far I'm not hearing anything so credible on your end—"

"Look, I followed them one night," I said, cutting him off. "I know that might not be so kosher. But I did. Just to see where they went. And it was to this German beer hall on Second Avenue called Marienplatz. You know it?"

"No." Monahan shook his head. "Should I?"

"It's a known hangout for Nazi sympathizers and organizers up there."

"It is, huh? And how do you know that?"

"It just is. . . . Look, you guys just arrested twenty-six of them, for God's sake. I'm not making this up. I followed them there and saw the Bauers embraced by the owner and then go back to this meeting room, where they were all doing that Nazi salute they do. *Sieg Heil*-ing. With a Nazi banner on the wall behind them. So for all the effort they're putting into denying any association with Hitler, here they are being welcomed like heroes at a meeting where they're all saluting him. Tell me why?"

"I can't tell you why. Could there be any other possible explanation?"

"Well, I suppose I should mention they were in the beer business at some point," I said. "That they apparently had a small brewery."

"Yeah, that was good to mention," the detective said, "this being in a bar and all. . . ." He jotted it down. "That all?"

"No, it's not all," I said. It was clear I wasn't exactly knocking him over, and now this next part of the story got even trickier. "I don't want to say how—at least not right now—but I saw something the other day. In their apartment."

"And what is that?"

"A radio transmitter . . ."

"A radio transmitter?" This time his eyes did grow wide. "And you're sure of this?"

"I can't be one hundred percent sure, but that's what it appeared to me. It was about this big . . ." I stretched my hands about eighteen inches apart, "and black, had what looked like a frequency gauge on it and two knobs. An antenna and a headset. What else could it be?"

"I don't know what it could be." The lieutenant shrugged, looking at me. "I didn't see it."

"Look, like I told the officer downstairs, I'm not a crank. I was in the doctoral program in European history at Columbia. I'm not making this up. Or trying to waste anyone's time."

"And you found this transmitter exactly where?" The detective tapped his pen on his desk.

"In a closet. Inside a trunk."

He looked up at me again. "Inside their apartment?"

"I told you I didn't want to get specific on how I found it. Just that I did. And it should be of interest to someone. It's not legal to have that, is it?"

"I don't know if it is or it isn't. No more legal than maybe how you found it. And everything you're telling me pretty much hinges on the specifics, if you know what I mean? I assume they didn't invite you to rummage through their belongings. This trunk . . . it was locked?"

I blew a deep breath out my cheeks, knowing how this was going to play. "Yes."

"And you opened it somehow? Like with a key?"

I nodded again.

"And you obviously knew where this key was. Where did you say this trunk was? In a closet?"

"In the hall closet next to the front door," I said. "Yes."

"In the hall closet. And not in plain view, I assume?"

I took in another deep breath and shook my head. "No."

Now it was the detective's turn to exhale. "So you see what we got ourselves here, don't you? If you got this fancy degree like you say, you probably heard of a thing called unlawful search and entry. Was their front door locked as well?"

"No."

"It was just *what* . . . open?"

"Not just open," I said. "Kind of cracked."

"Cracked or kind of cracked?"

"Cracked," I said. I twisted in my seat.

"But the owners of the apartment . . ." He consulted his notes. "This Mr. or Mrs. Bauer, they weren't there at the time, I presume?"

"No." I cleared my throat. "Of course not. They weren't there."

He nodded with sort of a troubled frown and tapped his fingers into a steeple, kind of pensively. "You're sure it was a radio transmitter though? That's important."

"I'm pretty sure. Yes. And coupling it with the coded message I found . . ."

"You're the one who's claiming it was a code," the detective said.

"*And* the meeting with the Nazis at Marienplatz . . . ," I said, adding emphasis, "*and* this business about *Lebensraum* . . . It does all add up, doesn't it?"

"I don't know what it all adds up to, Mr. Mossman. I'm just listening. So anything else you want to add . . . ?"

"Yes. One more thing. There was a book in the trunk as well.

Charles Darwin's *Voyage of the Beagle*. In German. There were a lot of words and numbers circled and underlined. I think it might be the key to the code I spoke of."

"Again with the code," he said.

"Look, I'm laying something out that I think anyone who looks at these things would find troubling," I said, my voice rising an octave.

"Gimme a second," the lieutenant said, seeming to grow equally annoyed with me. He made some notes on his pad. "You got dates for all these . . . ?"

"Dates for what?"

"All these things you're describing. For the report."

"Not exact dates, no. I wasn't exactly taking notes. But yeah, I think I can put that together. Or at least close."

"Good." He scribbled something again. "That should do it for now. Oh, just one more thing from me. . . . Earlier, you said you were away." The detective looked up. "Where?"

I knew it was bound to come up. Sooner or later. And I knew it wasn't going to make the rest of what I'd had to say any more convincing. "In prison," I cleared my throat and said.

Now the detective's eyes really stretched wide. "In prison? You're on parole?"

"My sentence was commuted. I had a situation. You can look it up. I got into a fight. Outside this bar in Midtown. It was the night of the German Bund rally at Madison Square Garden two years ago. You remember, when all those Nazis got together. Anyway, someone got hurt. Killed. Accidentally. A kid."

"A kid?"

"Sixteen. I got into a tussle with a bunch of Nazi sympathizers who barged into the bar, and he was just passing by and got sent into a plate of broken glass. I spent two years up at the penitentiary in Auburn, New York, for it. Third-degree manslaughter." I sat back and let him absorb what I'd said.

"So now it's kind of making sense to me," he said.

"What's making sense?"

"Seems to me you got this thing against Nazi-lovers."

"What do you mean, a thing? I don't have a thing against them. Any more than half the world does. At the bar, I'd had a bunch to drink. The witnesses will tell you, this crew of them who barged in, they were an ugly group. Instigating and insulting. I went off. The poor kid just happened to be in the way. It's all in the trial proceedings."

"I'm sure it is." Monahan jotted some thoughts on his pad. Like he had me sized up.

"And this time, if you're even interested, this time it was all purely happenstance. While I was at Auburn, my wife moved to this apartment in Yorkville. This couple happened to be across the hall. I visit my daughter twice a week. That's all."

"Other than you followed them to that Nazi bar and broke into their apartment."

"I didn't break into their apartment," I huffed, my frustration rising now. "They left the door open. And this isn't about me, Officer. I'm reporting something serious here. The right people should know about it."

"Lieutenant," he said, glancing up at me.

"Huh?"

"It's Lieutenant," he said, pointing to the nameplate on his desk.

"Yes, Lieutenant," I corrected myself. "Sorry."

"So just one more thing. . . ." The detective tapped his pen on his desk and looked at me. "You still drink?"

I leveled my eyes back at him and looked at him squarely. "No."

"Not at all?"

"It's a condition of being with my daughter. So no."

"Good. Glad to see you're on the mend. So I think I got all I need. . . ." He finished scribbling a few notes, tapped the pages together, and then slid the stack across the desk to me. "Look it over and put your John Hancock on it. I want to thank you for coming in and doing your civic duty. That's how we find these people. People like you."

The way he said it made me think he would never look at it again.

"Will the FBI even get a look at this?" I questioned. "It's still valid, everything I've said. Whether I followed them or not, or went inside their apartment. There's still a transmitter there."

"See that file . . . ?" He twisted around and pointed with his thumb to a bulging file on the shelf. It was maybe ten inches thick, and barely covered what looked like a hundred reports stuffed inside. Maybe five hundred. "People in Yorkville who think they uncovered Nazi spies."

People who hadn't spent two years in jail; and who didn't have a history of drinking, he didn't have to add.

He chuffed, "If I only had a nickel, right . . . ?"

"No one's going to even see this, are they?" I looked at my own report, discouraged. Desultorily, I added my signature and address at the bottom of the last page.

"Don't worry, everything gets reported," the lieutenant said. "You can take that to the bank. Your Swiss grandparents will be on someone's desk. The right people. Mr. . . ." He glanced down, double-checking my name on the report. ". . . Mossman, right?"

18

For the next week, I didn't hear anything back on the police visit, nor did I expect to. Or from Liz *or* the Bauers about how I had made my way into their apartment.

Still, I did my best to steer clear of them. I'd done what I could about what I'd found. The rest . . . law enforcement and the government would have to take it from here. If they even heard about it. My day job was expanding. A Marymount colleague had a friend who needed some help in his appliance store down on Houston Street. And I found I actually liked the work. Assistant manager in the repairs department. It was becoming increasingly clear I was never going to get a job teaching anytime soon.

And something else happened that same week that changed my life.

I met someone.

Without even meaning to. Isn't that the way it happens? I was heading back from the shop to the elevated trains on Third on my

way back to Brooklyn. I was thinking maybe I'd take in a film tonight. On my own. *Suspicion* with Cary Grant was at the RKO on
Grand Avenue. The weather was particularly chilly for November,
and all of New York was bundled in winter coats.

I was walking, glancing at the headlines of the afternoon *Her-
ald Tribune.*

Suddenly a gust of wind rose up, and in front of me, crossing
Houston, a young woman cried out as papers she was carrying in
sort of a bundle flew into the air. Six or seven of them, perhaps,
scattering onto the street.

"Here, let me help," I said, springing into action. I kneeled
and, one by one, picked them up off the sidewalk. One literally
right from under someone's heel as they passed by. They were a
little soiled now, whatever they were: typed, in some kind of order.
But they all seemed salvageable.

"Oh, that one too!" The woman pointed to another blown like
a leaf into the busy traffic on Houston.

I sprinted after it.

"Careful!" she called after me, hugging herself with worry.
"You'll be—"

I darted into the street, raised my hand to stop an oncoming
truck, which put on the brakes and gave a honk at me. Quickly,
I picked up the sheet. A car had run over it and turned it into a
dirty mess.

"Here," I said, hopping back onto the sidewalk, presenting
them back to her. "I hope they're okay."

She was around thirty, and pretty, in a dark cloth coat, her
curly brown hair tucked under a flat wool cap. Her eyes were olive,
but bright, and sparkling, mostly with gratitude. "You could have
injured yourself," she said. "Thank you so much." She placed all

the pages back in a folder. I detected an accent. Dutch. French. In any case, not from around here.

"A little soiled." I shrugged. "But a little grime from the streets will only give them character," I said. "Whatever they are."

"My *dissertation*," she said. French it was, it seemed. "How do you say it, I think . . . my thesis . . . ?" I now saw the papers were all written in French. "I am having it translated."

"Your thesis? What's it on?" I asked.

"What it is on . . . ?" She seemed surprised at my question. Cars honked as they went by. "Why, Jung. And it's my only copy. If it was gone . . ." She showed me a folder with many more pages in it and shook her head, as if to say, *a real mess.* "You see, I had the address I was going here. . . ." She adjusted her bundle and showed me a piece of paper clipped to the first page. *144 East 2nd St.* "A tutor. He is helping me to get into a graduate program here. And . . ." She flung her hand in the air. "Then suddenly, *le vent! Disaster!*"

"*Le grand vent,*" I said. "Though Jung might say you were sabotaging your own efforts to gain admission," I said, "by carrying your work that way." I grinned sheepishly.

"Jung, maybe . . ." She laughed. "More likely Freud. Anyway, you have saved me from such a fate. These streets, they are all new to me."

"You're French?"

"*Oui.* From Honfleur. A small town in Normandy. Do you know?"

"I was in Rouen once. At the cathedral."

"Yes, the Monets are in your museum here. I saw them. Yes, that is nearby. Anyway," she glanced at her watch and her eyes went wide with alarm, "I must go. To my appointment. The time. I was late to start. . . ."

"Of course. It's only around the corner anyway." I pointed out the route for her. "This is Lafayette, and the next street over is Bowery. Then you make a right on Second Street."

"This person is very important, I am told, so I must hurry. But maybe some other time . . ." She hesitated. "We . . ."

"We could meet," I said, delighted, picking up on what I was hoping she was trying to say. Who wouldn't be, gazing into those vibrant green eyes.

"Well, I suppose, yes. We could. I owe you a proper thanks for being so brave."

"How long is your appointment?" I asked, suddenly having an idea.

"My appointment?" She hesitated. "Why, an hour. If I can even make it." She smiled guiltily with another glance at her watch. "I'm so late."

"Then go. But how about I wait for you afterward?"

"Wait . . . ?"

"Why not? Look, I don't mean to be too forward. But I've just finished work and I've got nothing planned. Say in that coffee shop over there. . . ." I pointed to one across the street where I'd had lunch a few times. "We could have a coffee."

"Well, we could have a coffee, yes. Why not?" she agreed. "You have been the savior of my day. I'd be happy to have a *café* with you. In an hour . . . ?"

"Great. I'll be waiting then. Don't you reconsider now. Dr. Jung would be angry."

"No, I won't." She laughed. Then she glanced at her watch and her eyes went wide again. "But for now I must go! Goodbye."

"Yes, go," I said. "I'll be there. In an hour." She waved and rushed off into the crowd. "Hey, what's your name?" I called after her.

She turned. *"Pardon?"*

"Your name!"

She had one hand grasping her bundle and the other holding on to her hat as the wind picked up. An image of her that I would always picture in my mind.

"Noelle."

For the next hour I sat in the coffee shop, not wanting to miss her in case she came back early. It had been years since someone smiled at me that way, and it felt truly uplifting. Years. Since that altercation at the bar—no, going back to since Ben had died the year before—it seemed only tragedy had followed me. I thought of Liz. *I've moved on, Charlie.* She'd left no doubt of how she wanted to make our separation final. So, why not? I thought. Why not open myself to someone. I'd paid my penance. I was trying to do the right things in my life. I deserved a little happiness too.

Meanwhile I cautioned myself not to get ahead of myself. A cup of coffee was a long way from a real date.

First, let's see if she even comes back, I told myself.

The hour passed. I glanced to the front door maybe a hundred times, and each time it flooded my heart with expectation. But still, no sign of her. I checked my watch over and over. At an hour and fifteen minutes, a little doubt began to set in. Maybe she'd reconsidered. Perhaps I'd been too forward. Meeting someone on the street that way, so happenstance, though I might have a feeling about it, the possibilities, who knew if she felt the same? Or if she was married? I never even looked for a ring. Or had a guy? I began to feel sure she wouldn't show, thinking, how did I even deserve such good fortune? A girl as pretty as her. Still, fate *had* intervened in that moment.

After an hour and twenty minutes, I looked at my watch one last time in discouragement and decided maybe I should just go home. She wasn't coming. I could still catch that show at the Orpheum.

Then the café door opened, and to my delight, in walked Noelle, still clutching her manuscript like a baby in her arms. My heart soared. She looked around awkwardly, those large emerald eyes searching the tables.

I stood up.

She smiled as she came upon me. "I am so sorry." She hurried over, putting her bundle down. "He would not stop and I did not know how to leave. He kept asking if I would like coffee. I'm glad you're still here."

"I'm glad you came," I said. "Here . . ." I helped her off with her coat. She had a pretty beige sweater underneath and a colorful scarf tied around her neck. A petite, appealing figure. "Please, sit down. I admit, I was starting to have my doubts."

"Well, I couldn't just let your mind go off in the wrong direction with all those thoughts of Jung and Freud, could I?" she said. She took a seat. "So, I am Noelle," she announced formally, and put out her hand. "I think we said that."

"And I'm Charlie," I said, shaking it.

"Charlie, Charles . . ." She had a warm smile like Ingrid Bergman and I was immediately swept under it. "Very nice to meet you, Charlie."

Over coffee she said how she was new to this country. She'd been here for just five months. A refugee, from France, through

Lisbon. She lived in a women's boardinghouse on Thirtieth Street. "I was very lucky to get a visa to be here," she said. "The circumstances of my trip were not straightforward."

I didn't ask her to explain.

She said she'd been in graduate school in Paris before the war. In psychology.

She asked about me and I told her I was separated, and that I had a daughter. "She's six. A real young lady," I said, beaming. That I had been a university instructor myself, in European history, but the job came to an end. I declined to go into just how. The market for such positions was very tight now, I said. The economy had still not fully come back. "But I still read papers for my old department head at Columbia."

"You read papers?"

"Exams. *Dissertations*," I said in my best French accent. "Like yours."

"You mean they are in *French*?" she said, wide-eyed, then broke into a smile. It was clear she was teasing me.

"No." I smiled back. "Though sometimes they might sound that way. And mostly they manage to stay out of the street."

She laughed.

"It is very hard to start over here in school," she said, exhaling. "My records, they do not exist anymore. Due to the war. Do you think America will come in?"

"Into the war? Yes," I said. "I do. In the end, it will be hard to stay out."

"Good. I hope so," she said, pinching her cheeks. "I have no love for the Bosch."

The mention of the war seemed to make her downcast. "But

let's not talk about such topics. Please, tell me about your life here in New York. That would interest me very much."

The next time I saw her, only a few days later, for dinner, she told me how she was alone here in the United States. That her parents were in a Nazi prison back in France. "Political prisoners," she explained. "My father was the mayor of our town. He was very important there, how you say, a dignitary, but he would not welcome them." That was over a year ago. She knew nothing of their fates. "There is no one who can tell me anything," she said. "It is very hard."

A brother, in the French army, had died in the German blitz-krieg, defending the Maginot Line.

"I'm sorry," I said. "Are you Jewish?"

"Jewish? No." She shook her head. "Though sometimes I feel like one."

"Why?"

"Because the Bosch," she shrugged, "they've taken everything from me."

Her eyes averted downward and I reached across the table and touched her hand. "I'm Jewish," I said. "And I lost a brother too. In the Spanish Civil War." I told her about Ben, and how I felt a bit responsible.

"Your brother fought in Spain?" she asked, surprised.

"For the Republicans, of course. He was really a fellow of prin-ciple. A doctor. I think you would have liked him."

"There are heroes all over your family," Noelle said brightly, I think referring to my dash into the street to rescue her papers. "To your brother, then." She raised her glass.

"And to your parents," I added. All I had was my cup of coffee. But it was enough. "I hope you find out they're okay."

"Thank you very much, Charles. I do too. Do you mind if I call you Charles?"

"No, Charles is fine. That's what my mother calls me."

"I see you don't drink?" she asked with an air of curiosity. "We French, we wouldn't know how to eat supper without a glass or two of wine."

"I used to. Not so much now," I said, hedging a full explanation. A topic for another time. "Maybe one day I'll have a toast with you."

"I will look forward to it." She smiled.

"As will I."

I hadn't felt so at ease with another person since my early years with Liz. I'd almost forgotten what it was like to feel the basic joy of human connection. Of someone interested in me. Who treated me with kindness and warmth and not judgment for what I had done. I said, "Maybe I can speak to someone at the college and see if they can help you continue with your studies."

"Is that possible? If you could, I would be in your debt forever," Noelle said, her eyes bright and alive.

Brickman still had some clout at Fordham. "I'll give it a try."

"I am very glad to have met you, Charles Mossman," she announced, and nodded.

"And I, you, Noelle."

"So now, please tell me about your daughter."

I had a photo of us in my wallet and I brought it out. "She's great. She draws like a champ and loves to do puzzles." How grown-up she had become. How she lived in a brownstone in Yorkville with my wife. My soon-to-be *ex*-wife. "In fact . . ."

It was clear from what she had told me that she had no love for Germans. They had imprisoned her parents and killed her only brother. I felt sure I could trust her with what was going on.

"In fact . . . I have a little situation," I decided to share with her. "There's this couple that lives next to door to them. They're Swiss, or at least that's what they claim to be. . . ."

"What do you mean they claim to be Swiss?"

"It wouldn't surprise me," I decided to spill the beans, "if they were straight from Berlin."

"Berlin?"

"That's right." I laid out the story of the Bauers.

I didn't see any reason to hold it back. I'd done all I could on the matter. It was out of my hands now. And it would be nice to hear someone else's view on it, a European, even from strictly a moral perspective of what to do.

So I went through it. All of it.

"It's hard to say." Noelle listened to my story intently. "Swiss, German, even French, the borders are all not very far apart there."

"All right, I admit that. But then why would they need a transmitter," I asked, playing my trump card, "if they're indeed Swiss?"

"A transmitter?" Noelle said, shocked. "You didn't tell me that. You mean, to signal someone."

"Why else, I figure." I told her about what I'd found in the closet, deciding for now to leave out the details of exactly how I had come upon it, which didn't sound so dashing in America or France. "Apparently, they're not illegal, still . . . It's not even a crime to be a Nazi sympathizer here in America. We're not at war. I mean, look at Charles Lindbergh. To you French he's a hero, but you know he visited the German High Command in 1938 and even received a medal from them. But for most people, getting back to the Bauers, the telephone seems to work just fine unless you have matters you want to keep secret."

"What matters?" She leaned forward as if I was telling her a great spy story.

"Well, I don't know for sure." But I told her about watching them go into the Nazi meeting at the German beer hall, though I painted it as more coincidental, that I had simply come upon them on the street and saw them go in. "It doesn't sound like people who share the same view of Germans that you do, does it? Masquerading as the kindest, sweetest couple in the world. My daughter can't get enough of them. And it would hurt her terribly if they were proven to be something else. My wife tells me to just stay out of it. She's got her head in the sand. But I'm certain . . . I'm certain I'm right about exactly what they are. It all adds up, doesn't it?"

"It does. Yes. The way you tell it. In France this would not be allowed to go on without a discussion."

"I even went to the police."

"*Le milicia*. You did?"

"Turns out, there's a hundred cases just like this they're already following up on. They even showed me the file. Most of them are cranks, of course."

"*Je ne sais pas,* cranks, Charles?" she asked, shrugging.

"Sorry. Meddlesome grandmother-types who hear noises next door. Or crazy people. They just don't lead anywhere. I don't know what to do now. I'm not crazy, am I?"

She shook her head. "No, I don't think you are crazy, Charles. The Abwehr have their tentacles in many countries. I assure you. I have seen it firsthand."

"My brother was killed in such a way. By one of his own staff, who was actually an enemy saboteur. Anyway, I can't just go around making accusations not backed up by fact. I'm afraid I've got some things in my past."

Noelle looked at me sympathetically. "We all have a past, Charles. In war, we all do."

"These things are big, Noelle. I'm actually afraid to tell you."

"But you can tell me," she said, touching my hand.

"You're sure? You won't think less of me?"

"You have my word."

So I did. I told her about what happened in the bar two years ago and my time in prison. Which was also why I no longer was teaching at the university, I had to admit. Or married. Or drank alcohol, I finally said.

"Oh, I see."

I waited. I half expected her to get up and excuse herself and leave.

But she didn't leave. She stayed. In fact, she reached out and took my hand in hers. Softly. And I felt real tenderness in it. How long it had been since someone actually touched me that way.

"I know this must be very painful for you, Charles."

"There isn't a day that goes by when I don't see that kid. When I'm not haunted by his face, and wish there was a way I could make it up to him."

I wrapped my thumb around her fingers.

"But there's not. He's dead. I tried contacting his parents several times, but they're not interested. All I can do is live my life the right way now. And this is part of it. Doing what's necessary. Though I have to be careful. I can't make any untrue accusations. It will finish me. With Liz. And Emma."

"Look, you offered to help me, Charles." She took in a breath. "Maybe I can help you as well."

"Help? How?"

"I may know someone too. Someone in this line of work you are looking for. In fact, he works for your own State Department."

"The State Department?" My eyes widened with surprise.

"Yes. In Washington, D.C. He is a friend of mine."

"How do you know this person?" I asked. Someone who had only been in the country six months, having this kind of contact?

Noelle's eyes shifted downward. "The circumstances of how I got here were not straightforward either," she said. "We all have things in our past. Getting to this country required some assistance. He helped me with my visa to remain here. He has many contacts. I am sure he would know precisely what to do with what you know. If you can trust telling him?"

"Let me think about it," I said. A high-ranking contact at the State Department. I had better be one hundred percent right in whatever I accused the Bauers of.

"I promise, Charles, he is discreet as well as resourceful. You will see."

I was dying to know what she was keeping to herself—what lay behind the veil of this beautiful woman. *We all have things in our past.* But she had fled from a country at war. A refugee. Things happen in war. And it wasn't my business.

"I promise he will know what the right thing is to do. Will you talk with him?"

I looked at her. Her wide eyes locked on me. Emerald and liquid. Her innocent face said all it had to about earnestness and trust. The truth was, with my past, I didn't have anyone else to go to.

"Why not?" I nodded. I'd wanted what I knew to reach the right people, and this beautiful, mysterious girl, in this country for only months, how fitting she would be the one to get me there.

"How did I get so lucky as to bump into you?" I said, and smiled. "I guess we have kind of a pact then." I put out my hand to shake.

"Yes, a pact." Her smile was broad and beaming. I think she felt joy, real joy, that I would even trust her. "We can help each other, Mr. Charles Mossman."

"To each other." I lifted my water glass. We shook hands.

19

At exactly eight P.M. that same night, the Boston Philharmonic radio program went on RCA and Willi Bauer adjusted the knob of the transmitter to the correct frequency.

Over the sweet tones of Tchaikovsky (String Concerto in D Major), a message came in from the embassy in Canada in a series of staccato beeps, and he meticulously jotted them down.

Not the Swiss embassy, of course. In truth, there was nothing even remotely Swiss about the Bauers other than their passports.

But from the German legation in Ottawa.

From a source inside the embassy known to them only as Freddy, who was in direct contact with Admiral Canaris's office at Abwehr headquarters in Berlin.

And with their chief spy apparatus in the United States.

These were the remnants of the Duquense group. Who had passed secrets from the Nordon plant in New Jersey and even the United States Military Academy itself, on their new Sherman tank design and the Nordon bomb site back to Germany.

The Bauers' so-called customers—actually accountants and engineers—were in the employ of these companies.

Many had been rounded up, but a second cell was still in operation. Willi and Trudi's cell. With an even more important mission to perform. Once war was declared. Which was inevitable.

Willi took the numbers down and just as quickly Trudi referenced them against the Darwin book, which was the key. One by one she leafed to the indicated pages and located the appropriate lines and words.

Soon she had it all written out in German. *Onkel Teddy kommt immer noch planmaessig an von London.* Uncle Teddy still arriving from London on schedule.

Just as planned. The same date and time. What they'd already transcribed from a similar message just a month ago. The one Charlie had stared at in the trash. That Trudi had failed to destroy completely:

128 3 7. 14 12 3. 0300.

We'll be drinking lots of beer together, the message continued. Which, of course, meant something important to them as well.

Finally, when there were no beeps to come, Willi tapped back that the message was received.

"Two weeks." Willi looked at Trudi with satisfaction. "And we'll be fully operational."

"Yes, it's all going as planned," Trudi said.

Operation Prospero.

Now there were only the beautiful notes of the Tchaikovsky in the background. They prepared to put the radio back in the trunk.

"It's time to move this out of here," Trudi said, indicating the transmitter. "Just in case. We can't be too careful." They had still not determined if Charles Mossman had rummaged through the closet, given the misplaced key.

"Maybe to the brewery," Willi said. There were a hundred places they could conceal it there. "Tomorrow."

"Yes, tomorrow," Trudi agreed.

She tore off the message from the pad. Tore off the sheet underneath it as well, as Willi's heavy hand had slightly indented the message onto the following page. She ripped the two pages into strips as Willi struck up a match and lit them.

"Shall we?" Together, they watched the strips burn to ash in the ashtray.

"This time," he patted her arm with a smile, "we will watch them burn to the very end."

Suddenly there was a knock at the door.

Trudi's gaze flashed toward Willi. They always lived with the fear of unexpected visitors, but now, since this business with Emma's father, even more. And with everything about now, at just the wrong time.

Trudi grabbed the transmitter and took it into the bedroom, while Willi broke up the charred embers of the burnt message into unrecognizable ash. Then he ran and dumped the ashtray into the garbage.

"Yes, in a minute!" he called.

Trudi came back out and they each gave the other a look of reassurance as Willi went to the door. "Yes, who is it?" He brushed the wrinkles out of his vest and unlatched the door.

To his relief it was little Emma in her pajamas. And Liz.

"By all means, come in, come in . . . ," he said with a smile.

"We didn't mean to bother you," Liz said. "I hope it's okay.

Emma just wanted you to see what she made at school, before she went to bed." It was a drawing of a green valley with snowcapped mountains and a pretty blond girl in a long skirt.

"It's Heidi," Emma said.

"My goodness, how beautiful!" Trudi exclaimed. "And just like I described it to you."

"*Wunderbar!*" announced Willi, clapping his approval.

Emma beamed.

"And maybe some hot chocolate before bed?" Trudi said. "For the deserving artist."

"Can I, Mommy?"

"Sure, honey, I don't see why not," Liz said.

Trudi headed to the kitchen. "Right in here, my darling."

On her way, Emma's eyes seemed drawn to the hall closet, which was open. To the steamer trunk inside it, the top of which was open too.

"With a dollop of *schlag* just to put an exclamation point on it," Trudi said.

Then Emma said something that made Willi turn and Trudi come back out. And then look at each other. Out of the mouths of babes, Trudi thought. Their question answered.

Emma was pointing toward the open trunk. "Did you ever find my daddy's hat?" she asked them.

20

"Mr. Mossman . . ." There was a knock at my boarding room door.

My tiny room. The few clothes I had filling up the small closet. The handful of books on the night table. *The Rise and Fall of the Roman Empire*. Dos Passos. A shared bathroom down the hall. "Call for you. Downstairs."

I rolled off the bed and threw on a shirt. I went downstairs to the one telephone used for the three boarders here. I didn't receive many calls. My lawyer. A teaching prospect or two that never panned out. My boss at the store. I hadn't given my number out to too many people. I was hoping it was someone replying to my applications for a teaching job.

"Hello?" I got on with anticipation.

"How could you, Charlie?" Liz's voice said, with ire in it.

"How could I what?" I said, though in fact I suspected what she was referring to.

"Involve Emma in this insane little game of yours."

"What game, Liz?" Though I hardly had to ask the question, and waited for her to lay it on me.

She said, "We were across the hall at Willi and Trudi's earlier tonight. Their hall closet was open. Emma looked in it and you know what she asked them . . . ?"

My stomach plunged like a heavy weight tumbling from the top of a skyscraper.

"She asked them if they had found your hat, Charlie."

I sucked in a breath and winced as if a bolt of pain shot through me. "Shit."

"Your daughter, Charlie . . . You used your six-year-old daughter as what, a prop to break into our neighbors' apartment? You can't stop yourself with this irrational suspicion you have of them. And who do you have to bring into it, but Emma. . . . You ought to be ashamed of yourself, Charlie."

It stung.

And I barely had an answer.

"That's not exactly the way it happened, Liz," I said, stammering to defend myself. "I didn't break in. At least not like you say. The door was left open. And I didn't bring Emma in with me. She happened to come in later while I was in there. I swear. And as for the hat, I had to come up with some excuse so as not to get her any deeper involved."

"In covering up this unfounded vendetta of yours . . . Then you break into a locked trunk of theirs. Do you know they could call the police on you? Do you know what the consequences would be of that?"

"I do know." I exhaled and sat down in a chair. I didn't have much to say in defense of that one.

"Don't you have some condition of your parole that speaks

to the commission of a crime? You could go back to jail, Charlie. And for the record, I just want you to know, the fucking trunk was open when we got there. They showed me what was inside. Nothing. Just some old blankets and sweaters. Unless you think they're actually hiding something from *us* now. So my six-year-old doesn't turn them in."

"Then they emptied it, Liz, 'cause there definitely was something in there when I looked. A radio transmitter. I saw it with my own eyes. You could even ask Emma. She saw it too. And for the record, I actually already went to the police."

"You did what?"

"What was I supposed to do, Liz? This isn't a game, as you call it. It's real. Just tell me, why don't you, why anyone would need a radio transmitter except to send or receive messages they don't want anyone else to read?"

"I don't know, Charlie. I don't know why someone would use a transmitter. I don't know that they actually had one." Her voice raised in frustration. "That's what you say. So tell me, what exactly did the police have to say on this?"

What did the police say? I couldn't tell her what the police said. I didn't answer.

"I'm not surprised," she said. "Since there was nothing fucking there."

"Well, they moved it then. They must have gotten suspicious when they found Emma and me on the landing. Which speaks volumes in itself, Liz. Why would they get it out of there? I'm only sorry that Emma had to be in the middle of it."

"You know what she said, Charlie? She looked around at us, our blank faces, and said, 'Did I say a wrong word, Mommy?'"

Like *Lebensraum*.

I'd told her, *Let's keep this between us, darling.*

"I feel terrible about that, Liz. I'll have to talk with her. I promise, from now on—"

"There's not going to be a 'from now on,' Charlie. At least, not on this. I don't want you here anymore. Not for a while. If you are, I'm going to call the police and tell them exactly what happened from my point of view, and have you taken off the premises. If Trudi and Willi are too nice at heart not to do that themselves, I'll do it for them. You can't go around breaking into people's homes."

"Liz, don't. I told you, I didn't break in."

"Then snooping. Whatever you want to call it. And using your daughter as a cover to gain entry."

"I told you, I didn't use her as a cover." I knew how I was beginning to sound. "And what's important isn't that I did some irregular things, but that these people who you think of as your friends are not who they say they are—"

"I don't care, Charlie. They are to me. I only know that if I told your parole officer what you did I don't think he'd be particularly happy with you."

"Don't, Liz. Please . . ." She was right. I could end up back in jail for this.

"Charlie, listen to me. I don't want you seeing Emma right now. Hear me? I'm going to talk to my lawyer. And I think you should talk to yours. From now on, we play it by the book."

"Liz, please . . ."

"Don't 'Liz, please,' me, Charlie. Just don't come by. If you do, I'll call the police on you myself. I'm not going to deny you access to Emma. That would hurt her too much. And through it all, you're a good father. I know that. But I will insist that certain conditions be put on it. And from a personal perspective, Charlie, you've got to put this craziness behind you. You're starting to act like the old Charlie. And it's scaring me. For the moment, I'll tell her you had to go on a business trip for a job or something. Until we work something out more permanent. But I'm begging you, Charlie, for the sake of our daughter. Stop. I mean it. Stop."

21

I was disconsolate and stayed to myself over the next few days. My time with Emma was the most important thing in my life for me. I talked with Sam Goldrich, who agreed to handle things for me and save me the cost of a divorce attorney. Which I honestly couldn't afford. It's not like we had tons of assets to fight over.

But my afternoons without Emma were empty, like being back in prison again for me.

A few days later, Noelle called and said that her friend from the State Department happened to be in New York, and he could see me if I still wanted.

I didn't know what was right anymore, but the right people ought to know about them, the Bauers, I figured. If I told them what I knew then I could wash my hands of it. So I said yes, that would be great. Noelle was now about the only good thing happening in my life.

"His name is Warren Latimer," she said. "I'll arrange it."

So we met in Latimer's hotel room at the Chesterfield Hotel

in New York, a quiet, unassuming place with a smoky wood-and-brass lobby in the West Forties. After a few moments all together in small talk, Noelle said she would leave the two of us alone. "I'll see you tomorrow," she said to me, and reached up on her toes and gave me a peck on the cheek.

"Thanks for doing this," I said, and squeezed her arm affectionately.

The State Department man was tall and slight, with thin lips, wire-rimmed glasses, distinguished-looking gray hair on his temples, and narrow deep-set eyes. His handshake was firm and decisive. He had on gray pin-striped suit pants, the jacket draped over a chair. His striped tie was clasped by a pin. Suspenders over his blue shirt. His cuff links were shiny and gold. He directed me to a small table, and from a gold card case inside his jacket pocket he took out his card. *Director. Department of Immigrant Affairs*, it read, *U.S. Department of State*, in blue, important lettering.

"I wish I could give you one of mine," I said with a sheepish grin, shrugging.

"No matter," he replied. "Please sit down. Noelle tells me you have a story to tell me."

"Thanks. I think I do."

We chatted, about Noelle at first, and while he was vague on how he knew her and what their history was, he did remark how she was a "charming and beautiful woman," and how "any friend of hers would be considered a friend of mine as well."

"I feel the same," I said, though in truth I barely knew her.

Latimer struck me as the kind of Ivy League blueblood who was fed from the top college straight into the top realms of government, specifically the State Department. Measured, tight-lipped, played it close to the vest. Still, he was relaxed and easy to talk to.

He went to the rolling bar in the room and picked out a bottle. Glenfiddich. "Scotch?" He checked his watch. "It's after five."

"Coffee would be great," I said. Though a scotch would have made this a whole lot easier for me. It wasn't every day I pointed the finger at someone to the U.S. government. I admit I was feeling some nerves.

"Relax," he said, brushing it off with an offhand wave, "it's just the two of us." He poured my coffee and sat down. He opened his tie clip and loosened his tie. "So start from the beginning," he said. "Assume I know nothing. Let me hear what you have to say."

I kept it all as vague as I could, not fully knowing who Latimer was and how he fit in, and not wanting to have this boomerang back on me, if my accusations were somehow wrong or if he gave what I said to the wrong people. Until I knew I could trust him. So I painted the picture of this Swiss couple I'd met in my ex-wife's apartment building.

"You're divorced then?" he asked. He took out an Old Gold from another gold case and pulled the ashtray over to him.

"Shortly. And it's probably best to get something else out of the way up front. . . ." I shrugged. "I've recently spent some time in prison."

"Yes. Noelle did brief me on that. She didn't want me to be surprised. She said you got into a scuffle a while back with some Nazi supporters . . . ? And someone was hurt."

"Not hurt, killed. He fell through a glass window. Man two. I was released four months ago. Though it's not really pertinent to anything I have to tell you. I just wanted it out up front." I ran him through the events that happened the night of the Madison Square Garden rally and the drunken punch I'd thrown; my time at the Auburn penitentiary, and how it had cost me dearly—how

I used to teach history at Columbia and now I was barely able to find a job.

"Columbia. I studied there myself," Latimer said. "Under Arnold Krause. Know him?"

I knew Krause's name, of course. He was head of the economics department when I was there. A Nobel Laureate. He might as well have been John Maynard Keynes. Miles and miles above my pay station. "Then I went on to Yale for a law degree," Latimer said. "But getting back to your story . . ." He beckoned me onward. "You don't drink?"

"Not anymore." I took a sip of coffee. "In light of what happened."

"Commendable." He nodded graciously, and put his scotch down.

"Please, go ahead. And I should also admit up front, in what I'm going to say, I've done some things that may not sound one hundred percent kosher. . . ."

"Kosher . . . ?" He squinted his narrow, reed-blue eyes.

"Legal. By the book. But what's important, I hope you'll agree, is what I've found, not precisely how I found it. I fully admit I'm not exactly the FBI here."

"Yes, exactly, Mr. Mossman," Latimer said, and smiled. "You're not the FBI. I get it. So let's begin."

I looked at him and leaned forward, elbows on knees. "There are these people who live across from my ex-wife up in Yorkville," I started in. "On East Ninetieth Street here in New York. They're Swiss, or claim to be, around sixty maybe. Could be older. They've been in this country a while. They even once had a small brewery in town. Called Old Berliner. My wife and my daughter think they're the nicest, most charming couple in the world, and when

I met them, it was easy to see why. I did too." I took him through everything that had happened. Starting with the word *Lebensraum,* which he didn't need explained. Then the people always showing up there—"customers," Trudi called them, even after it turned out their business had closed a year before. And then the one I happened to see at The Purple Tulip, a known pro-Nazi hangout.

"And how do you know this place is pro-Nazi?" Latimer asked.

"It's just known to be," I said. "Even back before I went to prison. We used to live in the neighborhood."

"All right." He took out a small notepad. "You mind if I take some notes?" He peered above his wire-rim glasses.

"No," I said at first, then upon reflection: "Well, on second thought, maybe I do. How about this first go-round, you just hear what I have to say?"

"All right, Mr. Mossman, that's fair." He blew out a plume of smoke and closed the notepad. "I'm all yours."

I told him about the undestroyed strip of paper I had come across in Trudi's trash bin that because of the sequence of numbers on it I presumed was some kind of code; carefully describing the look I'd received from Trudi Bauer while caught standing over it, conveying it was clearly something I wasn't supposed to see. And unlike with Monahan at the police station, he didn't interrupt me a dozen times with his skeptical barbs. He just let me go on, taking it all in in a measured, thoughtful manner. "That got me curious," I said, "so one night I followed them when I knew they were heading out. I know that sounds a bit cloak-and-dagger. . . ." To that, he merely smiled. And I told him about the Marienplatz restaurant and the *Sieg Heil*-ing group of men in the back room there, and why would they go to such effort to hide their Nazi sympathies if they weren't up to something? "But I still didn't have anything really concrete," I admitted. "We all read about these twenty-six Nazi agents the FBI arrested. . . ."

"Yes." Latimer nodded. "A good haul."

"Engineers and accountants, marketing people . . . Right under our noses."

"Fortunate how that all worked out," Latimer said, "but, as I'm sure you know, sympathy for the Nazi cause, even now, is not a criminal offense in this country."

"Yes, I know, of course. Even in our own government, it appears. That's been made clear to me a dozen times. That's why I felt I had to go one step further."

"Further . . . ?" Latimer stared at me.

"Yes. I was at Emma's a few weeks ago and saw they had left their apartment door ajar. I know it's maybe not what I should have done. I said before I'd done a few things that weren't kosher. But I snuck inside."

"You broke in?" Latimer's narrow eyes went wide.

"Snuck in, is more like it, I would say. Maybe there's a difference. But I did go to the police with it, though they seemed to not have much interest."

"You went to the police?" He blinked, surprised. "That was before or after you snuck in?"

"Well, after." I shrugged. "With what I had. Anyway, I found this old steamer trunk inside and in it . . ."

"You found a trunk *where*, Mr. Mossman?"

"In the hall closet."

"In *their* hall closet. Open . . . ?"

I shook my head. "No. I managed to find the key. It was in a small bowl in the bedroom."

"I didn't imagine it was. Anyway, you certainly made your

way around the place." He sniffed, amused. "Kind of like the Three Bears."

"Look, like I said, everything I've done may not have been a hundred percent by the book. Still, I looked inside it and I'm pretty sure I found something really important."

"I'm listening, Mr. Mossman. What?"

"A radio transmitter," I said.

Latimer's gray eyebrows arched wide. "A radio transmitter? You say you're *pretty* sure?"

"I mean, I've never seen one before. Only in the movies. But yes, I'm sure. I mean, it had knobs and gauges and an antenna and a headset. And what would anyone need a transmitter for unless they had something to hide, right?"

"One might draw that conclusion." Latimer seemed to agree. "But I see what you're saying here. And why it would be concerning."

"See? These people may pose as Swiss, but everything about them shouts German. Which they're going to great lengths to hide. And I even think I might have a lead on how they communicate."

"What do you mean by a *lead*?" Latimer asked.

"I think it's possible I may have broken their code."

I explained about the book on Darwin. And the State Department man leaned back in his chair, took off his glasses, and blew out of stream of smoke. "There are concerns, of course," he said measuredly, "about what you might call a fifth column, if you're familiar with that term? About Nazi agents, embedded deep into the fabric of life here, who might be spies. Or worse?"

"Worse?" I said.

"Potential saboteurs. Should our nations ever be at war. Which is looking increasingly more likely these days."

Everything he was saying fit together for me. Music to my ears. I explained I did know the term. That my brother had fought and died for the Republicans there. "So I was right?" I said. "To pursue this? To do what I did?"

"I'm not the expert here, you understand. That's for others to decide. I can't say what would be admissible and what would not be in a court of law. But I think it's something the right people would definitely want to know about. Are you prepared to be a little more specific with me? About who these people are. Give us an affidavit in writing?"

"An affidavit . . ." I hesitated. I thought, *What if I'm somehow wrong? Then what? And what if Liz holds it against me?* She already warned me to stay out of it. I now had to get my daughter back through custody. Was it worth being further withheld from Emma just to prove my instincts on the Bauers had been correct? Would this prove that what I did was right to Liz or would it only make it worse? Without solid evidence. "You know, my personal history doesn't exactly make me the most compelling accuser," I said.

"I assure you whatever you say will be held in the strictest confidence."

"Witness Number One, huh . . . ? Still, they'll know it was from me. Liz would know. And anyway, I'm told whatever was in the apartment has been moved."

"Moved. Told by whom?"

"By my wife. Or my soon-to-be ex-wife. My daughter admitted we were in there. How about you let me think on it," I said. "Regarding the affidavit. Maybe at our next meeting."

"And how do you propose we set that up?" he asked.

"I have your card." I picked it up and looked it over again. Immigrant Affairs. "Or through Noelle."

"I've found it's best to nip these budding networks before they have a chance to take root," Latimer said. "There's no telling how long they've been at it. How many are involved. Or what their ultimate goal is."

"I understand."

"But that transmitter does suggest to me they have a larger network supporting them, of course."

"You mean like what, Berlin?" I asked.

"Who's to say? But I assure you they didn't purchase it at Macy's, that's all."

"No, of course not," I said. "So you believe me?" I felt a rush of validation spread through me. At last, someone did.

"Let's just say you don't strike me as a crackpot in the least. But just to be clear," Latimer probed one more time, "you're saying the New York City Police know all this?"

"They have a file there as thick as the phone book." I stretched my fingers apart as wide as they'd go. "Filled with people making similar accusations. My sense is, no one will ever even read my report. The detective I met with—"

"You met with where?"

"At the Nineteenth Precinct. He just looked at me as some kind of Nazi-hater because of my past. That I was trying to build some kind of case against them, because of my run-in at the bar and my time in prison."

"And are you?"

"Am I what?"

"Are you simply just trying to build some kind of case . . . ?"

I looked at him directly. "You heard my story."

"Yes, I did. I did hear your story." He stamped out his Old Gold. "And for the record, Mr. Mossman, that's not what I think at all. You can be sure." Latimer rubbed his jaw. "And do you recall this detective's name?"

"I do. But maybe we can keep that for the next meeting as well," I said.

"All right. I guess I can understand your hesitation. Anyway, it's been eye-opening to talk to you on this, Mr. Mossman." Latimer stood up. "And I hope you do decide to come forward. Shortly. I think you've done your country a great service. Shall we agree to stay in touch?"

"Yes. Of course," I said, placing his card in my pocket.

"Then I look forward to hearing from you. At a time when we can be a bit more specific." He walked me over to the door. "It's important. And please wish Noelle my best. And by all means let me know if you come up with anything more."

"Anything more?"

"Why, evidence, of course," he said. He put his hand out and with the other, patted me firmly on the back.

"I will," I said, and shook his hand. Then I headed out the door.

22

I was elated. I felt vindicated. Someone finally believed me. Someone who could actually do something about it. And take this to the right people. People who could prove my suspicions. I left knowing I had done the right thing.

Though it occurred to me, other than through Noelle, I knew nothing at all about Warren Latimer.

That night I stared over and over at his fancy card. *United States Department of State. Director. Immigration Affairs.* It was all on the up and up.

And I wondered, just how had he and Noelle met?

If I did what he asked me to do, "get more specific" on what I had said, put names to my story, give up the Bauers, I realized I'd be putting a lot of my life in his hands. Foremost, my relationship with my wife and daughter. Noelle claimed he was discreet, and I trusted her. In his job you'd have to be. And that he was someone who would know precisely what to do. Which I trusted too.

But what if the whole thing fell down in pieces all around me?

What if Feds rushed in, put the Bauers in cuffs, and rummaged through the apartment? Turned their whole lives upside down, and then found nothing?

Nothing but two law-abiding people who, regardless of their political opinions, had not committed a crime.

Surely Liz and Emma would never forgive me for that.

For the embarrassment caused to their friends.

For ignoring Liz's warnings to put my own cocksure theories aside.

So the next day I called the number on Latimer's card. 202-331-4000. I needed to know that the State Department man was even who he claimed to be. That I wasn't dealing with a fraud.

After three short rings, an operator answered. "United States Department of State."

I asked for Latimer's extension. "3219, please."

"Hold the line while I connect you."

I still didn't know exactly what he had done for Noelle, and I admit, that had me thinking. She had said, *You are not the only one whose past has been difficult, Charles.* She was a person of secrets too. How exactly had their paths crossed? What had Latimer done for her? I wanted to know everything about her. I had to admit, she was beginning to captivate me. *In war, we all have stories. . . .*

"Department of Immigrant Affairs." A secretary finally picked up. "Mr. Latimer's office."

"Mr. Latimer, please."

So far so good.

"Mr. Latimer will be out of the office today," the secretary said, putting me at ease. He had told me he would be in New York another day. "He's not expected to return until tomorrow. Can I take a message, please?"

I was about to leave my name, when suddenly a wave of cautiousness hit me. That perhaps I was getting ahead of myself. That in bringing in the Feds, I'd be putting myself on the line. With my history and all the things I'd done wrong. I grew scared. Just like Monahan, they might not believe me. So I merely cleared my throat and said back, "No, I'll call him then, thank you," and put the phone back on the line.

I was sweating. I felt like I had one foot dangling over a ledge and only caught myself at the last instant.

But at least now I knew that he was for real.

That night I took Noelle out to the Old Heidelberg café in Yorkville. It was about the only place I knew, other than the Horn & Hardart near my room in Brooklyn, where I stood the chance of being treated like a big shot. I wanted to thank her for setting me up with someone as important as her friend in Washington. And I admit, I was hoping to impress her as well.

We sat at a table manned by my old waiter, Karl.

We met outside the restaurant, and this time the kiss on my cheek when she came up to me seemed a lot more real.

"Thank you for introducing me to Mr. Latimer," I said after we were seated. She was wearing a fitted green dress with a floral brooch above her breast. Her short hair was brushed out with curls around her ears.

"It's my pleasure. He's a very important man," Noelle replied. "I am sure he can help you. We can help each other like we said. I'm happy to."

"I'm thinking about what he asked of me. I held some things back from him," I admitted. "It's difficult."

"I understand, Charles. It is difficult to find yourself in a situation where you are giving evidence against someone."

"That's not it. Not exactly. It's Liz. My wife. She's made it clear she thinks I've crossed the line on this. She's asked me not to see my daughter for a while. Doing this would only make things worse."

"Oh." Noelle's brown eyes grew halting. I could see sadness in them. "Why?"

"Because I involved Emma. Because I'm pointing the finger at their friends. Who she believes in strongly. I know she'll eventually give in. I mean, at some point she has to see—Emma needs me. She adores our time together. But it's a part of the divorce proceeding now. I just wish I could put something indisputable in front of her that proves I'm not completely crazy."

"You will." Noelle reached across for my hand. "You're not crazy. It will all work out, Charles. I have a sense about these things."

I squeezed her hand back. "Well, so far you certainly seem to."

That made her smile.

"So how did your wife find out," Noelle inquired, "about being inside her friend's apartment, if you don't mind me asking? Maybe it was that snoopy housekeeper you mentioned?"

"Oh, did I tell you about Mrs. Shearer?" I said. I honestly couldn't recall.

"Yes, you told me about her when you described being inside your neighbor's apartment . . . ," Noelle reminded me.

"Oh. Anyway, no, it wasn't her. It was Emma. She was in their apartment the other day and asked whether I'd found the hat I was looking for, which was the flimsy excuse I made up for why I was snooping around in there. Anyway, I appreciate your optimism, Noelle. It makes it easier for me."

"A daughter needs her father, Charles. And I'm sure she loves you. So have the police not been back in touch with you?" she asked.

I hesitated. I truly didn't want to involve her in any more of this. I wanted to keep her separate. Look how that had gone with Emma. Still, I guess Noelle was already involved. Through Warren Latimer. And in truth, I was dying to know how their paths had crossed too.

"You know you can talk to me about this too," she said, looking deeply at me. "I can keep a secret. And sometimes a woman's perspective can go a long way to make things clearer."

"Yes, on that I agree. Anyway, no, the police haven't been back in touch with me yet. I have the feeling my report is on the bottom of a large, undisturbed pile."

"Well, they will." She nodded and squeezed my hand again. "You'll see. This will all work out. I know it. And you will be a big hero, Charles Mossman." She smiled. "You will get more 'specific' soon."

I stared at her. The adorable curls around her ears. Her sparkling and liquid green eyes. I felt myself falling a bit. Maybe more than a bit. And I couldn't grab on to anything to stop myself. I didn't have much of a job, I was getting divorced, and my past didn't exactly recommend anyone for me. Still, I felt Noelle was looking past all that. "Can I do something forward?" I asked.

"Forward?" She smiled. "And why not?"

"You won't take offense?"

"Offense? From you, Charles? Of course not."

I leaned toward her and placed a kiss softly on her lips. They parted slightly, willing, and she didn't pull back. Not one bit. I realized I'd wanted to do this since the first time I saw her. I didn't want it to end. When I finally pulled away, she just looked back at me and smiled, eyes twinkling. "And why would I take offense at just a kiss?"

"I don't know. I thought maybe it was too early. This is only our third time together. And people might be looking."

"Well, I think we should do something to celebrate this time, don't you?"

"Excellent idea. What?"

"How about a toast of champagne. You said you would have one with me one day. Tonight would be perfect."

I hesitated. I hadn't had a taste of liquor in over two years. Still, one little glass of champagne. . . . On such an occasion.

"Why not?" I agreed. I raised my hand and motioned to Karl, who came over.

"Two glasses of champagne," I said. "And try not to break the bank, Karl. But something nice."

"Yes, Mr. Mossman." He smiled, pleased. "I know just the thing."

"And no one is looking, Charles." Noelle smiled, her hand over mine.

Our champagne came. We toasted. "France's loss is my gain," I said. And of course, one became two. It was inevitable. I didn't want this dinner to end. I felt my head swimming a bit. Not just from the alcohol, but from the moment. Being with her. The tingling I was feeling all over. Afterward, we nuzzled up close to each other in the cab. She looked up at me and I gave her another kiss.

"Where shall we go?" I said. I was embarrassed to invite her home to my sparse room. A chair, a dresser, and a bed. A bathroom down the hall. "Maybe a nightclub?" I was prepared to spend all of my savings if it could keep this night going.

"My roommate is away." She looked up at me and smiled coyly. "Twentieth Street and Second Avenue," she told the cabbie, before I could even agree.

23

We were kissing as soon as we got into her apartment.

Before.

On the street, as soon as we got out of the cab, entwined in each other's arms. Stumbling up the two flights of stairs, laughing and giggling more than saying anything. Unlocking her door and then tripping awkwardly around in the dark, and finally tumbling onto the couch.

"I don't want to do the wrong thing," I said, my hands all over her. Noelle's body was small and tight and I felt the contours of her breasts under her dress and she didn't stop me. "I don't know anything about you," I said.

"You know all you need to know, Charles Mossman," she said.

Though part of me looked back at her and thought, *That isn't true.*

I unzipped the back of her dress. She put up her arms and let it wiggle to the floor.

"You're not, Charles. You're not doing the wrong thing at all," she said in her bra and girdle. Her body was just as inviting as I'd imagined. Diminutive and shapely and tight. She put my hand on her breast and met my eyes, a glimmer of mischief sparkling in them. "You're not."

I hadn't been with a ton of women. Just three before Liz, and two were drunken one-night stands in college. Liz had been my best friend, but she was still a little shy and reserved when it came to sex. As was I, if truth be told.

But Noelle . . . She opened my belt and took down my drawers. She reached down and put her hand on me. I sprang completely alive. She eased me over to the bed and stood in front of me.

I wanted to know every secret she held; every piece of her she had withheld from me; every part of her past that had brought her here and brought us together.

"Charles Mossman . . . ," she murmured, looking into my eyes, inviting me on.

"Noelle Brisson." I looked back at her. I sat, pulled her girdle down, held her by the waist, and eased her onto my lap.

"Wait," she said, with a cat's-eyed smile, putting up a finger. She stroked me gently, urging me on, then smiled, nuzzled herself knowingly between my legs, and bent her head down over me.

After, we lay there, in the tousled sheets. I felt her steady breathing next to me as she napped. A pure, silent sleep. I wrapped my arm around her breasts and felt the sheen of sweat on her sleeping body and nuzzled myself against her rump.

I was falling for her, I knew.

Falling—and nothing to catch hold of me as I did.

I had no idea how fate had interceded to bring Noelle into my life. A life that had been barren of love and empty of feeling for so long. In which I felt unworthy to allow myself to feel anything good. How was I so lucky? *Le grand vent* . . . I thought back with a smile. A gust of wind, her pages scattering. "My *dissertation*," she'd cried out. And I was there.

I looked around at the sparsely decorated room. It was strange, I didn't see any personal belongings anywhere. Of course, she shared it with a friend, and clearly they rented it as transients just as I rented mine. Month to month. Everything in it came with the lease. She had probably come here with only a small suitcase of clothes and her papers. Still, I was surprised not to see a single photograph, not even of her parents back in France. Who were now in a camp somewhere. All I knew was that she had come into my life and reignited it with joy and now passion.

With possibility.

And I didn't want to sit in judgment of even a sliver of it. I was just happy, grateful, that it had happened.

I thought back on the evening we'd just spent. That first kiss when she came up to me on the sidewalk. Did she know then where it would lead? Had she wanted this too? I thought, I'd broken my vow with those toasts of champagne, my first drinks of alcohol since that fateful night in the bar. God would forgive me. I smiled. He had to, if He knew it would lead to something this perfect. Snuggling next to her in the cab, barely uttering a word, our bodies tingling with hushed anticipation of what would happen next.

Still, something nagged at me. A tremor pulsing deep inside. Like that devious voice of temptation that had long been silent, reappearing back on my shoulder. Telling me it couldn't last, what I was feeling. I'd screw it up. Somehow. Like I always did.

No, I won't, not this time.

Maybe it was no more than just the simple fear of trusting that this was truly real.

Lying there, I let my mind drift, and it left Noelle and her sweet, sleeping body, and seemed to settle like a nagging weight on the question of just how much more deeply I should get involved with Latimer. I'd already told the New York police everything I knew. I held nothing back. I thought maybe I could just merely refer Latimer to them and not get myself any deeper.

They could handle it any way they wanted from there.

I was sure that if Liz could only see I was right about the Bauers I could regain her trust. She'd have to let me back into Emma's life. The Bauers clearly had already moved the transmitter I'd found. And the book by Darwin. *The closet was empty, Charlie.* That transmitter was the only tangible piece of evidence I had on them. The rest . . . The rest could all just be put off to my prior run-ins with Nazis, the overzealous machinations of my own vengeful mind.

I knew it was too late for Liz and me. Here, at long last, I finally felt free of her. Free to pursue happiness again. But I did need to make her see I wasn't making it all up. That I really wasn't "the old Charlie" again, the one who had let her down so many times. The one who she had grown to distrust.

Yes, it was indeed too late for us . . . But it wasn't too late for me and my daughter.

And I had to do whatever I could do to get that back.

Next to me, Noelle stirred, murmuring. "Are you okay, Charles?" she asked.

"Yes, yes, I'm okay," I said. "I'm perfect. Go back to sleep."

I wrapped my arms around her tighter and inhaled the fresh scent of her perfume.

Whatever I could do.

But as I allowed myself to drift off, a welcoming sleep to calm my worries, something did snake its way into my mind. Like a hidden electrical line, woven through rooms of a large house, something buried deeply in me that maybe Noelle had awakened, which now came alive. I sat up and opened my eyes. Oddly, it took me all the way back to those strips of paper I'd seen in Trudi's kitchen. Torn, with the edges burnt.

Numbers on them.

Numbers.

And the ones I had stared at that hadn't been destroyed. That I now saw again clearly.

128 3 7. 14 12 3. 0300.

I thought back to paging through the Darwin.

December 6. What if it was a date, after all? And a time.

0300.

Three A.M.

What if something was set to happen then? Something big and that only I knew about and could put together.

Why else would they hide the book in the trunk and destroy the message?

What if it was just me who had seen it and knew?

I had two choices, I lay there thinking. I could turn over what I knew to Latimer—and he could pass it on to his people. People who could do something about it. *He's a very important man,* Noelle had said.

But in the end, what did I really have? A possible code with nothing tangible to support the charge. The trunk was empty now. The book gone. The burnt strips of paper were long disposed of. I realized that there was no way Latimer could turn this over to anyone, have them review my testimony, in all likelihood have to interview *me*, then start an investigation into the Bauers—even if they did believe me; even if they did accept my story as told—in time to stop whatever might be happening from taking place.

Today was *the 4th. December 6th* was *in two days*.

"You'd be a damn fool," the voice on my shoulder warned. The voice of reason. Suddenly reappearing. "Look where it's got you before."

"Oh, do it," countered his opposite, my little devil, always urging me on. "It's the only way to know for sure."

The Bauers might be up to something. And I was the only one who knew anything might be happening.

Next to me, Noelle nuzzled against me, emerging from sleep again. "Charles, your mind is elsewhere, I think?"

"No, it's not," I said, tightening my arms around her. "It's right here. With you."

"Good." She smiled. She wedged her knee between my legs and began to rub it in a slow rhythm against my thigh. In seconds I came alive. She smiled, recognizing it, and eased her hand under the sheet. "In that case," she said, her eyes twinkling, "perhaps we can consider doing that again."

24

Two nights later, I stood across the street from Liz's brownstone once again, huddled in the shadow beneath the staircase of the brownstone across from them. It was 10 P.M. If something was indeed taking place that night, I knew the when, but not the where, and I wanted to make sure I was early enough to witness whatever took place.

If something was indeed taking place.

This time I had a small camera I had plunked down forty dollars for, in order to document whatever I found.

It was raw that night—a chilly, damp, early December evening, and I huddled in my wool barn jacket and bounced on my toes to ward off the cold. Across the street, on the third floor, Liz's lights were still on. I knew Emma was asleep in the next room; her shades were dark. I hadn't seen her in two weeks now, and this was as close as I'd gotten in that time, alone, outside their apartment, in the dark and rain. Thinking of my little girl.

The Bauers' lights were still on as well, but dimmed.

I waited.

At ten thirty, Liz's lights went out, but the Bauers' stayed lit. The sound of footsteps clattering on concrete came up beside me suddenly and I stepped back underneath the stairs as a couple, huddled under an umbrella, hurried by. I conjured up the fear of someone from the government spotting me standing outside the Bauers' building. Someone who would come up to me and ask for my ID. Who was maybe watching their apartment as well. How would I explain that one away? But it was always only the footsteps of ordinary people passing by. A woman in a long cloth coat heading back to her apartment in the very building I was using as my cover. Making me step back into the shadows to keep from being seen. Or a couple, arm in arm, walking down the street, slanting into the rain. The occasional taxi whooshing by.

Around eleven, four Chesterfields into a new pack, a dark sedan drove slowly up the block.

I stepped back into the darkness.

It slowed for a second in front of the Bauers' brownstone and then went on, and I thought nothing of it. Two minutes later, it came around again. No one got out. I watched closely, trying to make out whoever was inside. A Ford, it appeared to me. Dark gray. All I could see was the shape of a man in a hat behind the wheel. So I waited. A minute or so later the lights in the Bauers' apartment suddenly went out.

I was either right about this—that something was indeed afoot—or they were merely turning in and I was in for a long, cold, unrewarding night.

The man in the car rolled down his window and flicked a cigarette onto the street. He turned toward me and a shiver traveled down my spine. I was sure he had spotted me there and was staring right at me.

I ducked back in the shadow of the staircase.

To my relief, he simply turned back and looked away.

In another minute or so, the front door of the brownstone suddenly opened and the Bauers came out on the landing. My heart sprang alive with vindication. Without even acknowledging the car, they took a long, watchful look up and down the block—I was sure, to make sure no one was observing them leaving. Spotting nothing suspicious, Willi took Trudi's arm and they quickly came down the stairs and climbed into the backseat of the car.

It was 11 P.M. and they were heading out for the evening?

Something *was* happening.

The car door closed and the Ford drove off at a slow pace. Maybe making sure they weren't followed. I tucked the camera inside my jacket and came out from under the staircase, about twenty yards behind. I followed it to the end of the block, where their car stopped at a red light on Lexington, signaling a left turn. I quickened my pace and grabbed a photo of the license plate as best I could. At the corner I spotted a free taxi slowing and put up my hand for it to stop. Before the light changed, I hopped in. "You see that car over there?" I pointed to the Ford.

"I see it," the cabbie replied.

"Follow it. Wherever it goes."

"You a cop?" The driver turned around, in a flat wool cap, plaid shirt, and woolen vest, and looked at me. "A gumshoe maybe?"

"My wife." I looked back at him and shrugged, unable to come up with anything better. "Any problem?" I asked. "Money's the same."

"I don't got no problem," the driver said, turning forward. "No problem at all."

"Just make sure you stay a ways behind," I said, waiting for the light to change.

"Don't get all antsy. Ain't the first time someone's asked me to play detective," the driver said.

On green, the Ford pulled out and made a left onto Lex and then to Third, and at the corner, its turn signal went on again, signaling another turn. East.

My cab accelerated slowly, waiting for the Ford to make its turn, and when it did, the cabbie stayed about thirty yards behind and turned on Ninety-second as well, just making the light. When the light changed again, we followed him across to Second, and then all the way to First Avenue.

"I know what it's like, buddy," he said, seeing me lean forward, trying to get a look at it ahead of us. "I drove days, till I came home one day with a leg of lamb for Easter and found my wife with my . . . Well, why would you wanna hear all that? You got your own issues."

"Sorry," I said distractedly. I wasn't listening. "Look, they're turning. Stay behind them."

"Don't worry, don't worry," he said. "Not my first dance, mister."

Crossing First, they continued toward the river. The cabbie waited till they had gotten halfway down the block, then he accelerated to make the light after them.

"Bad to let this thing take control of you, buddy," he said. I ignored him. "It'll turn your blood to rotgut. Next you'll start drinking, and—"

"Look." I saw the car pull up in front of a building halfway down the block toward York. "Let me off here," I instructed him. We had just pulled up at the light. I stuffed a five in his hand for the one-fifty ride. "Thanks, buddy. Appreciate it."

"Hope you work it all out," he called after me. "If you don't you—"

I jumped out of the cab and shut the door.

The Ford had stopped in front of a large building and I hurried across the street against the light, staying well out of sight. It was 11:20 P.M. now and traffic was sparse. I cautiously made my way down the opposite side of the street. I was able to see the Bauers climb out of the car and quickly head inside the building. Whoever was driving got out as well, in a hat and long coat, but he remained on the sidewalk by the entrance, hands in pockets, as if standing guard.

Something clearly was going on. A sixty-year-old couple didn't head out at a time when everyone else was heading to bed. I only prayed I could get close enough to the building to see what it was.

I crept as close as I could without attracting attention, my heartbeat going rat-tat-tat, trying to stay out of the beam of the bright streetlamps across the street. Every time the lookout turned away—it was a cold and damp night, and he didn't look happy to be there—I crept a little closer.

In front of the building, there was a folding, corrugated metal door to what looked like a delivery zone for two trucks.

I made out large, chiseled letters engraved in the stone above the entrance. *ATIA*.

ATIA?

It looked like a firehouse. Then I recalled what Trudi Bauer had told me about their business.

We still rent it out.

Creeping forward, I was able to make out the entire name. *HELVATIA.*

We were at their old brewery. What was going on here now?

Suddenly, the metal door shot up with a loud clatter and the lookout spun around. There was a delivery truck sitting in the loading bay, facing the street. The lookout, satisfied there was no one about, took a last 180-degree scan at the seemingly deserted street and went inside. Which gave me the freedom to run up a little closer, snapping a photo of the Ford on the street and the delivery truck's license plate as well. I ducked behind a car parked across the street.

I felt my heartbeat thumping at twice its normal rate. What else could I do but wait?

A short while later, two men emerged from the building, rolling a pushcart with what looked like two large metal kegs on it.

Beer kegs, they looked like to me.

What were the Bauers up to here?

The truck had a loading ramp hooked up behind it and the man and the lookout wheeled the heavy kegs up the ramp and into the truck's cargo bay. In the dim light of the loading area I finally got a glimpse of the second man.

My heart slammed to a stop.

It was Curtis. The brownstone's janitor.

Nicest people in the world, he had said of the Bauers.

What the hell was he doing here?

Curtis and the lookout reemerged from the truck, the rolling cart empty, and headed back inside the brewery. No sign of the Bauers.

For a moment, the truck was left completely unguarded, the coast clear.

I was dying to know what was inside. By the time I'd be able to tell Latimer about this, whatever they were loading would be long disposed of, and I was pretty confident in saying this wasn't your normal beer delivery.

Anyway, the brewery had been closed for over a year.

Crouched down, I scampered across the street and into the loading area, where I put myself behind a wall of boxes and crates that were piled high about ten feet away. From there, I tried to get a glimpse inside the open truck. I heard voices again. Bending low, I saw Curtis and the lookout, who was a large, dough-faced man, come back out wheeling another two kegs.

"You first," Curtis instructed the man.

Dough-Face climbed up the ramp. They both grunted in exertion as they rolled the two heavy kegs inside the truck. Then, their footsteps heavy, they offloaded them inside; I heard the clang of each one striking the truck's floor as they obviously stood them upright. Then they wheeled the rolling cart out again and after another couple of minutes, came out a third time and did it all over again. Now there were at least six kegs in the back of the truck. Beer? I doubted. It made no sense to me. All I knew was that it was after midnight, the Bauers were here, Curtis was somehow helping them. Something was going on.

As they went inside the building one more time, I decided I had to take a closer look.

I knew it was crazy. I had no idea how to explain it if they found me here. But I needed proof of what they were doing. And I was more caught up in knowing than I was thinking about the danger. I heard their voices trail off inside the building. My heart picked up again with anticipation. *Now.* I scurried out from my hiding place and up into the cargo bay of the truck. I was looking at two rows of four beer kegs and then another row of two, taking up about a quarter of the cargo space, with a large tarp resting on them. I racked my brain—what could they be doing delivering beer at this hour? The only answer I came up with, the only thing that made sense to me given the secrecy about what they were doing, was that they weren't filled with beer—especially with Curtis and Trudi Bauer here. So what was it then? And why would it need to have been communicated in code, a code that only I had stumbled onto? Unless it was something far more sinister? I snapped off three shots of the inside of the truck and prepared to run back out and scoot back to my hiding place.

Suddenly the door to the adjacent office opened and I heard voices again. Close by.

This time, Willi's and Trudi's voices.

I froze.

If they found me here, I was cooked. I'd never be able to explain.

"You ride in the car, my dear," Willi said. "Freddy will drive. I will go with Kurt in the truck."

Kurt? No longer Curtis?

"As long as we all know the way," Trudi replied.

"Kurt knows the way. He's been there. Please, we have to get along now," he said to all, loudly clapping his hands. *"Schnell, schnell!"*

Friedrich. Kurt? Schnell? *What was going on?*

I glanced at the truck's open cargo door and knew I had no chance to get out now. I was trapped. Careful not to make a sound, I ducked behind the farthest row of four kegs, nearest the driver's cab. There was a narrow window for the driver to peer into the cargo bay right above me. Hugging my camera, I took the edge of the tarp and lifted it over me.

I heard Curtis come back out and stand just outside the cargo cab, not ten feet away. "Ready, Herr Bauer." *Herr Bauer.* He slammed the rear doors shut and suddenly everything turned completely black. Fear sprang up in me. I was trapped inside. No way out. I heard him wrap a chain around the outer latch of the door. For a moment I heard nothing but the pounding of my own heart, which I thought would give me away to anyone within twenty feet.

Wherever we were going, I was along for the ride.

A moment later, Curtis hopped in the front cab and got behind the wheel. Willi Bauer pulled himself into the passenger seat.

"Not made for people of your age, Herr Bauer," I heard Curtis say, somewhat blithely.

"I'll be fine. Do you have your gun, Kurt? Just in case? Though I doubt we'll need it."

His gun.

"Right here," the janitor said, patting his chest. "Just in case."

In a second the truck's engine coughed to life. The vehicle inched a few feet into the street, where it stopped again, Curtis hopped out, and I heard the corrugated metal door to the brewery's loading bay slam behind me.

Curtis got back into the cab.

"Two hours," Curtis said. "Sit back and enjoy the ride, Herr Bauer. Operation Prospero is under way."

25

OPERATION PROSPERO

What was he talking about? Prospero was rightful King of Milan in Shakespeare's *The Tempest,* whose plotting brother abandoned him at sea for twelve years on an island.

An island like Manhattan?

I curled up there, the tarp over me, trapped. And petrified. Still, not so petrified that there wasn't a tiny but insistent urge inside me to see what they were up to. Curtis had a gun. Clearly, if they found me back here, spying on them—spying on *spies*—he'd have no choice but to use it. Wherever we were going, I had no doubt Prospero meant something important.

And sinister.

The truck lurched and sputtered its way down the street. York Avenue, I assumed. It made a series of turns, until I felt certain, even without seeing, that we were heading south, maybe on Second Avenue. We continued for a while, pulling up at the occasional light. I couldn't hear anything said in the cab above the engine, though it was only feet in front of me. How was I ever going to get out of here?

Do you have your gun, Kurt?

Whatever they were up to, the taciturn, muscular janitor with what I'd thought was a Scandinavian accent seemed like just the type who'd have no compunction using it on me.

It was a long trip, wherever we were heading, and I settled in. We stopped and started over what I took to be the Fifty-ninth Street Bridge into Queens, then on all kinds of bumpy city streets in Queens until the truck accelerated and the ride smoothed out on what I took to be a highway. Forty minutes had gone by. It was now going on twelve thirty in the morning. At some point I crept out from underneath the tarp, careful to keep low in case one of them looked back through the window to check on the cargo, took a furtive glance through the small window into the front—and saw a green road sign ahead. *Eastern Long Island.* Were we on the Southern State Parkway? It was bumpy in there. I had nothing to hold on to but the tarp. I was tossed around. And it was cold. The floor of the truck made it feel like a meat locker. Behind the wheel, Curtis kept up a steady pace.

I looked at the door. How could I get out of here? There was an inside latch that I could possibly open, but the chain Curtis had affixed outside made trying pointless. Instead, I tried to think what I would do whenever they opened the door. Could I possibly hide in here? What would I say if I was caught? How could I alibi myself out of this? The inescapable fact was that I was trapped and there was no way out. And my captors were armed. It was clear whatever they were up to, the last thing they'd want was a witness blabbing about it to the police.

I started to think Liz or Emma, or even Noelle, might never even know what happened to me.

The one thought I played with was to immediately bolt out the back and take off the second the door was opened. Catch them by surprise. Wherever we were, it would be dark. By the time Curtis drew his gun I could be twenty to thirty yards away. In the dark, he might not be able to hit me. That seemed my only chance, I resolved. And then what? Where would I go afterward? Who would I tell? Latimer? The police? And what would I say? What would I actually have witnessed? Nothing. What had they actually done? A beer delivery in the dark of night? I was the one who was spying on them. Truth was, I'd still have nothing.

A greater fear pulsed through me as I also realized that our final destination could well be inside, in an enclosed space. And then where would I run? There were at least two of them larger than me.

I wouldn't get ten feet.

This could be my last ride.

An hour passed. Close to 1 A.M. The truck rumbled on. When I took another peek I saw road signs for Lake Ronkonkoma, and then the dual towns of Mastic/Shirley. Curtis and Willi seemed to have no plan to stop. Farther out, there were only beach towns on the far end of the Island. I had been out here only once before, to Southampton, to a fancy party on a huge estate a few summers ago, given by rich Gentile friends at Columbia. Everyone was dressed in blazers and white slacks and the women in nautical dresses and wide, white hats. Liz and I had never felt so out of place.

Until now . . .

At some point, the truck downshifted with a heavy jerk and we seemed to leave the main road. The road got bumpy, and suddenly one of the barrels toppled over and rolled on its side. Now it was rattling around under the tarp, making noise. I tried to reach over and stop it.

I lowered back down, sure that Curtis or Willi would be looking back through the window at it.

Instead, to my horror, Curtis pulled the truck over on the side of the deserted road.

"Be right back," I heard him say up front.

I froze, huddled there. I heard him go around the side, unlatch the chain at the rear, twist the outer handle, and then the back doors swung open. Cool air rushed in. I crouched, hidden by the row of beer kegs—thank God the one that had fallen over was in the row closer to the door—and covered up by the tarp.

"Christ, this thing weighs a fucking ton," Curtis grunted, hopping up into the truck and taking the keg by its sides and righting it. Huddled there, I could literally feel him not five feet from me. I prayed my pounding heart wouldn't give me away.

He set it back up, pulled the tarp back over it, and seemed to pause a second or two—or what seemed to me like a full minute—where I was sure the next sound I would hear was the hammer of his gun being pulled back and the command: "Whoever you are, come on out of there now!"

I stayed as still as I could. Without releasing a breath.

But to my relief, I heard him shout up front, "Back in business," and felt the gaze of Willi Bauer probably nodding through the small window, and then I heard Trudi Bauer's voice from outside—they were obviously following closely behind—"Is there a problem, Kurt?"

"No, Frau Bauer," Curtis said, jumping back down onto the road. "Just a little housekeeping. We'll be back on our way."

He jumped out, then the doors slammed again, the chain was reattached, and I took the deepest breath of my life in relief.

The temperature in the frozen cargo space couldn't have been more than forty degrees, but I had sweated completely through my clothes.

"Let's go," Willi said. "We've fallen behind schedule."

I heard Curtis jump back in the front and felt the engine release back into drive. I felt both relieved and nervous. Relieved that I hadn't been discovered; nervous, that wherever we were heading, we would be there soon.

Continuing on, I crawled out from under the tarp again and caught a glimpse as we passed some small towns. An old church. Shops. Old clapboard houses. All were dark. Empty. Barely a light anywhere. It was almost two in the morning.

As the truck slowed on one street, I finally caught a glimpse of a sign.

Bridgehampton General Store. *Bridgehampton?* Farther out than even Southampton. What were we doing all the way out here? Not any beer delivery, I was sure. I checked my watch. Certainly not at two in the morning.

As I was thinking that, the truck slowed and made a right turn. It continued along a long, bumpy road, the kegs bouncing. This went on for at least a mile and seemed to take minutes. I kneeled up and peered out ahead and all I saw was darkness all around and the thin, smoky beams from the truck's headlights barely illuminating the road ahead. Then we slowed once more and made a right turn, bouncing along at a slow pace, until it jerked to a stop. I felt the emergency brake catch.

We were here.

If you're going to make a run for it, Charlie, now's the time.

Curtis came around back and undid the chains. My heart started to race. He turned the latch and flung open the back doors.

Again, cold air rushed in. Hidden under the tarp, I didn't move a muscle. I sucked in a breath, worried that this was it for me. They were going to unload the kegs, pull up the tarp, and find me there.

I waited to hear Willi or Trudi shout, "Unload the cargo."

But they didn't.

Not just yet.

Instead, I heard the crunch of gravel and Curtis and the Bauers engaged in conversation a short ways away. "Out there," Willi said. I lifted my head out from underneath the tarp.

And smelled something.

Something that I didn't expect. But that now made sense.

Close by enough that I could reach out and touch it.

The ocean.

26

The door was left open. No one seemed to be around. The Ford I had seen earlier had driven up and parked directly behind us. Trudi and the dough-faced driver, Freddy, had walked on past and were with the group. Everyone was huddling, out of view. I could hear their voices, dimly now, several yards away.

I knew this was my chance.

I crept out from under the tarp and crawled to the open doors. No one was on guard. Taking a breath, I lowered myself onto the ground, a mixture of pebbles and sand, careful not to make a sound.

A short ways away I could hear the Bauers and Curtis engaged in conversation. But they were no longer speaking English. It was German now. No more pretense.

We were at the shore. They clearly weren't making any beer delivery.

I stole around the edge of the truck and caught sight of them around twenty yards away. Willi was pointing out to sea. It was dark, but the shore had to be right behind them. I could hear waves lapping up on the beach. I knew I had this one moment of opportunity to get away while everyone was distracted. Before they came back for their cargo. I could probably sneak away now, find my way back to the main road, and they would never know I was ever here. But what had I seen? What could I tell anyone was going on? Nothing. On one side of the truck, I spotted a wall of hedges and bushes I could easily hide behind. Behind me, I saw an old clapboard house, not a light on. And no other houses in sight. This was about as quiet and remote as it could be. Hugging my camera to my chest, I tiptoed over to the hedge and slipped behind it.

The night was moonless, completely dark. We were literally on a beach in a totally deserted location. Through the bushes, I could see Curtis and the other driver smoking. Willi Bauer took out his pipe. I checked my watch. 2:30 A.M. Why were we here? What was going on?

Then I remembered—whatever was happening, if my code held up, and so far it had, it would take place at three. In half an hour.

0300.

I waited.

Twenty minutes passed. I spent it crouched, observing, watching Willi Bauer and his group preparing, though I couldn't tell what for. So far they still hadn't unloaded the kegs. I was no longer even afraid. I had to see what was happening. The four of them were all the way down by the water now, which I could hear lapping onto the beach in small waves. They had a lantern affixed to a rope, which they lit, and occasionally swung back and forth as if signaling someone. Willi Bauer intermittently looked out through a pair of binoculars. Always staring out at the sea. Waiting.

I crept a little closer along the row of bushes, taking care not to make any noise against the pebbles. I snapped a photo or two, though I had no flash, and given the lack of light, I was doubtful anything would come out. There wasn't even a moon.

All of a sudden, Willi shouted out. *"There!"*

He pointed out to sea. Everyone got up and looked. To my shock, far out in the darkness, I saw a light flashing back at them.

They all cheered.

Excited, Curtis swung the lantern back and forth. I saw what looked like a dark shape crest through the surface, black on black, like some long serpent rearing its head.

Until I realized it wasn't a serpent.

"Mein Gott!" Trudi Bauer uttered in awe, her hand to her mouth.

It was a submarine.

A German sub, I had no doubt.

Far out in the water. But here . . . in American waters. Maybe a quarter mile offshore.

I stood there, watching, just as awestruck by the sight as they were.

And also at the fact, which was slowly dawning on me, that I was right. Right, since my very first suspicion.

The Bauers *were* spies. They were plotting something. Operation Prospero. And Curtis was part of their group.

I checked my watch. It was 0300.

27

About fifteen more minutes passed, the group on the shore actively preparing for something. Curtis waved the lantern in sweeping turns. Willi kept scanning through his binoculars.

Finally, Freddy pointed out at the dark tide and shouted, *"Hier! Hier!"* Waving into the void. Joyously patting Curtis on the shoulder. *"Uber hier!"*

Out of the darkness, a small craft began to appear, riding the waves in. *My God* . . . I focused my eyes. I leaned forward, snapping as many photos as I could. One, two, three, four . . . But I only had three or four left.

A sub.

To my shock, a team of dark-uniformed Germans jumped into the surf and made their way onto the shore. There were four. Two had submachine guns strapped over their shoulders. The others seemed like workmen. Trudi, Willi, and Curtis ran out to help them in. The sailors pulled the boat ashore; it had a tarp in it covering up something as well. A bearded senior officer in a black leather jacket shouted to his men, *"Schnell. Schnell!"*

They jumped out of the boat and started to unload. German soldiers. On American soil. The senior officer warmly shook Willi Bauer's hand.

I looked beyond them out on the water. The sub they had come from had submerged.

Prospero.

Abandoned on a distant shore.

I crept closer and kneeled behind the hedge to snap another shot. I heard a twig snap beneath my foot. I froze. Twenty yards away, Trudi Bauer turned toward me. On the shore, everyone was excited and filled with purpose, unloading the craft. Perhaps a spark of suspicion lit up in Trudi as she looked my way. I crouched, perfectly still, my heart pounding, as her gaze knifed right through me. If she chose to come over and investigate, with all these characters around, no way I could get away. I'd be shot on the spot. I held my breath, till someone called to her from the shore and she looked toward me one more time, but then Willi introduced the senior officer to her and her attention became diverted back to the task at hand.

I let out a breath of relief.

They lifted the tarp and I saw what I took to be supplies. Two of the sailors dragged onto the beach what looked like a heavy crate. They pried it open to show Willi and Trudi, and I could make out it was full of guns. I snapped a shot of it through the bushes. But there was something else in the boat too. Something big and shiny. That must be what they were bringing in.

A bomb was my first thought, and I readied my camera. But

when they lifted the shiny objects from under the tarp and rolled them onto the shore I saw exactly what they were.

Beer barrels.

Just like what had been loaded into the truck.

Except these, I was sure, didn't have a mug full of beer in any of them.

Snap.

Gradually, the German seamen plus Curtis and Freddy, the driver, lugged the barrels back to the truck and hoisted them up into the cargo bay. I watched them arrange the new kegs, four steel barrels, into the rear of the bay, behind the ones they had brought with them from the brewery, as if the ones they had brought were merely meant to conceal these new ones. Right where I had been hiding.

What was inside them?

Time was of the essence. Everyone worked quickly. I raised my camera and hit the shutter at German sailors on American soil. *Click. Click.* Suddenly I was out of film. Damn. When they were done loading, Curtis covered the kegs up with the tarp and relocked the truck. He wrapped the chain back through the latch, this time using a padlock to keep it secure. He put the key in his pocket. Then they all headed back to the beach. There, they said their goodbyes. More hearty handshakes and hugs, and a *"Sieg Heil"* from the bearded senior officer. Willi and Trudi and the others raised their arms in return.

Then the Germans climbed back into their launch. Curtis and Freddy helped them push back into the surf. They pushed off, rowing against the tide, back out to sea. In minutes, the boat melded into the darkness, the Bauers continuing to wave. No one left.

In the distance, I heard a deep whooshing sound and saw that the sub had reemerged, an amorphous black shape against the equally dark sea and sky. In about fifteen minutes, the launch made it back to the mother ship, and a minute or two later, after the men climbed aboard, I heard the same whooshing sound, and in a flash it was gone. Only silence remained, like it never was there. Crouching behind the bushes, I watched as Curtis and the other driver lugged the crate of weapons back to the car and placed it in the trunk, while Willi smoothed out the sand where they had been, erasing the footprints. Only then did they all say their goodbyes.

Willi and Curtis climbed back in the truck; Trudi and Friedrich into the sedan. In seconds, the two vehicles drove off. Not even a trace that any of this had just happened. Not even tire marks and a cloud of dirt and dust, or footprints in the sand.

Only then did I step out from my hiding place.

But something *had* taken place. An enemy sub had come ashore and dropped off a secret cargo. And I had seen it occur. Maybe not the enemy—at least, in a literal sense. We weren't yet at war. But illegal, for sure. Seditious. Something the government had to know about immediately. I'd been right all along. The Bauers weren't Swiss. I had wandered into a nest of German spies. Spies who were executing a mission, whatever was in those kegs, and had to be stopped from carrying it out.

28

It took me the whole next day to find my way back to the city. I got away from the house on the beach as fast as I could and walked in the direction I assumed would lead me to the highway. But the road wound around and, in the dark, I became lost. I fell asleep on the porch of a deserted house, huddled in my coat like a blanket. I woke up after 9 A.M., exhausted, cold, and started on foot again, finally catching a ride from a worker on a farm truck, who said he could take me all the way to Southampton.

"You look like you could use a coffee, pal."

I grabbed that coffee in a café on Main Street, as well as some breakfast. Then I waited for the next train at the station. It was a Saturday, and this time of year, they only ran every couple of hours. It was a cattle car, chugging to a stop at every town on eastern Long Island, and I didn't get back to the city until four in the afternoon.

I wasn't sure what to do with what I had seen the night before. I reminded myself over and over that only a couple of hours ago I'd seen Willi and Trudi Bauer make contact with a party from a German submarine on American soil. And that a secret cargo was unloaded, possibly weapons.

The best plan, I decided, was to try to reach Latimer. But it was a Saturday; I tried his office in D.C. from the phone outside my apartment, but no one picked up. I guess the Department of Immigrant Affairs didn't work weekends. I also tried the main switchboard at the State Department but the weekend operator said she had no idea how to raise him. "There are over two thousand employees at the State Department," she said, to my frustration. I thought about going back to the New York City police. But I already had the sense where that would lead. Nowhere. And now, I'd be raving about some German submarine that had come ashore, and have to explain everything all over again: The Bauers. How I figured the time and date out. My own past. I'd look as suspicious as they would. That no, I didn't know what was in the beer kegs they'd dragged ashore, how could I? Or how crucial it all was. They could well be explosives. But I gave it till Monday. Till I got my film developed. I prayed a couple of days wouldn't matter much. The fact was, Germany and the United States weren't even at war, so there should be time. Latimer seemed my best bet.

When I woke there was an envelope for me. I didn't get much mail these days. My bills were paid in cash. This one was light blue. It didn't take much effort to figure out who sent it.

My name and address were in large, basic cursive with a crayoned heart on it and the return read *Emma Mossman*.

I opened it, my heart filling up a bit. It was a card. Hand-drawn on drawing paper. Mountains with white peaks and a blue river and bright green fields. Two stick-figure persons, one pint-sized with blond, curly hair, Emma; the other tall, smiling, with an arrow pointing to it saying *Daddy*. And with what looked like a Saint Bernard.

They were holding hands.

I miss you, Daddy, the card read in bright red print. It brought tears to my eyes. It had been over two weeks since I'd seen her. "I miss you too, peach," I said.

I looked at the mountains and river and the Saint Bernard and figured it was Switzerland.

Then I turned the card over and saw Emma had written: *Aunt Trudi helped me make this.*

A chill ran through me. It was almost like a message. Like they were digging their clutches deeper into her and letting me know. Especially with what I had witnessed last night. I was on the outside, not even able to see my daughter, and they were drawing with her, playing with her, spending time with her. Were they telling me, We have her? You'd better be aware. You'd better stay out of our business.

She's ours.

I had a date with Noelle that next day. Sunday. It was a cold but pretty day in New York. Bundled up, we went for an afternoon walk in Central Park. Though it was December and the wind was biting us in the face, the sun was shining and it felt warm. Noelle had on her wool coat and a green beret. She latched on to my arm and made me feel whole again, walking around with the time bomb I was carrying inside that I was keeping from her.

It helped put the past day and night behind me.

We bought some bread crumbs at a stand and fed the ducks swimming in Central Park's pond.

"You seem distracted, Charles," she said.

"No, I'm fine," I lied. "Here . . ." I kneeled down and handed her some crumbs "I am."

"Good." She smiled and squeezed my arm. "I want you all to myself, Charles Mossman, and your mind to be completely with me."

"Tell me how your thesis is going," I asked.

But she was right, of course. I was distracted. I was quiet and insular and focused on what I was keeping from her, what I had witnessed the previous night, and barely lived through, that I dared not share. Reminding myself that it wasn't some crazy dream I had made up, but something real. Chillingly real. And happening. Now.

"C'mon, let's get a bite to eat," I said.

We went to a little brasserie in the Drake Hotel. They had a café there, with dark wood walls and low-hanging brass lamps. I thought Noelle would feel at home. We each ordered a beer. I figured I deserved one after the previous night, and took a pretty deep swig.

It was the first time I'd seen her since the night we'd slept together, and I wanted to tell her how much it had meant to me.

"Charles, there *is* something bothering you, I can see. If perhaps you wish that we hadn't done what we did the other night . . . I understand. It was only—"

"No, that's not it." I cut her off. "In fact, it's the opposite. The other night was swell. The best thing to happen to me in a couple of years. It's just—" Maybe it was best that I did tell her. As much as I wanted to keep her out of this part of my life, it was hard to simply put it aside. It was Noelle, after all, who was the one who had introduced me to Latimer. So she was a part of it.

"Look, something happened yesterday. . . ." I sucked in a breath. "It's nothing to do with us."

She covered my hand with hers and gave me a look of concern. "Emma?"

"No. No. Emma's fine." Reflexively, I glanced at my watch and took note of the time. It was a little after 3 P.M. *Here goes* . . . "You remember I said I'd found a book locked away in the Bauers' closet? That had previously been on the coffee table."

"Yes."

"And it had some writing in it. Words and numbers circled and underlined . . ."

She nodded. "Yes. You told me of this."

I was just about to tell her how I came to the conclusion that it was a time and date, when I heard a commotion coming from the bar. People were crowded around a radio, the bartender tuning it in. He raised the volume so everyone around could hear. They were shouting with anger, shaking their heads with what looked like dismay.

"Something's happened." I grabbed Noelle by the hand. "C'mon . . ."

"Charles, finish, please . . ."

"No. Someone's making an announcement. We should hear." I pulled her up to the bar, pushing our way in close. A man slammed his fist onto the bar in rage. "Those bastards . . ." A woman in a purple suit shook her head with tears in her eyes. "My God . . ."

"What's going on?" I asked.

There was a news flash. Everyone leaned in close to catch the scratchy report, which sounded like it was coming from a long ways away. There was suddenly also a lot of noise outside, cars honking, police whistles blowing.

"The Japs just sneak-attacked Pearl Harbor," the bartender said. "Lots of ships lost and people killed."

"My God!"

I turned to Noelle and a whitened cast came over her face. Like, *Here it is all over again.* Within a day, we'd be at war. Not with the Germans as I'd hoped for and everyone expected, but with the Japanese.

"Dozens of the most powerful ships and carriers lie broken and in flames in Honolulu Bay . . . ," the newscaster intoned.

In the restaurant, the crowd grew solemn. The bartender lined up glasses on the bar. He poured a shot of whiskey in all. "Here's to our boys," he said, raising his glass.

We all raised them. "To our boys!" we all shouted.

Even I gulped down a shot. People started singing "God Bless America."

This changed everything for me.

I knew I had to get to Latimer fast. That with what I'd seen, the Germans infiltrating our shore, bringing something in that I knew was meant for harm, things were only going to get worse. A lot worse.

"I know what this is," Noelle said, looking at me. "I've already lived through it once, and now here too."

I put my arm around her. "But this time you're not alone."

She didn't answer. Just gave me a brief smile and kissed me.

By the following afternoon, America and the kingdom of Japan were at war.

29

It took until Wednesday for Latimer to get back to me. A declaration of war had a way of turning the State Department upside down, he said. We met at the same Midtown hotel where we had met the first time. A porter let me in and he kept me waiting in his suite a while, and when Latimer finally came in, he looked tired and somber and there were lines of strain on his face. The attack on Pearl Harbor had given way to two days of national mourning. Flags everywhere hung at half staff. People broke out in patriotic songs spontaneously in public. No one could comprehend how our defenses had been so ill prepared for such an attack, and the casualties were numbing. The effect on our navy was just as bad. The draft was being reenacted and young people all over the country were kissing their wives and moms goodbye and leaving home and school and their jobs to sign up.

The country was at war. Just not with the people I had evidence against.

"Thanks for seeing me," I said to Latimer. "I know your time's important. Especially . . ."

"I'm here," he said, his lips thin and flat, his hair slicked back, and adjusted his wire rims. "I'm interested to hear what you have."

"I think you'll find it important," I said, and took out the packet of photographs I had had developed the day before. I laid them out on the table. "The people I told you about last week are named Bauer," I started in. More "specific." I pointed to a black-and-white photo of Willi and Trudi as they stepped outside their brownstone. "They live at 174 East Ninetieth. Apartment 3B. The other night, on a hunch, I followed them as they left their home at eleven P.M. and went to the brewery they once owned. On Ninety-second Street." I put down another photo. "I know it's dark. I'm hardly a professional, you can see. Here, you can see the truck. . . ."

"You say you followed them?" The State Department man stopped me. "How did you know to do so on this particular night?"

"You remember I said last time I thought I had stumbled upon their code?"

Latimer nodded. "Those strips of burnt paper in the trash. With numbers on them."

"The numbers corresponded to a book I also found there. Darwin's *Voyage of the Beagle.* In German. I put together that the numbers I saw in the trash corresponded to December 6, three A.M."

"You broke their code?" He took out a cigarette from his gold case and lit it with a lighter. "You're a very resourceful man, Mr. Mossman," he said admiringly. "You've been quite the eager beaver, I can see."

"This is only the half of it," I said, setting up what would happen next.

Latimer pulled the ashtray over to his side. "You have my attention."

I told him about the truck ride. About finding myself trapped inside while inspecting the cargo being moved in there, and then being unable to get out. Latimer's narrow eyes grew wide. I told him that the Bauers' accomplice, actually the janitor in the building they lived in, drove, and had a gun with him. That I'd spent the two-hour ride certain that when they arrived at whatever destination they were headed to, they would open the doors, find me there, and I'd be killed.

"I can only imagine," he said, flicking an ash. "So what was in the truck in the end?"

I laid down another photo. It was dark, a little blurry, but showed shiny objects taken from inside. "Beer kegs," I said, as he squinted closely at it but couldn't seem to make out what it was.

"Beer?" Latimer wrinkled his brow.

"At least barrels. From the brewery. I don't know what they were filled with. This wasn't exactly a delivery, if that's what you mean. The brewery is shut down. It was after midnight. Trudi Bauer was along for the ride. It took a couple of hours, but we finally came to a stop in the town of Bridgehampton."

"Bridgehampton . . . ?"

"It's a town all the way out in eastern Long Island," I explained. "We pulled up to this house with nothing else around it. Directly on the beach."

"A little late in the season to work on your tan, I suspect," he said. He seemed surprised at the destination.

"You might say."

"And obviously you weren't discovered. When you arrived."

"They opened the cargo door, but never unloaded what was inside," I said. "Which gave me the opportunity to escape. They all gathered on the beach. I was able to sneak out and hide behind a hedge. That's where I took these."

I put out two more photographs. Willi, Trudi, Curtis, and the other driver as they waited for what they were there to meet.

He looked at them and stared at me.

I said, "At just before three A.M., the exact time I recorded in the code I broke, I saw this dark shape appear out on the water. It rose up, pretty much out of nowhere. Maybe a quarter of a mile offshore."

He looked at me quizzically. I showed him what I had taken, the dark outline of the ship barely distinguishable from the black of the ocean and the dark, moonless sky.

Latimer took off his wire-rim glasses. I could see an air of importance spark to life in his hooded, gray eyes.

"It's a sub," I said. "A German sub."

"You can be sure of this?" he said.

"I'm sure, because approximately twenty minutes later check out what came ashore. . . ."

I laid out two more pictures. Neither of them were particularly clear or revealing. Mostly just dark, blurry shapes. But clear enough that he could make out the launch coming ashore, Curtis and Willi helping to pull it in through the surf, and the four German seamen climbing out onto American soil.

"This is completely incredible," Latimer uttered dully, his jaw slack. "I can't believe what I'm looking at. You just stayed there? You could have been killed."

"By that time, I have to admit I was far more mesmerized by what I was watching than I was afraid for my life."

He pushed away from the table, seemingly shell-shocked. "A German submarine. On U.S. soil. There is no dispute, this is highly provocative material," he said. "People must see this. And what are they taking out . . . ?" Latimer put his glasses back on and brought one photo up close. "It seems to me it's . . ." Then he looked at me again.

"Beer," I answered.

"Yes." He blinked blankly. "More beer."

"I'm no intelligence agent, Mr. Latimer, but I would suspect there's not a single drop of beer in any of these canisters, whatever they might contain."

Latimer put the photographs back on the table, his face ashen. "Yes, I would have to agree."

"Now you know why I needed to see you so urgently," I said.

"Yes, of course." He nodded peremptorily. "You've done well, son." He reached across the table and squeezed my shoulder. "And at great risk to your own safety, I can see. And . . . there is something you don't know—how could you, that's just taken place, barely an hour ago—that only adds to the urgency of all this. It's why I was late joining you."

"What's that?"

"Germany and Italy have joined Japan and declared war on the United States."

"My God."

"Tonight, President Roosevelt will address the nation and respond in kind."

"Jesus . . ." I sat back. My heart pounded like a drum. We would be at war.

"A day ago it was no crime to believe in National Socialism," the State Department man said. "Half of Congress was pressing FDR to stay out of things. But today, it's no longer someone's convictions, but outright sedition we're looking at here. There's always been the concern that some kind of fifth column was conducting espionage behind our backs. . . ."

The Bauers were traitors now.

"I assume you'll let me keep these . . . ?" he said, and tapped the photographs together into a pile. "I promise they'll be safe. You have the negatives? We'll need to make copies."

"Of course. They're in there." He put the prints back in their envelope from the photography store and stuffed them inside his jacket pocket.

"So who have you told about this?" he asked.

"Not a soul."

"Not even Noelle?"

"Not even Noelle," I said.

"Keep it that way." He rubbed his face. "You just stay out of it at this point. It's far too dangerous. This is in our hands now. And for God's sake, don't breathe a word of it to the police. That's all we need, the press or the wrong agencies getting wind of it and coming down our backs."

"I understand."

Latimer stood up. I got up too. He put out his hand. His grip was firm and resolved and I felt gratitude in it.

"You better give me a way to reach you," he said. "We'll likely need to speak again."

"Of course."

"You understand you've done a helluva good thing for your country, son. . . ." He placed his hand on my shoulder. "A brave and a helluva good thing."

"Thank you," I said, a glow washing through me.

The glow of having done something for my country. And at last, corroboration for Liz.

30

At the brewery, everything was in a state of readiness.

Willi's nerves were on edge. The Führer's declaration of war against America suddenly put their plans on the front burner. What was once merely organization and planning was now elevated to action. The kegs they had unloaded off the sub were hidden amid many similar kegs from the brewery that were filled innocently with beer, so that if their truck was stopped they could show it was only a normal delivery. Only they knew which was which. Each had to be handled with the most extreme caution. If opened improperly and spread, the contents of each could kill half the people within a mile radius. They had the plans, the commitment; they'd put in the training. They had met and gone over their roles a hundred times.

All they had waited on was the final go-ahead from back home. And now it had come.

Operation Prospero was to commence.

Germany and America were at war.

All they had been missing for weeks was an unwitting stooge to blame it all on, someone on the ground here who would look like a fitting "dupe" when the investigators looked into it, and now blessedly one had come their way.

He thought he was so smart, Willi and Trudi agreed, with his highbrow education and his vast knowledge of things, but in the end, what would officials find, when they looked into it: no more than an angry and unpredictable young man, someone who had been trampled on by society, denied his own dreams, who had scorn for all. Someone estranged from his wife and now his daughter. A life in ruins. Only a memory of what it once was. Alone.

Willi had to laugh; they couldn't have come up with a better fall guy for their plans if they had called up Hollywood and gotten in touch with central casting.

"Willi," Trudi called. She had the maps spread on the office table. She noticed his nerves. "You seem agitated."

"Just excited, my dear, now that everything is now in work," he said reassuringly. "I am fine."

"Good," she said. "Stay strong."

Curtis, or Oberleutnant Kurt Leitner as they knew him, in overalls and heavy workman's gloves, was prying the lids off the new "beer" canisters.

"Be careful," Willi warned him. "The wrong move and we will all be dying the worst death imaginable."

"Everything is perfectly secure," Kurt said. He had been sent here two years before for this very purpose. "But they need to be loaded now."

"Just be careful, for God's sake," Trudi said. "You know what you're dealing with."

"I know precisely what I am dealing with," the oberleutnant

said. As a chemical engineer who had once worked at IG Farben, where the contents of the canisters were made, he had been trained for this very task for years.

The phone rang. Trudi went to answer. Very few people had the phone number here, now that the business had closed, so it could only be one of a handful of people.

"Uh-huh, uh-huh . . ." She nodded soberly. "I see. . . ." Her color turned gray. "We know what to do then," she said. She caught Willi's eyes. "Thank you. We'll be in touch."

She put down the phone.

Willi looked at her, agitated. "What's wrong, dear?" he asked.

"Have you taken your stomach pills this morning?" Trudi looked at him.

"Of course." Though he already felt the acid starting to burn. "What is it?"

"Take another then, Willi," Trudi said. "And get Kurt and Friedrich in here. It seems a situation has developed. It's time to speed up our plan."

31

"Charlie . . ."

I had just gotten back from work, around six, and was trying
to keep my mind off the events of the past weekend and Latimer,
which I could no longer do anything about. The entire country
was abuzz with the news that we were at war. Headlines blasted all
over the papers. Radio broadcasts. From the president! I grabbed
a soft drink, settled on my bed, and unfolded the afternoon *Trib*:
"COUNTRY LURCHES INTO PREPAREDNESS," when the
landlord knocked on my door and said there was a call for me.

Because I didn't get many calls there I thought maybe it was
Latimer with news about Willi and Trudi. I went downstairs,
closed the door to the parlor where the phone was, and turned
away from the door. "Hello."

"Charlie, it's me," a harried voice blurted. I heard immediately
that it was Liz. She sounded upset.

"What's going on?" I said, though I already knew the answer
to my next question. "Is everything all right?"

"No, everything's not all right, Charlie. Something's happened. Emma is missing."

"Missing . . . ?"

"She never came home from school. Mrs. Shearer and I made a time to have her back here at four today—she had a dentist's appointment. And it's six now and they're still not here. I've called the school and everywhere I can think of. No one's seen them. I'm worried sick, Charlie."

"Calm down, Liz. We'll find her." I sat down. Nausea balled up in my gut. "What about Mrs. Shearer?" A thought ran through me. "Is she around?"

"No, she's missing as well," Liz said. "The school told me they left as they do every day, more than two hours ago. I went around on the street, on the route they usually take, and I can't find her anywhere. No one's seen them. Oh Charlie, I know something bad's happened. I can feel it. You know I'm not like this—I don't get all out of sorts—but we spoke about her appointment just this morning. They're never late. It's over two hours now. I'm just letting you know, I'm calling the police."

"No, don't call the police, Liz." I stopped her. I knew the Bauers were bad. Something popped into my head. Mrs. Shearer. *She's missing too.* "You once told me the Bauers found Mrs. Shearer for you, isn't that right?"

"Yes. They did. But what do Willi and Trudi have to do with this, Charlie? I knocked on their door too. Trudi said she hadn't seen them today."

"Liz, just listen to me, I want you to go to your sister's, please." Her older sister, Sophie, lived with her husband on East Forty-seventh. I had to get Liz away from there. "Just go, *now.* I know what to do. I promise. I'll be in touch with you shortly."

"My sister's? Charlie, you're honestly not going to start this again with Willi and Trudi, are you? Didn't you hear me, Emma's missing. I can't bear this right now."

"I know Emma's missing, Liz." And if Mrs. Shearer was as well, and not in touch, I felt certain the two events had to be connected. "And I have an idea why. Just promise me you won't do a thing till you hear from me."

"What are you saying, Charlie? *Why . . . ?* Look, maybe I shouldn't have called you. I'm going to hang up now and contact the police. I just wanted to let you know."

"No, Liz, don't!" I begged her. "Don't contact the police. Not just yet. Just hear me out—I'm going to get her back, Liz. Just go to Sophie's. Don't do anything. Promise me. I'll be in touch."

I could hear the consternation in her voice. Laced with panic. She was confused, petrified. As was I. Who wouldn't be? "Charlie, I don't know . . . I think I should be at home. What if they—"

"Mrs. Bainbridge can call you if they come home. Just leave the number with her. But they're not, Liz . . ."

"They're not what?"

"They're not coming home today." I was sure of it. I was sure I knew where they were.

Her voice shook. "What are you saying, Charlie?"

"Just give me a chance to resolve this. Promise me you'll go there," I pressed. "Please."

She finally gave in. "Okay, I will."

"Trust me, I'll find her for you, Liz. I will. I'll be in touch."

32

How do they know?

I didn't know the answer to that, but they did. I felt certain. Things like this didn't just happen. They'd found out I was onto them. Something had happened.

Liz had said, *They even found Mrs. Shearer for us, and what would we do without her?* If Mrs. Shearer was missing as well, I had no doubt the two had to be connected.

My first thought was to call Latimer. But it was well after six now and I knew the State Department switchboard was closed. I grabbed a cab into the city and instructed the driver to East Ninetieth. To Liz's brownstone. My blood pulsed like a steam valve thrown open on a train, flooding my veins with simmering anger. Half out of my mind with worry. Half boiling with rage. Liz was right on one thing. I'd let my little girl become caught up in this.

I had the cabbie let me off on Third and I sprinted the block and a half to 174. I bounded up the stairs and threw open the door. I pressed the buzzer over and over for Willi and Trudi, and when

Willi finally came on, I said, "It's Charles Mossman. Let me up."
He buzzed me in without even asking why.

My blood racing, I bounded up the two flights to the third
floor, not even stopping at Liz's apartment. I was set to pound on
the Bauers' door when it opened.

Willi Bauer stood there. In a sweater vest and loosened tie.
"Come in, Herr Mossman." He looked around. "We've actually
been expecting you."

Expecting me.

Trudi stood there, her gray hair pulled back in her bun, her
eyes fierce and glaring. Next to her, wearing his work uniform, was
Curtis. No pretense anymore: He pulled his jacket back to reveal a
gun in his waistband. Seated on the couch was an older man with
a bushy white mustache. It took me a second to realize who it was.

And as I did, I began to see precisely where this was unfolding.

It was Karl, my waiter from the Old Heidelberg. I shook my
head at him with disappointment and confusion. "Karl."

He didn't answer.

I looked around in anger, going from face to face. I settled on
Willi, who had followed me in, and who stood facing me with a
hand on the rounded arm piece of the couch. Trudi sat on the love
seat with a saucer of tea. "Swiss, huh . . . ?" I sniffed at them with
contempt.

"I think we can dispense with all the pretense at last, can we
not, Herr Mossman?"

"Yes, please. I dispensed with it long ago," I said. "Where's my
daughter?"

"Emma is quite safe, I assure you of that." He made no effort
to even hide that he had her. "We have no thought in the world of
harming her. You have my word on that. At least for now. She is

with Mrs. Shearer. We would like nothing less than to hurt her in any way. But that is up to you, Mr. Mossman. Should you decide to do anything foolish."

"I've already been plenty foolish," I said. "By ever letting her and Liz trust you. And you." I turned to Trudi and Curtis. "All of you . . ." My gaze ended up on Karl, my kindly German waiter, sitting there with his hands folded in his lap. "You're traitors. All of you. Whatever you're up to. That witch Mrs. Shearer, too."

"Traitors . . ." Willi Bauer smiled. He came over and stood by his wife. "I would hardly use that word, Mr. Mossman. Soldiers, perhaps. One is never too old to do one's duty. We are all natural-born Germans. Even Herr Leitner here." He nodded to Curtis. "Oberleutnant Leitner, as he is better known to us. From the Abwehr. All of us living in a country we now find ourselves at war with. And now, at last, doing what has to be done."

"Spies, then," I said. "If that sits better with you. Have it however you wish. And just what do you mean, doing what has to be done? What does it have to do with my daughter?"

"Why, the first blow in the war against your country, of course. From our side. A war I assure you our country did not seek. And a decisive blow, you will find out soon enough. And I'm afraid that is why we had to enlist your lovely daughter in this enterprise."

"My daughter? What does Emma have to do with any of this?"

"Why, nothing." Willi Bauer shrugged with a contrite smile. "She has nothing to do with any of this, of course. She was merely a necessary step for us to guarantee your participation. You see, it is *you* who we need, Charlie."

I looked around at the coven of Nazis. *"Me?"*

"Indeed. Look, Charlie . . ." Bauer led me over to their eating table outside the kitchen. A large map was spread on it. Armonk.

Chappaqua. Towns I recognized that were north of the city. In Westchester County. And a part of the map circled in red. It appeared to be a body of water.

I looked closer and saw that *Kensico Reservoir* was printed on it.

"You see, Charlie, the drinking water of New York City is fed by a network of reservoirs. Here, north of the city." He tapped on the map. "And in Queens. Near Aqueduct Raceway. You can only imagine how many millions of people use that water every day. And how harmful it would be, the panic it would cause, how very distrusting people would be of their own government, were something to be put in to contaminate it. Not just contaminate it, in fact, but to make it lethal to drink. And for it to be made clear to all that agents of the German government had the means to have done it."

I looked at him and it became clear to me what they had in mind. I flashed back to the beer barrels. The ones they had taken off the launch. From the sub. What I now knew they were filled with. "You're planning on poisoning the city's water supply," I said, my jaw slack. The thought hit me like a sledgehammer to the chest. "It was poison in those canisters, not bombs."

"Sarin, to be exact," Curtis said, in an accent I could now hear clearly was German. "At least, a liquefied form of it. Very, very lethal. A product of the IB Farben Company. A pinprick is sufficient to cause instant death. A hundred-liter keg . . . Four of them, in fact. Introduced into the city's water supply . . ." He shrugged with a roll of his eyes. "Well, one can only imagine . . ."

"You're all insane." I glared. "And you think I'm going to help you in this plot? I'd rather die."

"Maybe you would." Willi nodded. "As might any of us. If you had the choice. But yes, we do expect it, Herr Mossman—that is, if you value the health of your pretty daughter. Or unless you'd like to think of her taking a healthy dose of it in her morning orange juice," Willi Bauer said. He had lost his smile.

"I don't believe you would do that."

"You don't, do you? But would you be willing to wager it? You see, you have made yourself a bit of a nuisance, Charlie. I admit, more than we thought. That's for sure. What we Germans call *ein Ärgernis*. And as such, I'm afraid, you've made yourself quite expendable as well."

Curtis reached inside his jacket and took out the gun he'd had there. "Don't doubt me, Mr. Mossman." He held it firmly in his hand. "I have no compunctions about using this."

"Now, now, that won't be necessary, Kurt," Willi said. "Herr Mossman perfectly understands the situation. I'm sure he knows if there is any resistance on his part, even the slightest, or if he decided to bring anyone in on this, it would have the utmost consequences for Emma. Painful as that would be for all of us. She is like part of the family to Trudi and I."

"Yeah, a part of the family." I sniffed, looking at Trudi. "Look, I don't care about me. Just give me Emma. And I'll go through with it. What does she have to do with any of us?"

"I wish I could, Charlie. I truly do." He wagged his finger. "But that wouldn't be getting us what we need."

"Me?"

"Who do you think will be responsible for all this? Long after Trudi and I, even Herr Leitner, have left this beautiful country. Where do you think the curtain of blame will fall? Certainly not on two kindly Swiss grandparents. Without an enemy in the world." He patted Trudi's shoulder. "Who do you think would have the intelligence and the resentment against how his life had treated him to pull something like this off?"

"That's crazy."

"Is it, Charlie? Not as much as you think, I'm afraid." Willi smiled.

Was it? It started to dawn on me. How, yes, they'd set me up. I was going to be their patsy. And there were things, yes, that fit their description of me. They had me trapped to play the spy, the saboteur, or lose Emma. I thought it was them, as I tried to hunt them down, uncover evidence, but it turned out that I was the fifth column here.

Me.

"How did you know?" I asked dejectedly.

"Know?"

"That I knew."

"It's our job to know, Charlie. How did you think you could act so foolishly and not be found out?"

I still didn't know what Karl was doing here.

"Okay. Say I agree," I said. "But there's only one little problem. You see, the Feds already know about you and your plans. They know about everything, Willi. Your Nazi ties, the radio transmitter that was in your trunk over there; the code I came upon in your trash. Even your little delivery the other night. Your countrymen in that sub. If you ask me, they've probably got the place under surveillance right now, just like they had those other spies under surveillance and," I snapped my fingers, "the whole thing went up in smoke. All I have to do is call them."

"Do you, Charlie? Is that right?" I expected to see panic in their faces, their plans falling apart. But there was no sign of any. "Call them, you say . . . ?" Willi Bauer said, looking at Trudi, seemingly holding back a smile. He went to the side table and picked up the phone and extended it to me. "Then by all means, go ahead, call them. Here . . ."

Something wasn't right. I didn't move.

"Please, go ahead."

"Anyway, that won't be necessary, Mr. Mossman . . ." Another voice rang out. Not from the living room, but from inside. A familiar voice. "I'll make the conversation painlessly easy for you."

The door to the bedroom opened and Warren Latimer stepped out.

In a gray pin-striped suit, no jacket, suspenders, his dark hair slicked back. Wearing a smug, even slightly embarrassed smile on his face.

My jaw fell open and a surge of vomit formed in my gut and started to climb up my throat.

He was here? How? He was part of the State Department.

What was he doing here?

My knees buckled and my legs almost gave out. My head started to spin. I reached out to hold on to something.

In a flash, I thought back to everything I had divulged to the man. The transmitter. The code. The sub. Everything I thought had been passed on to the right people.

The pictures I had given him. The negatives . . .

You've done a helluva brave thing here, son . . . A helluva good thing, he had said. *For your country.*

And he was one of them. A Nazi. Part of this plot.

A traitor.

I felt a burning in the back of my eyes, as I held back the urge to lunge at him and grab him by the throat.

I'd told him everything. Everything I knew about the Bauers, I'd given him my proof. And all the while he was feeding it right to them, working with them.

Half the State Department wants FDR to stay out of the war. . . .

"You sonovabitch," I said.

Then suddenly my body felt like a weight was crashing through it, as an even more painful truth became clear to me. My thoughts swirled in a daze as I slowly put it all together.

Not just Latimer—but how he had first come into my trust. How I had met him. And the answer I was getting felt like a ledge had given way out from under me and I was suddenly in free fall, in a disappointment and confusion so deep I was being swallowed up in it. Crushed by it.

I recounted precisely how it had been: Who had introduced us. Who had vouched for him.

He's a very important man, Charles. He'll know precisely what to do.

"God, no . . ." I shook my head.

And I knew then that I had been set up from the very beginning. Going back to the chance meeting on Houston Street. From the moment those pages flew in the air. "My *dissertation,*" she had uttered so perfectly.

Taking me in.

And I had to reach out for the table next to me to even remain on my feet, as, following Latimer, just steps behind, Noelle stepped out from the bedroom too.

"Hello, Charles."

She was wearing a navy polka-dot dress, her lips blanched and pale. Her eyes hung in a downcast patina of guilt and shame, no life in them, almost a different person from the one I knew.

"How?" I looked from face to face, my body concussing in a wave of shock and foolishness, realizing in that instant everything that the sight of her, here, in this room, with these people, meant.

It had all been set up from the start. Those papers rustling in the wind. Our laughter together. Our lovemaking. Noelle, who I'd fallen for. Whom I had shared it all with. *All.* And which I now saw in the ghost of her wan, downcast face meant nothing to her. Nothing.

She was part of them too.

"I'm sorry, Charles," she said, her cheeks blanched, her lips pale, looking at me with deeply hooded eyes.

"It was all just, *what* . . . ," I said, shaking my head. "A lie? All a lie? Everything you told me. About how you got here? Your family back in France? How you hate the Bosch?"

"Ms. Leperrier did her job admirably," Willi Bauer said. "No less than what was expected of her as a member of the French *milicia.*"

"*Milicia?*" Pawns of the Gestapo, she had said. "Even your name . . . ?" I said, shaking my head with a grudging smile. "Was any of it true?"

"You must know, I had no love for any of this, Charles. I told you." She shrugged, and I detected a tinge of sadness in it. "The circumstances of how I got here were not straightforward either."

We all have our pasts, she had said.

"Yes. I guess that's perfectly clear now," I said. I turned back to Latimer. "And *you* . . . ? Do you even work for the State Department? Or is that a ruse too? Is that your real title, Head of Immigrant Affairs? Or are you just a run-of-the-mill, everyday traitor?"

"Don't be so naïve, Mr. Mossman." Warren Latimer sat down on the rounded arm piece of the couch. "Half the State Department doesn't want this war. We may not agree with the Nazis on every-thing, but we both recognize who the common enemy we face is. Where the real threat to our democracy lies. The Bolsheviks and the Jewish interests aligned with them—that will be the real war, after this one in Europe is resolved and our own government is brought down and we sue for peace. It's the Russians, any clear thinker on the world will agree. You're a student of history. Surely you can see. Communism is the dark, lurking danger. The one true existential threat. Not what's going on in Germany now. That will all sort itself out."

Sort itself out . . . The bombing of London on a nightly basis. The horrific persecution and relocation of the Jews.

"I'm truly sorry you've been forced into becoming a small cog in the formidable wheel of history, Mr. Mossman. But that is where you are now, at this moment, and I want to impress upon you that your daughter's safety is purely a matter of what you choose to do about that."

"You harm one hair on her head and I'll kill you myself, you can be sure of that," I said.

"Rest assured, Herr Mossman," Trudi Bauer finally spoke up, "no one here has any desire to see her harmed." Her eyes were deep and hardened in a manner that was nothing like the caring, grand-motherly way I always saw her before. "Still, you must also know we would not hesitate one second to do what needs to be done. Her fate lies with you, Herr Mossman. Not with us."

"With me . . . And what if I go straight to the police," I said, with a glance to Curtis's gun, "and tell them all I know about all this? What happens then?"

"Besides that result being a very unfortunate turn of events for your daughter, you would tell them exactly what, Mr. Mossman?" Latimer stood up and said. "Exactly what would they find? If they looked into things. A rootless ex-con unable to hold a job, with a history of drunkenness and violence. Who, when his daughter was taken from him by his wife, had resumed his drinking again."

"That's a lie."

"Is it . . . ?" Latimer widened his eyes. "Is it, Herr Habenshaller?" He turned toward Karl. "You've waited on Herr Mossman and Fraulein Leperrier at the Old Heidelberg café several times, have you not?"

"I have." Karl nodded enthusiastically. "He always asks for me."

"And what have you seen? You've served Mr. Mossman drinks there?"

"We had a champagne toast," I said. "Once." I looked at Noelle. "To celebrate our relationship. With someone who I thought cared for me."

"Not according to Herr Habenshaller, I'm afraid," Warren Latimer interjected. "Karl, you've seen him many times at the bar there, have you not? Over the edge."

"Many times," the heavyset German waiter with the ruddy cheeks replied. "Once, where he could simply not even walk out on his own. Another time, he almost got into a fight with another customer over his political views. Have you not seen the same . . . ?" He turned to Noelle.

Again, she merely clenched her jaw and nodded acceptingly. "I have." Her face blanched again with shame.

"How could you?" I glared at her.

"How could she? You mistake her," Willi Bauer said. "Miss Leperrier is bound to do her duty."

She averted her eyes.

"And that transmitter? Would you like to check the closet, Charles?" Warren Latimer gestured there with his hand. "Clearly a figment of your own overactive zeal to find some kind of cause against them. And what was it you claim you saw on the beach the other night? A German submarine? Please. Your drunkenness clouded your senses once before in a very unfortunate way. And now, no doubt again, it's sad to say. Try opening any of those barrels you claim to have seen rolled in and what would you find, Herr Bauer?"

"Why, beer, of course." Willi Bauer shrugged with a grin. "Good German beer. We have not fully disposed of all our inventory since we shut the brewery's doors. Perhaps you would like a taste, Herr Mossman? I'm happy to show you, if you like? *Bitte . . . ?*" He lifted up a mug from the table to me.

"No, that won't be necessary," I said, seething with anger and frustration. I saw where all of this was leading.

"And even the Bauers themselves . . . ," Latimer went on, gesturing toward Trudi and Willi. "Such nice, upstanding people. Who doesn't have a kind word for them? And yet you questioned them right from the start. From the first day you got out of prison. Mrs. Shearer overheard you many times. In fact, I think your own wife would readily admit to that if pressed. No . . . ? Bad-mouthing them. Following them when they went out. I think you even admitted such to the police. Looking into their affairs. Were you simply jealous of them, Mr. Mossman, having replaced you in your daughter's affections while you were in the state penitentiary? Or maybe it's just that you've built up this antipathy toward anything that even speaks of fascism. After your brother's unfortunate death in Spain. For which apparently you carry a deep sense of responsibility and which you haven't forgiven yourself for, isn't that right, Mademoiselle Leperrier? I mean, Noelle?"

"No, that's not true," I said, my temperature rising.

"But it is. It is true. Didn't he tell you all this, Mademoiselle Leperrier? Didn't he unburden his soul to you?" Noelle was pale. It was almost like he was trying to rub it in to her as well.

"Yes," she said, swallowing and bowing her head.

"What was that? I didn't hear."

"Yes." Noelle said again, nodding more firmly.

"So you see, Mr. Mossman, you really have nowhere to go with any of this. Not if you truly value your daughter's safety. You can't harm us any more than Emma can. Because nothing you've seen or uncovered points to anyone but *you,* I'm afraid. To your own irrational contempt for those who have stolen your daughter's affection. Finding plots under every rock simply because the Bauers' accent is Germanic. The truth is, we don't even need the pistol Herr Leitner is holding there. Please, Kurt, feel free to put it away. There is no need to keep our guest one minute longer than he likes. If he wants to make trouble, which I'm sure he will come to his senses and see for himself is the foolish path, he'll regret it for the rest of his life."

I clenched my fists. He was right on one thing: I would have liked to have leaped on him and buried him with blows. But I did see it. Plainly now. The taste in my mouth was so bitter I could barely wet my lips. I'd been set up. From the start. And they were right, I was trapped. Trapped by my own foolishness and stupidity to think I was more cunning than them. To want to believe I could be loved again. Trapped even more completely than when I was in my own cell. In Auburn. The only thing that mattered now was to get Emma back, and Latimer was right, if I blew that, if something happened, I'd live with it for the rest of my life. And I could see they were prepared to do what they had to do to get their plans accomplished. The rest . . . The rest, my own safety, as Latimer said, would sort itself out in the end.

"First, I need to know that Emma is okay. She must be terrified," I said.

"I assure you, Emma is perfectly fine," Willi Bauer attested. "She is being well taken care of. Just look at it as if she was spending a day at camp."

Camp. I scoffed.

"But if there is not a call from us every day, at a particular time . . ." Willi shrugged. "Then I'm afraid she will not feel that way at all. You understand me plainly, don't you?"

"I understand." I took in a breath and seethed, looking at their blank faces staring back at me. "So tell me, how do I know I can trust you?" I said to Latimer. "You tell me you're prepared to kill my daughter. If I do what you need me to do, how do I guarantee we will get her back?"

"Please, we are not savages, Charlie." He sniffed with some pride. "No matter what you think of us, no one here wants to hurt an innocent child."

"Emma is like a granddaughter to Willi and I." Trudi put her teacup on the table. "Never in a million years would we choose to hurt her unnecessarily."

Unnecessarily . . .

My chest was tight. Futility and helplessness swirled in me. Mixed with rage. I'd never had the urge to actually kill someone before, but now . . . "So when . . . ?" I looked at Latimer. "This beer party of yours. When does it take place?"

"Thursday," Willi Bauer said. He looked to Latimer and Curtis. Kurt.

Thursday. Thursday was two days.

Two days till I became a traitor against my country. Two days to get my daughter back in Liz's arms.

I looked back, defeated, accepting. I let my gaze fall from Trudi to Willi and then to Latimer, and ultimately to Noelle, where it remained until she looked away herself.

"All right." I nodded and took in a breath. "What is it you need me to do?"

33

Deflated and spent, I left Liz's brownstone and started to walk down Lexington Avenue, my mind in a daze. I was trapped. They had laid out what they wanted me to do. Participate in poisoning the water supply of New York. They said they needed a fall guy who could talk his way out of trouble. But more like someone they could pin the whole thing on. And I was the perfect candidate for that. My life had already crumbled to where no one would doubt I could do anything. Anything stupid and irrational. Even turn on my country.

Something called liquified sarin gas. I didn't know how many might die from something like this.

But however many it was, now I'd be complicit.

And if I didn't agree, they'd made it clear Liz and I would never see Emma again. And that was a possibility I couldn't face. I had no idea where they had her kept. *If we don't make a call once a day at a particular time . . .* Maybe Mrs. Shearer could be traced somehow. Maybe their calls could be traced. I heard they could do that now. But *Make no mistake,* Latimer had made it clear, *if you choose to go to the police, I'll know. I have my own contacts high up at the FBI, which is precisely where they'll go. You get any foolish ideas, Mr. Mossman, I'll know.*

Emma's fate is entirely in your hands.

They didn't even try to follow me when they let me out. I had no choice but to comply.

So what were my options? I tried to reason them through. Help them in their plans, I'd be a traitor. In shame for the rest of my days. If I even survived the night. Maybe Liz would get our daughter back again. Turn them in, as Latimer laid out, I still may not be able to prove a thing. I didn't even have the photographs I'd taken. They'd preyed on every weakness I had. And I was still reeling from the thought that the person I thought I was falling in love with just a few hours ago had duped me from the first moment we met.

Heading downtown, deep in my own thoughts, I saw those pages fly all over again.

My dissertation . . .

On Sixty-seventh Street, I saw a police car turn down the street and realized I was a block from the station.

I could go in and ask to speak with Monahan again. Lay it all out for him. I didn't have the photos or the Darwin book or anything, but I could try to convince him that I wasn't some kind of lunatic who once came in about Nazis down the hall and secret codes and now had graduated to German subs unloading weapons on American beaches and rogue State Department traitors. Would he believe a word that I was saying?

Certainly when Willi and Trudi, Latimer, Noelle, or even Karl the waiter pointed the finger at me, no one would.

Latimer had warned, *If you go to the police or the FBI, we'll know. . . .*

I looked behind me. I didn't see anybody following. A couple, arm in arm, went past. A man on the other side of the street ducked into a doorway as if avoiding being seen, but then I saw him go into the building and a light go on in the hallway.

It was all clear. They didn't even think it necessary to put someone on my tail.

I turned, huddled into my jacket, and went down the block to the station. I didn't know what was the right or wrong thing to do, only that Emma's life hung on whatever decision I made and I was scared to make it alone. I stopped in front. Two uniformed officers stepped out, nodded my way, and continued past me. *Go on in,* I exhorted myself. It was my only way out of this mess. Let the professionals handle it. I was just a pawn in this. Set up. Latimer couldn't have his tentacles everywhere. They'd see it. Liz could confirm Emma and Mrs. Shearer were missing. I could name names. People. Places. But, of course, accusations like this would have to be looked into. And investigations would take time. And time was something I didn't have now. And there was no guarantee, even if I did what they wanted, that Emma would ever be returned safely. I'd be risking her life, doing their bidding—all the while with no assurance of ever getting her back.

All these things were careening through my mind.

I asked my inner voice what to do, the one who always gave me the right advice, but he pulled himself out of the discussion fast, going, "I can't help you this time, pal."

I took a last look around, pretty certain that no one was watching me, then said, "Hell," and flung the station door open. My heart raced; I prayed I was doing the right thing. I took a breath and stepped up to the elevated front desk. A duty officer was sitting behind it, different from the one who had been there the last time I'd been inside.

"Help you, buddy?" he looked down and said. He glanced up from whatever he was reading.

My heart started to pound.

All I'd have to do was blurt out, "They've taken my daughter!" That's all I had to do. But my tongue was paralyzed.

"Sir, can we help you . . . ?" the duty officer asked again, peering down over his glasses.

"Yes. I need to—" I felt a swell of panic come over me. Monahan already thought I was a flake. The story I had to tell now would be even harder to accept.

"Buddy, are you all right . . . ?" The cop peered over, seeing me break out in a sweat.

I wasn't even close to all right. I wasn't sure if this was the right thing to be doing. Finally, it all made me feel like I was going to burst. "Sorry," I exhaled, and turned and ran back outside. My chest was tight and exploding and I needed air. As soon as I got out of the doors, I gulped the crisp night air into my lungs and my heart went rat-tat-tat against my ribs.

All I could conjure up was the image of the police knocking on the Bauers' door, and then what would happen? Or the FBI sitting me down in an interrogation room, trying to pick apart the truth from what appeared to be ramblings. German subs. Latimer.

All it would take was one call from Trudi and Willi and then what? About Emma.

I just couldn't take the risk.

Slowly I regained myself and felt the sweats start to recede. I blew a blast of air out my cheeks.

I had a day to figure something else out.

Something that didn't involve the police.

Something so I wasn't a traitor.

Emma, I'll find another way.

34

I headed down Lex to Forty-seventh and York to Liz's sister's apartment. The doorman rang me up.

"What?" Liz met me at the door with worry in her eyes, searching my face for an answer. "Charlie, tell me."

"She's all right," I said upfront, trying to calm her. "I promise." We went inside and sat down on the couch. Her sister Sophie poured some coffee. "But you are going to have to trust me on some things, Liz. Things that may be hard to believe at first. First, she's being held. By Willi and Trudi. Just as I told you. And by some others too."

"Held?" Panic lit her eyes. "What do you mean?"

"I've come upon some things, Liz. You're not going to like them."

"What things, Charlie?" She gasped and put her hand to her mouth. "What do you mean by that?"

"What I mean is I was right. About what I've been trying to tell you all along. The Bauers . . . they're German agents, Liz.

I know that's hard for you to believe, but it's true. Worse than agents, in fact. They're about to take some steps against the country now that we're at war." I took her through the entire series of events that I'd been a part of over the past week. From the truck ride out to Bridgehampton and seeing the German sub in the water and the launch coming ashore. To Warren Latimer. And how I met him. And who he was. To Curtis and Mrs. Shearer. All the people in her life. German spies.

She looked at me with the detached, slack-jawed gaze of a doctor trying to ascertain the mental health of a raving patient. "Charlie, you don't actually expect me to believe all this, do you . . . ?"

"Liz, look at me," I said. "This isn't fantasy. This is real. You know it is. They have Emma. We're at war. They have her in order to entrap me into helping them in some way."

"Helping them do what?" she asked.

"I can't tell you, Liz. You're just going to have to trust me on this. The less you know the better. I know you've been skeptical of all this. I know you thought I was making stuff up or was even out of my mind. But I also know you know I wouldn't do anything to jeopardize Emma. And that's what's at stake here. And why I need you to trust me on all this. I'll get her back."

"How? How will you get her back? What do they want you to do? You say they're spies, Charlie. Even if I believe you on this, then we have to go to the police. Now. Right this minute. What else is there?"

"No." I held her by the shoulders. "Part of trusting me is accepting that I just don't think that's the best way right now."

"What's not the best way, Charlie?" Panic flamed in her eyes, along with distrust. Distrust of me. "What's not the best way?"

"Getting the police involved. There are people in this who are already more well connected than the police. We might alert them if we go . . ."

"We might? Trust you? What are you jabbering about, Charlie? You're telling me our daughter's been taken. By this group of people we trusted who are now spies . . . That my own nanny is somehow involved. You say they're plotting something. They're holding our daughter for ransom. And that we can't even take it to the police? What about the FBI then?"

"No."

Her pupils were wide as dark moons, terrified. And I was doing my best not to be just as terrified. And to try to make sense to her, as much as I could. I described the meeting I'd just had with them. I even told her about Noelle. How the person I thought I was falling in love with had betrayed me.

She looked to her sister and her brother-in-law, Les, a lawyer, for support.

"How do we even know they'll keep their word?" Les muttered after I fully mapped it out, making me trust I had at least convinced them I wasn't raving mad.

"We don't." I shrugged kind of futile-like and helplessly shook my head. "But I think you're right on one thing, Liz. Trudi and Willi do have feelings toward her. I don't think they'd want to see her harmed. They'd have no reason to, except to punish me, if we don't comply. I'm banking on that."

"Comply with what, Charlie . . . ?" Liz finally asked, looking pale and terrified.

"If I do what they say. They have her hidden somewhere. I don't think they'll hurt her if I comply. But if I don't, if they feel threatened in any way, I also have no doubt they'll do what they say they'll do."

"Do what, Charlie? What do they want you to do?" she asked again.

It was best she didn't know. Didn't know what depths I had to sink to to try and save Emma. "They just need me to help them in something." I exhaled. "For Emma's sake, I'd rather not say."

Liz leaned back. Her red eyes raw and glazed. Trying to make sense of it. Of anything that was happening. "Willi and Trudi . . . ," she muttered, shaking her head. "I can't believe this . . . I can't . . . And Mrs. Shearer . . . I just can't."

She just sort of fell into me, not having anyone else to hold her, and I put my arms around her. I put my arms around my wife in a comforting way for the first time in more than two years. "I know . . . ," I said, stroking her while she sobbed. "You don't have to say it, Liz. I know. Just let me get her back for you."

"Please don't let her down, Charlie . . . ," she said, tears soaking my shirt, finally giving in. "It's our Emma."

I left, begging her to give me just two days. Two days that I prayed would give us back our daughter. And I prayed I could deliver her.

Then I'd worry about whatever might happen to me.

I took the subway back to Brooklyn.

All the way, the rattling train echoed in my brain. I ran through our situation, thinking that there had to be something they'd screwed up on. Where were they holding her? How were they getting into the reservoirs? Was anyone else involved? The only thing I did feel sure of was that I knew where the kegs of poison were being held. If only I could somehow tamper with them.

In Brooklyn, I walked the six blocks from the F train station to Powers Street in a kind of trance. In the end, I came to the conclusion I had no choice but to comply. Whatever the ultimate risk to me. I would either be seen as a traitor to my country or turn them in and possibly see my daughter killed.

It was a choice I had no answer for.

On Powers, I went into the house I rented a room in and up the stairs. Completely spent, I put the key in my door and opened it, tossed my hat on the desk, and flicked on the light, preparing to hurl myself on the bed and sleep.

A voice said, "Good evening, Mr. Mossman."

My heart stood still.

Someone was in my chair, his long legs crossed, in a double-breasted suit and tie, his hat on the table next to him.

I felt a throbbing in my chest.

"Sit down, Mr. Mossman." The man nodded me toward the edge of the bed. "Take a seat, please."

I remained standing.

Even in the dim light I realized I had seen him before. But where? And why was he here? And how?

And then, in a horrifying tumble of images, it came back to me. Like a bad dream forming shape and coming back into focus long after you've woken up.

It was the man who had been sitting across from me at The Purple Tulip next to the Old Heidelberg café the night I waited for Liz. With the thin mustache and the mole on his chin.

The same man I had seen on the landing that day outside Willi and Trudi's door. Who had tipped his hat to Emma and me when we had mailed Trudi's letters.

I realized he was one of them. One of the Bauers' so-called customers.

A Nazi.

My chest started to pound in fear.

"Let me explain the facts of life to you, Mr Mossman," he said, reaching his hand into his inside pocket for what I took to be a gun.

"I didn't say anything," I said. I assumed he'd been watching me and had seen me go into the police station. Maybe I was a dead man for doing that, and if that's what this was, so be it. But I couldn't lose Emma because of it. Not now. "Please, I just went inside, but I came right back out. I never spoke with anyone. I swear."

"I asked you to sit down," the man said again, nodding me toward the edge of the bed.

Warily, I let myself down.

Instead of a gun, he merely came back out with a cigarette case, and offered me one. "Smoke?"

I shook my head, the panic in my chest starting to subside. If he wasn't here to shoot me then what *was* he here for? Whoever the hell he was.

"Maybe a whiskey then?" he said. There was a bottle of rye on the side table next to him and he lifted it to me. "I brought along my own."

"No." I shook my head. "I don't anymore."

"Oh, that's right," he said. He filled two small glasses and pushed one toward me. "But just this once I think you might."

Oh, that's right. How did he know that about me? I reached across and took the glass, up, my hand still quivering a bit.

What he said shocked me.

"Bottoms up, Mr. Mossman. Here's to getting your daughter back."

35

"What are you talking about?" I replied, my chest still tight as a drum, my eyes blinking. I didn't know who he was, or who had sent him, whether he was from the Feds or the bad guys, but Emma's life hung in the balance of whatever I said or whomever I talked to, and I wasn't about to give that away.

All I knew was, I'd seen him going into the Bauers' apartment. This guy was a Nazi.

"I'm talking about your daughter," he said again. He reached into his jacket one more time and came out with a photograph. He handed it to me. It was of Emma and me, coming down the stairs of her brownstone. Hand in hand. On one of our walks. I wasn't sure how long ago it had been taken. We weren't wearing coats. So a while. I looked back at him, still not certain just what I should divulge. Her life hung on what I said. "She's missing, right?" the man said. "I have a daughter myself. I can only imagine . . . I know what it must be like for you. Not to know if she'll live or die. You do want her back, don't you?"

"Who the hell *are* you?" I stared at him closely, screwing up my eyes. "And just what the hell are you doing here?"

"I'm not one of them, if that's what you're thinking. Let me put you at ease. You're not the only one with questions about Willi and Trudi Bauer, or some of their associates. By that I mean certain members of the government who may have, how shall we say, confused their allegiances. Even," he said, taking out a lighter and lighting up his smoke, "in our own State Department."

He meant Latimer, of course. But still, I didn't give him an answer. They'd set me up once before, these bastards. They might be testing me again. And Emma's life was on the line. "How are you here then?" I pressed. "How did you find me?"

"You filed a report with the New York Police Department, didn't you?"

"A report . . . ?" I almost choked. Monahan. I couldn't believe what I'd just heard. The report that I was sure was on the bottom of a forgotten pile somewhere. But how else would anyone know about that? Unless the police had been infiltrated too, I thought. Which was possible. The State Department had. I wasn't sure whether to be elated by what he had told me or more concerned. But how could it get any worse for me? "You're with the police?"

"Not the police. But you're warm. My name's Fiske. You want me to show you a card? Just a bunch of initials. You wouldn't recognize them anyway. Latimer likely showed you one, and what did that accomplish? We've been looking into certain persons of interest for some time. What's perfectly legal one day becomes outright treason and sedition the next. And I don't blame you for being a little skeptical about things. Still, you won't have too many chances to help yourself, Mr. Mossman, or your beautiful little girl. Events are moving fast. And this is one of those times. I know they have you squeezed. So I suggest you grab it. This chance I'm offering you."

"Do you know where she is?" I finally gave in, hope rising in me. I went with my gut.

"No, I don't, I'm afraid." He took a drag on his cigarette. "But what I do know is we're the only chance you have to help her. Or yourself, for that matter . . ."

I just looked back at him. I hadn't even thought of what might happen to me in this. Only Emma. I guess that showed on my face.

"You don't really think they're going to let you just walk away from this, do you?"

"Walk away? Walk away from what?"

"Don't try to play too many angles, Mr. Mossman. It's not your game. You know what they have planned. I don't, to put my cards on the table. Other than it's called Prospero. But I do know it's something the United States of America can't let happen. And I also know they've squeezed you like a ripe lemon to be complicit in their plans. And that you have to make a decision now. Just who can you trust? And even more so, what's the best chance to get that lovely daughter of yours back safely? I'd take that drink now, if I were you. You'll need it."

I held the glass, a little unsure, and looked back at him. I was starting to feel he was right. Maybe a shot of rye wasn't the worst thing in the world for me right now. I chugged it back and felt the splash of liquor burn its way down my throat and into my chest.

"Of course I want her back," I said. "I want her back more than anything in the world. How do I know I can believe you? Who you say you are. One thing you've got right, they did set me up. There's this woman. She's French." I exhaled. "I thought she and I were—"

"Miss Leperrier." He cut me off with a knowing smile. "There's always a woman in these things, I'm sad to say. That's how they hook people. But trust me, she's just the tail of a very large fish on this. She was sent here by the Abwehr to hook people like you. Her parents are being held in a Nazi prison in Drancy back in France. Whether they ever walk out of there is up to her. So you see, she's as much of a pawn in this as you are, Mr. Mossman, if that's any consolation."

So it was true, what Noelle had told me. At least about that. *The circumstances of my trip were not straightforward.* . . . They had her trapped just like they had me. And we both had to work our way out of it. But I wasn't looking for consolation now.

I said, "She introduced me to this high-level government man from D.C." I put my glass down. "From the State Department. The Office of Immigrant Affairs . . ."

"Warren Latimer," Fiske said with a nod.

"You know him too?"

"We have a good part of the network under watch. You've no doubt heard or seen many expressions of sympathy with the Nazi cause in the lead-up to this war. Some, simply to keep America out of it. Which makes sense to some and wasn't even a crime until a few days ago. Others . . ." He flicked off an ash and balanced his cigarette on the ashtray. "Let's just say others have blurred the line where political ideology and good citizenship meet. And that's not exactly good policy now. We can't have it. Not in our own government. I'm sure you of all people can understand, given all you've been through."

Latimer. The head of the fish. Or maybe it even went higher up than him.

"They said if I went to the police, they'd know," I said. "Or to the FBI. I don't know who you're with. They said they have contacts there. Maybe people in your own organization. You said you had a daughter, so you know. You know the choice you'd have to make. I don't care about myself anymore. Whatever happens. But I can't put Emma in any more danger than she's already in. By talking to you. You understand that, right? You've already said you have no idea where she is. So how can you help me?"

"That is a choice to make," Fiske said, "I admit. And you're going to have to make it. Tonight even. But before you do, if I were you I might just think, just where have you seen me before, Mr. Mossman? Other than at The Purple Tulip. On the landing of the Bauers' apartment, if I recall. So they don't know about me. If they did, you can be sure I wouldn't be here talking with you. So that should comfort you at least a little." He kept his narrow eyes trained on me. Beady, nonconfiding. "You're smack in the middle of this, Mr. Mossman. You can help do something good for your country. And I'll do everything I can to get that girl of yours back safe and sound. I give you my word. Besides, to me, you're already ahead of the game as it is. . . ."

"How's that?" I asked.

Fiske took a last drag on his cigarette and stamped it out. "A minute ago you thought I was here to kill you." His thin lips edged into a smile. "And here you are having a drink with me. That's the best proof I can offer."

I gave him the thinnest smile in return. "So who do they think *you* are, since you've obviously gained their trust?"

"They recruited me. To them, I'm an electrical engineer with the aircraft research lab in New Brunswick, New Jersey. We're working on airplane engines. Jets, they call them. One day, they'll make a big difference in this war. I pass them schematics every once in a while, but rest assured, whatever we send 'em will make a whole lot of noise but never get off the ground. There's about to be a big bust. Their whole network is going down. And I don't want you to get caught up in it the wrong way. Or your daughter."

I stared at him a long time. The long, gaunt face. The suit that looked a size too large on him. On my own I was nowhere. With him I was just another pawn. But what choice did I have? "So what happens to me in this if I do help you?"

"You mean if you survive . . . ?" Fiske gave me a knowledge-able wink. "Look, you're a family man, Mr. Mossman. In spite of a few unfortunate items on your résumé, which we assume you're well past today, the United States of America would be grateful for your support, and would show that gratitude by pretending you never were even a participant in any of this. And hopefully, you get your pretty little daughter back, which I'm worried for you may not happen any other way. Not to mention you will have done something good for your country at the same time. Have another . . . ?" He lifted the bottle my way.

I put up my hand. "No. That's as much as I've had in two years. And if I've got a decision to make I'd like to keep it that way. So you know about the sub, I presume?" I asked, starting to give in, but still keeping my cards close to my chest. I saw no better option than to trust him.

"The sub?" His eyes grew wide. Clearly, he didn't.

"One came ashore a week ago. On eastern Long Island."

"A German sub, I assume you're saying?"

"That's right. A launch from it came ashore. They unloaded some cargo. I watched it all take place."

"Who unloaded cargo? The Bauers? Latimer?"

"Four German sailors. And two of the Bauers' henchmen, one who works in their apartment building."

"You say you saw this? Yourself?"

"It's a long story." I nodded. "But yes." Now I had something on *him*.

"I've got nowhere to go," he said, tipping his glass to me to go into it.

I told him how I had snuck onto the delivery truck at the brewery and had taken the ride all the way out to Long Island, where I saw them unloading what looked like kegs of beer from the launch that came ashore.

"What was it? Weapons?" Fiske looked at me, deadly serious now. "Explosives, maybe?"

I had no choice but to trust him. For Emma. I needed someone who could help get her back. "They've got some kind of lethal poison," I said. "They called it sarin."

"Sarin . . . ?" He shrugged. "I've heard they have something." I could already see his mind in gear.

"Bauer said just a pinprick can kill a man. They've got four kegs. Sit back, Mr. Fiske. Now it's you who may want to take another drink." He did. And I continued.

"They're going to try to introduce it into the New York City water supply."

36

The next day I went back to meet with Willi and Trudi at the brewery, which Fiske said his people already had under watch. It was Wednesday, the day it was all supposed to take place. Fiske assured me they wouldn't make any move until I learned exactly what Bauer and his team were mapping out. What their plan was. And where Emma might be.

I wasn't just a dupe. I was a double agent now.

"Charlie!" Willi Bauer said happily when I showed up exactly at noon. I rapped on the outer door in a series of knocks as they'd instructed me. "You remember our little brewery, don't you?" he said with a wry smile, dressed in a sweater vest and knit tie. "I believe you were in here once before. And I'm very glad you've seen the wisdom of seeing this matter through. Emma will soon happily be back with your wife. And with you, I hope, if all goes well. Perhaps we will all be pleased with the outcome."

"You're a murderer," I said, glaring at him and Trudi, who was dressed in a drab, gray suit with a floral hat, and who only glowered at me suspiciously.

"A combatant, as we choose to see it," Willi Bauer said. "A slightly different view. One is never too old to do one's duty for their fatherland."

"Call it what you like. If this goes through, you'll have thousands of lives on your conscience. I didn't take you for that kind of man."

"Don't spend your time dwelling on that, Mr. Mossman. I'd spend it thinking about your daughter and how you're helping to get her back."

"What do you say we just get on with it," I looked at him and said.

The same delivery truck I'd ridden in out to Bridgehampton was parked in the loading bay, its cargo doors open. I didn't see any kegs around, or whatever it was the sub had dropped off. They led me into an office through a side door. Curtis was there, or Kurt now; Oberleutnant Leitner, as they were now calling him. Leaning back in a chair with his foot up on the table. His shirt open at the top two buttons. "Mossman." He nodded brusquely, the "Mr." now gone.

I had the feeling everyone in the room expected I wouldn't survive the night.

Spread on a table was the large blueprint site map I had seen at the Bauers' apartment.

The Kensico Reservoir in Westchester.

"Where's Latimer?" I looked around.

"Probably back at his desk," Willi said with a smile. "In Washington. He has an important job to do, now that his country is at war."

"Yeah, we're lucky to have him on our side," I sniffed cynically.

And Noelle, I was about to add. Where was she? Having done her duty.

I didn't see her anywhere either.

"You don't mind, do you?" Curtis got up and came over to me and forced my arms outward. He patted me down brusquely, pulled open my jacket, felt my chest under my shirt until he was satisfied nothing was there. "Our man is clean as a baby." He nodded to Willi.

"Good, Mr. Mossman. We wouldn't want this to be over before you've had a chance to help yourself and Emma." He smiled through his white mustache.

"So when is all this happening?" I asked. "All I want is to do what I have to do and have Emma released. I want to see her before I go."

"Don't worry yourself with so many details," Trudi Bauer said. She was dressed in a dark suit and flat navy hat. "All will be revealed soon. Be assured. But I'm afraid what you ask won't be possible. Emma is safe and in good hands. Hands that have cared for her. As soon as we are safe, a call will be made, I assure you. As Mr. Latimer has said, we have no reason to harm her once we accomplish our goal. We're not exactly savages."

Not only did I have to help them, she was saying, I now realized their mission had to be successful for Emma to be released. I prayed I hadn't screwed it up by agreeing to work with Fiske. But what choice did I have?

"Let me speak to her then. I've done everything you've asked."

"Now?" Willi Bauer shook his head. "Impossible."

"Yes. Call her up. It's the least you can do for me. Please. You say you care for her. She must be scared out of her wits. I'm living up to my word."

My argument seemed to make a dent in Willi's hardened demeanor. He glanced toward Trudi, who, with the slightest shrug and hardened gaze, gave her husband the answer.

"Tonight, perhaps," he proposed.

"Tonight?"

"Yes. You'll be here at midnight sharp."

"Midnight? It's happening tonight?" Nerves sprang up in me. Midnight meant Emma's life and mine were on the line. A rat-tat-tat sped up in my blood.

"The less you know, the better, Mr. Mossman," Trudi Bauer said. I inched as close as I could to the table, hoping to make sure of the target. My eyes glanced down, taking in as much of the map as I could. Before Willi started to fold it up.

"Unless I know she's safe and unharmed, I'm not going through with it," I said. "That's not negotiable for me. I want to hear her voice."

"I can't promise, Mr. Mossman. You are certainly not in a position to be bargaining with us."

"Maybe. But you're the one who wants me to betray my country. What if you've already harmed her? That's what it will take if you want me. To speak with her."

Willi glanced at Trudi. She seemed to nod ever so subtly. "Just be here tonight. We'll see what we can do."

"I'll be here."

I looked around. Freddy, the dough-faced man who had driven the second car, was there too.

"Just one more thing . . . ," Willi said. "So what are you,

Mr. Mossman . . . ?" He seemed to size me up. "A fifty long perhaps?"

"Fifty long . . . ?"

"So sorry. I always still think in European sizes. Force of habit after all these years. An American size forty, perhaps? In a jacket?"

"I don't know. Forty. Yeah, I guess," I said. "Why?"

"Twelve sharp, Mr. Mossman," Willi said. "You can go now. But I must remind you, if you do anything stupid, if we feel even the slightest lessening of your commitment . . . if Mrs. Bauer or I don't make a call at precisely the right hour, no one will ever see your daughter again. So her fate is in your hands. Just so you know. You understand me, don't you?"

I looked back at him, and then at Trudi, with a coil wrapping tighter and tighter in my gut.

"I understand."

37

At six, I sat at a table at the Seligman's Kosher Cafeteria on Bushwick Avenue near my apartment in Brooklyn.

A few early diners, mostly older types, sat at about six tables in the restaurant, polishing off plates of kreplach, bowls of borscht, roast chicken in gravy, or a slice of pie. I picked at a plate of brisket, but I wasn't exactly hungry.

It was happening tonight.

By morning, I'd either have my daughter home and safe again and back with Liz, or, God forbid, I'd be dead, she might be dead, and a terrible thing would have happened to the country. I was thinking it might be better if I didn't survive the night.

A man in a fedora and raincoat stepped in.

"Take any table," someone from behind the counter said to him.

"Thanks." He found an empty one on the other end of the dining area, took off his hat, revealing a long, thin face with a mole on his chin.

"Brisket's lean," the waiter in a white shirt and apron said. "Everyone seems to like."

"Just a coffee for now, please. I'll come get it in a minute."

He looked my way with a subtle nod, got up, and headed back down a short corridor to the men's room. Another man I didn't recognize—short, dark—got up and put himself at the entrance to the corridor, as if blocking traffic. No one else even glanced up from their food.

I put down my knife and fork and got up as well. As I went past the man guarding, he merely motioned me along with a subtle flick of his chin. *In there.* A mobster setting up a hit couldn't have done it in a more mundane way.

In the men's room, Fiske was washing his hands. "We've got about two minutes before it starts to look fishy. What do you know?"

"It's happening tonight," I said. "Or early tomorrow morning. They've asked me to come back to the brewery at midnight."

"Midnight. Do you have any idea where?"

"The Kensico Reservoir," I said. "It's up in Westchester some-where. They had the site map opened up on a table, so I'm sure. They folded it up when they saw me looking at it."

"Kensico?" Fiske looked at me and questioned.

"Yes. I saw the same map once before, opened up in their apartment."

"Sixty percent of the city's water supply comes from the Ken-sico Reservoir," Fiske uttered gravely, in the manner a general might observe when coming upon a battlefield and looking over an opposing force double the size of his own.

"I didn't see any of the beer kegs. Maybe they have them stored somewhere where they used to keep the beer."

"Yes, certain gases need to stay refrigerated to avoid combustion."

"I think they actually said it wasn't a gas. That they'd found some way to treat it so that it wouldn't just dilute in water. They're going to kill me after," I said. "After I've done whatever they need me to do. I told them I needed to speak with Emma. They wouldn't let me. Maybe tonight, I was told. But I could feel it, the way they were all looking at me. The minute I've done what I'm there to do, I'm as good as a dead man."

"We're not going to let that happen, Charlie," Fiske assured me. "I give you my word."

"Your word, it's as good to me as theirs," I said. "Anyway, all that matters for me is Emma. They told me again if they don't make a certain call after this is over, there are orders to kill her, so, whatever you do, they have to be captured alive. Do you hear me? You're watching the brewery, right?"

Fiske nodded. "We are."

"And can you trace the call? If I get them to get Emma on the line. I've heard that's possible today."

"Maybe. If they let you stay on long enough. It's not perfect or quick. But . . . Our plan will be to take the Bauers alive at all costs. We need them ourselves, to dig out the entire network. I suspect in the end they'll be happy to trade the whereabouts of a six-year-old girl who means nothing to them for some reduction of what's in store for them."

"Your mouth to God's ears, Fiske," I said. "You say you're a father?"

He nodded. "A boy and a girl."

"Just know, if things don't happen like you say, if this goes south in any way, you'll have this in your mind every time you look at your own daughter."

"I don't need that as an incentive to do my job. I promise you, we'll be there, Mr. Mossman."

"You better be. Just remember, you're the ones who pushed your way in on this, Fiske. I was perfectly set to go at it alone."

"Don't worry, Charlie. You're not alone. You have my word. Still, maybe it's best we give you a gun to go in there with. Just in case. And a wire."

"No. Curtis, the maintenance guy, or Kurt, Oberleutnant Leitner as they refer to him—the guy's a German officer—frisked me as soon as I came in. I'm sure they'll do the same tonight. If they find something on me, they'll know I've been talking to someone. I can't take the chance."

"All right . . ." Fiske massaged his chin in thought. "Here's what we'll do. There'll be a white Pontiac sedan parked right outside the brewery entrance. Jersey plates. Under the rear passenger wheel you'll find a gun. Once they frisk you, say you want to go out and have a smoke. Or you need some air. Your nerves are making you sick. When you're next to it, toss your cigarette out and find a way to bend down and pick up the gun. Hopefully, they'll be busy with their own preparations and won't be watching you."

"All right." I blew out a breath. "I'll do my best."

"Ever use one?" Fiske inquired.

"A gun? No." I shrugged.

"The safety will be off. Just point it at someone who's trying to kill you and pull the trigger," the government man said with a smile. "Simple."

"Thanks. I'll try."

"All right, we better get out of here now. Listen, luck be with you later." He squeezed my arm. "You're doing a brave thing, Mr. Mossman. I know you're nervous about your daughter. There isn't a father in the world who wouldn't be. But I just want you to know, we'll get her for you. Just know we'll be at the target site. You won't see us, but we'll be in place. We'll take them down once we see who shows up and they're in motion. I assure you, one of them will give up her location, rather than face kidnapping charges and an espionage sentence that would mean the rest of their lives in jail."

"All right." My stomach started to churn with nerves. At both the thought of Emma and the resonance of the word "tonight." It was all playing out in a matter of hours. Even if Fiske's raid proved successful we still had the challenge of getting Emma, but if I didn't involve them, I'd have no control over it at all. Fiske put his hand on the doorknob.

"One more thing . . . ," I said.

"What's that?"

"Bauer asked me for my jacket size."

"Your jacket size?" Fiske said.

"I have to figure they're not fitting me for a tuxedo," I said.

38

I got back to my place around six thirty and called Liz at Sophie's. I told her it was going to be tonight that things were happening. That she should probably go back to her place and wait there. And that with God's help Emma would be returned safe.

"Tonight," she muttered nervously. I heard the tremor in her voice. "Charlie, just what are you going to be doing?"

I'd never told her fully.

"What I should be doing," I said. "Don't worry, we're going to get her back. And Liz . . ." I felt a lump in my throat.

"Yes."

"I'm sorry for all the pain I've caused you in this. I mean through everything. You know I always loved you."

She hesitated. I wished she could have come back with "I always loved you too, Charlie." Instead, she merely said, "You just be careful, Charlie. I trust you. Whatever you're doing. Bring our daughter home."

"I will, Liz."

I called my mom and dad as well. I hadn't spoken to them in months. And this might be the last time they'd ever hear from me. "I know I've disappointed you," I said to my dad. "I know I wasn't like Ben. And that you always held that against me."

"I never held it against you, son. It's just that . . ." His voice trailed off.

It was just that what . . . ? I waited. He couldn't finish it.

"Well, I wish that things had somehow been different between us," I said. "I wish I could take things back. I wish I could take a lot of things back."

"Charlie," he said, clearly hearing my trepidation. "Are you all right, son?"

No, I'm not all right, I should have said. *My daughter is being held hostage and I've gotten myself into something deep and dangerous, something that might make me look very bad when it all comes out. If I even survive. And I really have no one to say goodbye to if it turns out bad. Only people to say I'm sorry to.*

"Yes, Pop, I'm all right," I said.

"How's Emma?" he asked. As if mercifully changing the subject might lighten things with us. "How's our little girl?"

"Emma. She's doing great," I lied. "I hope you're doing well, Pop. Tell Mom I love her too."

"Charlie, wait—"

As I put the receiver down, I knew I might never speak to them again.

It was just after seven now. I went upstairs and threw myself on the bed. I had five hours to go. Five hours that may well be my final ones. I lay there, smoking a Chesterfield. For a while my thoughts drifted to Liz and Emma. How I'd let them down once and how I wanted to change all that in the next few hours.

Then they went back to that punch I had thrown in that bar. One reckless act that had changed everything for me. And the kid I'd inadvertently killed. Who never had a chance to become the person he was destined to be. How badly I would have liked to stand in front of his mother right now—and ask forgiveness from her. I had long given up any thought that it was all just a matter of bad luck and timing, but that it was me—my choice, my actions—that led to it. My responsibility.

And Liz was right, what came between us was far more than just that one punch.

And then I found my thoughts wandering to Ben. Whose fate for these past few years I'd taken on my own shoulders. And in the same way, I came to suddenly feel that it was his choice to go off and join the fight over there. Not mine. I'd blamed myself for it for so long, and now I saw, clear as my daughter's eyes, that it was his. I'd never once spoken with him about why he felt the need to go. Other than to do the noble thing. *Tikkun olam,* he called it. He always spent more time in temple than me. It meant "to heal the world." And it gave me strength, lying there. The courage that I was doing the right thing now. Healing my life in whatever time I had left. I had always admired him so much, and now, I was the one standing up for once. Fighting for what I loved and believed in. I felt a bit of a smile come onto my face. A peace. I felt lighter than I had in years. *Tikkun olam.* Heal the world. I was sure, if Ben was around, if I could share with him what was about to take place, he would admire me.

The clock on my night table now read 8:30. Still almost three hours to go. I shut my eyes.

Suddenly I was awakened by a knock on the door. I realized I must have dozed a little. The clock read 8:50. "Who is it?" I called out.

"It's me, Charlie."

Liz.

I jumped up and went to open it.

"Your landlady let me in," she said. "I hope you don't mind. I—"

"No, I don't mind at all. Come on in," I said, and opened the door. "I must have dozed off for a second. It isn't exactly the Ritz," I apologized, letting her in. My one room, a table, a chair, a dresser, the bed. Some clothes thrown around haphazardly. The one shared bathroom was down the hall.

"Thanks." She was in a wool coat and sweater. Her hair was pulled back. Her cheeks were peaked. She looked how I felt. Which was scared. I didn't want to show her that I felt that way too. She said, "I just couldn't be alone, Charlie. I had nowhere to go."

"Do you want anything?" I asked. There was still the bottle of rye Fiske had brought on the table. "It's not mine," I said, seeing her eyes go toward it. "I promise. It belonged to a friend. I was just lying down. I have to leave around eleven."

"Eleven?" Her face grew taut with worry.

"Yes. And you should probably head back to the brownstone around then yourself and wait."

"What's going on? I wish you would tell me, Charlie."

"I can't, Liz. I wish I could. Please don't ask me again."

She looked around. "I could lie down too." She shrugged. "If that's okay with you. You used to make me feel calmer when I would get all crazy about things. My thesis. Whether Emma was sleeping through the night."

I looked at her and saw she might fall apart any second. "With me? Of course, it's okay, Liz. That would be real nice."

She took off her coat and draped it on the chair across from the bed. "All those things we fought over, they don't seem really important right now, do they, Charlie?"

I looked back at her and gave her a bolstering smile. "No, they don't."

I went back to the bed and sat on it. Knees up. Liz was dressed in a gray sweater and slacks. She gave me a smile that showed she knew how awkward this was, and lowered herself down next to me. It was the closest I had been to her in over two years. I didn't know what to do. Hold her. Put my arm around her. At first she remained a foot or two away from me on her side. Then I put my arm out on the pillow and she rested her head on it and nudged a bit closer to me. Her head fit onto my shoulder and her body fit in the grooves against me as naturally as a missing puzzle part you've been looking for. We had done it a thousand times.

I squeezed gently.

"I know I've been mean to you," she said. "I know I've acted like I was unable to forgive you. And for a while, I'm sorry, Charlie, I couldn't. It was hard. Not forgiving you was the only way I could not feel pain. But I have forgiven you now. I just didn't know how else to be. Our life had changed so much."

"That's okay," I said, and pulled her slightly closer. "I see it now."

"I was just so fucking angry, Charlie. You hurt me. And I didn't know how else to be."

"I was angry too, Liz. At a lot of things. Not at you. Ben, maybe. What happened to him."

She nodded against my chest. "It's just not fair what happened. Any more than what happened to that boy at the bar."

"No, neither were fair," I said. "Any more than it's fair what's happened to Emma."

"You have to bring her back," Liz suddenly said. She turned to me. "That's the only way out of this, Charlie. Can you see? She. You. You both have to come back to me. Promise me that. I know you can't, really. I don't even know what you're going to do. But promise me anyway. Please."

"I promise," I said. I wiped a tear from her eye and let the moisture dampen my shirt. For a moment, everything felt like it always had felt with us. Like we always belonged this way. Only one thing missing. "I will get her back, Liz," I said. I lifted her chin and put my lips against hers. I didn't know how she would react, but she returned the kiss, needy and urgent and afraid. We didn't take it any further. It was enough just to feel her next to me again. Trusting me. She closed her eyes. In a minute, I felt the steady rhythm of her breaths against me.

If I could devise a serum that could give me the courage to do what I needed to tonight, infuse me with the conviction that I was doing the right thing and would somehow succeed, I couldn't have asked for more than having her there with me.

I stayed awake next to her. Thinking of my daughter. The daughter I was going to take in my arms after and bring home with me. Bring her back to her mom.

As well as the slim, but suddenly tangible chance—like the sun coming out amid clouds on a dreary day, spilling its warmth on all—that there might be a life for us after.

Two hours passed, until the clock struck quarter of eleven. I shook her and put my lips close to her ear. "Liz, it's time."

39

At the brownstone, Willi and Trudi were packing. Their valises were open, and they threw in whatever they would need for their upcoming journey. It would be a cold one on the open sea. An eight-day crossing of the Atlantic. By tomorrow morning they would be on the 8 A.M. train bound for Montreal, with new names and forged documents; two days hidden in a safe house there, and then they would board a Portuguese freighter bound for Lisbon. After that, in a neutral port, they would board a diplomatic flight bound for Berlin.

It would be new to them. They had lived in the United States for twelve years. Since 1928. Before that, three years in the Graubünden province in Switzerland. When they were first recruited by General Canaris himself of the Abwehr on a visit back to their homeland in '36, they had no idea how their loyalties would be tested. In a way, Willi felt like an American now. They had many friends here they would miss. But in the end, when the war was won on the Continent and America sued for peace on the second front and gave up the fight, they could come back.

No, Willi understood, as he sadly picked up the silver frame of the two of them visiting Niagara Falls, *after tonight we can never come back.* Their friends who were a part of their life here they would be forced to leave behind. It was always understood that might be the eventuality from the very beginning. A cost of war. The cost of commitment to their homeland. The cost of what they were doing, he knew. Trudi had always been the more committed.

"This . . . ?" He showed the photo at the falls to Trudi. They packed up all their important memories. Ones they had carried from home. That and their clothes. That was all they were taking.

The rest they would leave behind.

"Yes, I loved that weekend, Willi. Of course," Trudi agreed, and wrapped the filigreed frame in a protective cloth. "You remember, we had the best strudel with apple butter at that inn nearby."

"The couple who owned it hailed from Wutzburger, I believe, if I recall," he said.

"No, Morlbach, Willi," she corrected him. "Outside Munich, if you recall."

"Ah, yes, you are right." Willi nodded, corrected. "As always, dear."

Trudi smiled.

The brewery building had been sold and put in a trust for their grandchildren in Chicago. The radio transmitter had been dismantled and smashed into a dozen pieces and tossed into a refuse bin at a construction site. Over the past week, all their papers, documents, messages, anything that might tie them to their secret life had been burned and destroyed.

By tomorrow there would be no trace. No trace of the work they did once the door was closed. Only the kindly old couple who had suddenly disappeared. A mystery worthy of a novel. It would be Mossman they'd be thinking of, looking into. And once it was clear that was all a smoke screen and the questions came back to them, they'd be long gone, back in Berlin likely, and their adopted country would be reeling from its wounds. They filled their valises, folding their sport jackets and dresses carefully, smoothing out the wrinkles, until they looked at each other, satisfied they were done.

"Will you miss it?" Willi asked, sitting on the bedspread. "We have enjoyed our time here."

"Yes, we have," Trudi agreed. "But now it is our turn to do our duty. What we want for ourselves no longer matters compared to the good of the fatherland. You understand that, don't you, dear?"

"Yes, of course, I know, but—"

"There is no *but*, Willi," she said sternly. "I know you sometimes see it that way, but the path we have chosen is clear. History demands it. Do not waver, my husband. Much will be asked of us tonight."

Willi nodded, placing his palms on his knees. "I just think, all those people . . . Innocent people, Trudi. Like our little Emma. In some ways, it is a heinous thing we are doing, I think sometimes . . . Duty or not, they are still people. As are we."

"And look at the thousands of our own sons and brothers who will die if America enters the war. They cannot wage a two-pronged fight. The Führer tells us that. You will see, they will submit. And then you will be proud of the work here. So do not think so much on it." She came over and sat beside him. "Just do your duty, my husband. I know you are troubled, but you must be strong. Thousands and thousands will die in this war. In the end, no one will miss them."

He nodded.

"Our little Emma too, if it comes to that."

"Yes, you always say the perfect things, my dear," he sighed, "to bolster me when I grow a little weak."

"They are the *right* things, my darling." She ran her knuckles along his cheek. "Because they are true."

"Look . . ." He picked up a picture book of Havana. They had traveled there once to promote their beer. The beaches there were the nicest they had ever seen. "What do you say?" he asked her, holding it over his valise. "There is room."

"By all means," Trudi said, smiling. "Whatever makes you happy, *liebchen*. No memory is too small not to take it with us."

He gave her a kiss on the cheek, this woman who had been by his side for close to forty years, who strengthened him and always saw things clearly for what they were. He stood up and flattened his case. He was done. All there was to take. All there was to take of their lives.

They would live new ones now back at home, as heroes.

"Just tell me something, dear," Willi said. Trudi was folding the filigreed tablecloth that had been a treasure of her mother's back in Freiberg.

"Yes?"

"Just tell me she will live. I need to hear it. Assure me of that one thing, Trudi. I know you feel for her as much as I do. I will be fine tonight. I will do what is needed of me. I just need to know that one thing."

"She will live if her father performs his duty," Trudi said. He

had hoped for a trace of warmth from her but there was only harsh-
ness in her voice. Ice. "Otherwise, we will do ours, Willi. We will
all do ours. Margaret will not waver."

"Yes, darling." He took a breath, nodded wistfully. Willi closed
the valise and secured the clasps. "You are right as always." He put
the closed valise on the floor. "I see it now."

40

I dropped Liz off at the brownstone and told her to wait there. She gave me a heartfelt hug on the street that was hard for me to release. I pressed her extra close and watched her go inside, saying, "Be careful, Charlie. I know it's dangerous, whatever you're doing." I wasn't sure if I would ever see her again.

Then I walked the five blocks to the brewery, arriving there a few minutes before twelve.

I noticed the white Buick parked on the street outside, about two cars down from the entrance, just as Fiske had said. I didn't look to confirm what I knew was hidden beneath the rear passenger tire. I knew it was there. I looked around, and didn't see anyone on the street. But he said they'd be watching. I stood in front of the entrance and blew out a bolstering breath before rapping on the corrugated door in the same manner I had earlier, to indicate that it was me.

In a moment, the door cracked open a bit. Curtis peeked out and looked around outside. Satisfied that I was alone, he let me in.

"Charlie!" Willi exclaimed when he saw me. He was dressed in a tweed wool sports jacket, sweater and knit tie, and woolen Alpine cap. Curtis turned me around and patted me down as roughly and thoroughly as he'd done earlier that day. He especially felt over my chest and down my thighs for a trace of some kind of wire. Then he looked over at Willi and nodded, satisfied.

"I commend you, Charlie." Willi gave me a smile. "You didn't even make us wait it out as to whether you would come."

"Let's just get on with what we have to do, if that's okay," I replied. The delivery truck sat in the loading bay, but this time with a large gray tarp covering it. The rear cargo door was open, and as we went by, I could see several of the so-called beer kegs lined up inside. Next to it, the black Ford sedan from the other night was parked.

I said to Bauer, "You said when I came back I could talk to Emma."

"I said we'd consider it, Charlie. But I'm afraid that won't be possible. Not enough time."

"It better be possible," I said. "Otherwise, whatever you need of me, it's off."

"*Off*, Charlie . . . ?" Willi mused discouragingly. "Curtis, please remind Mr. Mossman he's not in any position to be setting terms with us. Not if he wants the evening to end happily for him."

The large German stepped closer and took out his gun.

"We don't need you, Charlie," Willi said. "We want you, but the events of this morning will go on, whether you're involved or not."

"So shoot me then." I shrugged. "We both know there's not much hope of me surviving the night as it is. I only care about Emma. And before I help you one iota, you need to give me proof that she's alive and unharmed."

"You mean other than our word?" Willi said.

"I think you can understand how your word doesn't carry much weight with me right now."

"Well, then . . ." He looked at me, then Curtis in a fatalistic way, and then shrugged, as if to say, *All bets are off then. Do what you have to do.*

Curtis put his hand on my shoulder.

"Please, Herr Mossman . . ." A voice called out from the inside office. It was Trudi. She stepped out wearing a blue suit and a feathered tulle hat. "No need for such intemperance. I have someone on the line who very much wants to say hello to you. It's very late. A child her age shouldn't be wakened from sleep."

"Always thinking of others," Willi said, "my Trudi."

My heart leaped and I ran toward the office. Trudi had the black phone on the desk and gave the receiver to me. Her hand remained over the mouthpiece. She said, "Go ahead, but only for a minute, do you understand? Just to hear she's doing fine and nothing more."

"Honey!" I grabbed the receiver and pressed it to my ear. "Emma? Are you there, sweetheart? Are you all right?"

"Daddy?"

"Yes, darling, it's me. It's me. How are you? I know you must be scared. Are you all right?'

"I guess so. I'm with Mrs. Shearer," she said. "But why do they have me here, Daddy? They won't let me go home. I miss Mommy. Why can't I see her?"

"You will see her, sweetheart. Soon. Tonight, I hope. You just be a big girl and hang in there for a little while longer and later you'll be in your mommy's arms. . . ." I felt myself starting to choke up. "I promise, baby. . . ." I turned to Trudi with a glare, for putting her, an innocent six-year-old child, through such torment. "You just tell Mrs. Shearer she has to treat you extra nice, okay . . ." I said. "They are treating you nice, aren't they?"

"Yes, Daddy, they are, but . . ."

Tears burned at the back of my eyes. Tears of helplessness and anger. I wanted to lunge at Trudi, all of them, and twist the phone cord around her neck and choke the life out of her for putting my daughter in such anguish. "You tell her from me, to make sure she is treating you nice, or I'll be angry with her. You tell her I'll come talk to her. You tell her that from me. Those very words, Emma. And—"

"That's all now," Trudi said, attempting to wrestle the phone from me.

"Daddy, I want to see you," Emma said. "They're telling me I have to go now. That I—"

"That's it, Mr. Mossman." Trudi's eyes grew firm.

"Just a second more. I'll be seeing you soon, hon. I love you, baby! You know that, right? I—"

Trudi pressed her finger on the switch hook button and suddenly the line went dead. There was just a dial tone. I had no idea if Fiske had been able to trace the call in that time. It had barely been a minute.

I glared. "You hurt that little girl, Trudi, and I promise, you'll burn in hell for it," I said.

"Please, please . . . She'll be fine," Trudi said dismissively. "By morning, your little angel will be back in her mother's arms. Just do what we ask you to do and you won't have to worry your mind about it. Now go, get ready. . . ." She stepped outside. "Oberleutnant Leitner, please have Herr Mossman try on his uniform."

"Uniform . . ." Behind the desk, I saw three leather valises on the floor that looked fully packed. The Bauers were clearly leaving tonight. Or in the morning. After everything was done.

Curtis came over and grabbed me roughly by the arm.

I tried to yank it away.

"In here, Mr. Mossman." He took hold of me again. There was another room to the side of the office, possibly a secretary's station. File cabinets and a metal desk. "We've gone to a lot of trouble for you, Mr. Mossman," he said, sniffing with a clipped, amused smile.

On a hanger, I saw a military uniform hanging from one of the file cabinets. It was army. Military green. Captain's bars were pinned to both epaulets.

"Try it on," Curtis said, taking the hanger off and removing the trousers.

"What do you all have in mind?" I asked.

"Don't you worry your head with what we have in mind. Just put it on. We want you to look nice. We've gone to a lot of trouble for you."

He leaned with his back to the wall, conveying that he wasn't leaving. I removed my jacket and started to unbutton my shirt. Curtis looked like he'd like nothing more than to use that gun on me, any excuse he could get. Like I was still alive only to do one thing, and once that was done . . . I knew I'd better arm myself as well, otherwise, the second I'd outlived my usefulness, whatever it was, he would likely do just that. Fiske was right.

I put on the khaki shirt and unzipped my pants and took them off. I threw them over a chair at the desk.

In a minute I had changed into the uniform, Curtis never once removing his gaze from me. It fit fine, a little large in the jacket. He tossed me the tie. "The whole thing, Mr. Mossman," nodding for me to put it on as well. There was a black leather belt with an empty holster attached. "The cap too," Curtis said. He took it off the hook and tossed it to me when I was done. I put it on my head. "Captain Mossman." He nodded with an approving smile. "You'll pardon me if I don't salute."

Willi and Trudi came back in.

"Nice. Very nice, indeed." Willi smiled, impressed. "So sorry we couldn't complete the outfit with a gun for the holster, but I think you understand."

I stood there like a groom in his fancy wedding tuxedo, everyone staring at me.

Trudi said, "It will do just fine."

"I hope you don't mind . . ." I transferred my cigarettes and matchbook from my own trousers.

"Now Kurt . . ." Willi Bauer swung the front door back, revealing another uniform. Much the same as mine, except it was for an enlisted man. "Your turn now. I'm afraid we couldn't get you the same rank."

Curtis removed his plaid jacket and started to change.

"So where are we going?" I asked. I tried to play dumb, though I already knew. "What is it you want me to do?"

"Oh, you'll know in due time, I promise," Willi Bauer said. "You'll be briefed on everything on the way north."

North. He checked his watch. It was 12:25 now. "Is everything loaded up?" he asked Curtis, once he had finished putting his pants on.

The German nodded, stuffing his shirt into his army trousers. He wore sergeant stripes. "It is, Herr Bauer. We just need to secure the cargo in place."

"Well, get it done. As soon as you can. I want to get out of

here. Make yourself at home, Mr. Mossman. Just a few more details to go over and we'll be leaving shortly. You're going to play a
very important part in history tonight."

"Yeah, great." I did my best to appear clammy and peaked. "As
long as you live up to your word on Emma, that's all that matters
to me. Look," I blew out my cheeks, "I'm actually not feeling so
well at the moment. You mind if I get some air?"

"I'm sorry, but I'm not sure if that's such a good idea," Willi said.

"It's a good idea unless you want me to bring up my lunch all
over your truck on the way to wherever we're going." I wiped my
hand across my brow. "This isn't exactly my normal routine."

Willi glanced warily to Trudi.

"You've got my daughter," I said. "What's the risk? Keep an
eye on me, if you like. Where the hell am I going to go anyway?
I came here of my own accord. But just decide quick, 'cause I'm
starting to feel queasy."

"All right, all right . . ." Willi relented. "Friedrich, keep an eye
out on Captain Mossman while he gets a little air." The German
nodded. "And don't let him go too far. Trudi, Kurt, please come
in the office. I need to go over something with you in here. . . ."

"Thanks," I said, sucking in a fortifying breath and heading
over to the front door.

The dough-faced driver, Freddy, now Friedrich, followed me.
I looked at him once as if to say, *Is this really necessary?* If I was going to run, why would I have even shown up in the first place? He
opened the door to the side of the loading bay and I stepped outside. Truth was, my stomach was doing somersaults and a breath
of air would do me good. I inhaled one deeply into my lungs. They
had me in an army captain's uniform. And they were going to
Westchester. Kensico, like the map I'd seen and like I'd told Fiske.

"Cigarette," I showed him, digging into my jacket pocket and coming out with a Chesterfield and my matchbook. He nodded for me to go ahead, and I lit it up, muttering thanks, and stepped away from the building, inhaling a deep drag of smoke into my lungs. The white Buick was two cars down.

I glanced behind me and gave a brief smile to Friedrich, to say, *Feeling better now.* He remained in the doorway, keeping an eye on me as Bauer had said as I took another drag and blew it out, and tried to look about as lost in my thoughts as I could. It was cold and I put my free hand in my trouser pocket to warm it, and bounced on my feet to keep my blood moving. My breath came out of my mouth.

I looked down. The shoes would give me away, I thought, my own brown leather ones and not a crisply polished set of blacks. They'd forgotten that. If someone even noticed.

Behind me, Curtis came over and muttered something to Friedrich in German. My watchdog nodded in my direction as if to say, *What about him?* And Curtis shrugged and said what I took as, "Don't worry. He's not going anywhere." In a moment, I looked back and the two were gone, back inside the brewery.

I blew out a plume of smoke as aimlessly as I could and glanced at the Buick, only a few feet away. I knew that whatever their plans, whatever their intent for Emma, they didn't need some witness blabbing about it, whatever took place tonight. Which only reinforced Fiske's belief that they would shoot me as soon as I was no longer useful. I glanced around again, and took another step up the street, to the Buick. I didn't see anyone watching. Fiske said the gun would be under the rear passenger's tire. My heart started to race. I looked around one last time. No one there. I wondered if any of Fiske's team was watching. Now was the time, I thought, if it was ever going to happen. And that weapon would come in handy.

I flicked my cigarette to the curb near the rear wheel of the Buick, took a step toward it, and stamped it out with my shoe. Sensing the moment of opportunity, I dropped my matchbook on the pavement, my heart starting to pound now, then kneeled down as close to the rear wheel as I could, as if picking it up, my hand reaching for the black revolver Fiske had assured me would be there.

Barely a foot or two away now.

I got my fingers around the handle.

"Mossman," a voice called behind me. The door opened again.

I jerked my hand back.

Friedrich stepped out. He looked at me with kind of a suspicious glare. "Lose something . . . ?" he asked, seeing me kneeling there.

"No." My heart nearly fell off a cliff. "Just this." I picked up the matchbook and showed it to him and stood up. The gun futilely remaining there. "Dropped it."

The big German merely shrugged and waved me toward him. "Come on, they're ready for you inside."

I stepped away, not sure what I should do. What could I do? The gun remained on the street. No way to get it now. I was going into a trap unarmed, one where I knew they intended to kill me. Other than Fiske and his crew. At the reservoir. *We'll be there*, he'd said. They'd be my only hope.

"Yeah," I said, blowing out a breath, with a last futile glance down to the Buick. "Thanks."

It truly was a trap now.

41

I went back inside. Friedrich closed the door after me and locked it. Trudi Bauer was heading back into the office. "Feeling better, Herr Mossman, I hope?"

"Yeah, much," I said. But inside, my heart was beating like crazy.

"Good. We'll need you fresh and ready for your big role," she said. "Willi, our guest is back. Prepare the truck."

"Go ahead." Willi nodded to Curtis.

The janitor and Friedrich went over and drew the canvas tarp down.

It was the same truck, only painted. No longer black.

It was now military gray. Like an army truck.

"What do you think, Captain?" Willi grinned at me. "Like it? I know you were familiar with the previous color. Friedrich, Kurt . . ." He clapped his hands. "Now we can leave."

Willi beckoned me into the front. In the middle. He climbed in next to me. Curtis, in his sergeant's uniform, jumped in behind the wheel.

He turned the ignition on and we pulled out of the loading bay as Friedrich hopped out of the sedan and shut the metal door behind us. We continued on, to York, and then, at the light, turned north. I glanced through the rearview mirror to see if anyone was following.

No car picked up behind us.

"Looking for something?" Willi Bauer said. I had no gun now, only the hope that Fiske would be at the scene, as promised.

"No." I shook my head. "Just nervous. Blame me?"

"You have nothing to be nervous about, Mr. Mossman. Do what we ask of you and everything will go as planned. And you and Mrs. Mossman will have your daughter once again."

"And a couple of thousand people will be dead," I said.

"Maybe a hundred thousand. Till they figure out just what is going on." We turned north and then headed back west at the Boyd's pharmacy on Ninety-sixth Street. "Think of it as the cost of war," he said. "In London, just as many have died for two years now, and your own government merely stood on the side and did nothing."

"Well, we're coming in now," I said grudgingly, "whatever you do."

"We'll see." He looked forward. "We shall see."

We continued west, the truck bouncing on the pavement through the park, to the West Side. There, we continued on through some traffic and picked up the West Side Drive.

"Where are we heading?" I tried to confirm, noting that we were driving north toward the bridge. "What do you need me to do?"

"As you know, to a reservoir," Willi said. "It's being guarded by a small detail. You'll need to advise them that a water-quality test is taking place. You'll say your instructions come straight from the Civil Defense Unit of the 9th Battalion of the Army Engineers. You'll outrank anyone on site, so it shouldn't be a problem."

"At two in the morning?"

"As I said, you'll outrank them. You'll see to it they don't object."

"What'll happen to the guards?"

"We'll take their weapons. Maybe lock them in the guard-house, till we're gone. We'll see."

"That's all?"

"That and make sure any other guard detachments are di-verted while we do what we are there to do. Curtis will be with you."

I glanced at him, driving. He had a gun in his belt.

"Kensico?" I confirmed. I threw it out there. "In Pound Ridge." Willi didn't answer.

"One thing that's bugged me," I said. "You mentioned this poison was a gas. What did you call it?"

"Sarin," Willi said. "Apparently an acronym of the inventors' names."

"A gas would normally dilute as soon as it blended with water," I said. "Especially in such a vast quantity of water. No matter how lethal."

"And now you are a chemical engineer as well . . . ?" Willi turned to me with a smile. "Don't burden yourself with this detail, Charlie. But to answer, it is not gas at all we are putting in, but the ingredients encapsulated in the tiniest of microscopic pellets. They will not dissolve in the water supply at all, but be carried like lethal messengers through the viaducts into the faucets, the food supply, and the drinking water into thousands of bodies. We have special gloves ourselves to avoid any contact; even the tiniest of contacts would be instant death for us too. But not to dwell on all this, Charlie. We have a special role designed for you as well."

My heart picked up. Tiny, microscopic capsules. Of this deadly poison. Contained in the beer kegs. There had to be millions of them. Who knew how many people would be affected if this came off.

Hundreds of thousands of people could die.

We drove on, passing under the George Washington Bridge, until we hit the Bronx. It was one thirty now. Traffic was nonexistent. I figured we had about another forty or forty-five minutes until we got to our destination. Kensico was in Pound Ridge. I'd never been there, but Fiske figured they would take 9A all the way up and cut over on some local roads up there.

"These guards," I said. "They're just going to let us in? They're going to believe we're doing a water test? At two in the morning?"

"They are enlisted men, Charlie. Probably their first assignment. You're a captain. They won't argue. Just make it convincing, whatever you do. When they're gone you'll help us bring the beer kegs up from the truck to the head of the viaducts."

"Then you'll make that call?"

"What call?"

"For Emma," I said, pressing.

"We'll make it once we're back. Not before. You'll be coming with us. Emma will be dropped off at a specific location. Don't worry, we'll advise you."

"So why did you need me? Curtis's English is good enough."

"Just do your job. You'll see, Charlie. All will be made clear."

The answer, I know, was that they were going to pin the whole thing on me. Dressed in a stolen army uniform. By the time anyone thought anything else, they'd be long out of the country.

I sat back and took a deep breath. I rested my head against the seat back. I would have felt a whole lot safer to have that gun in my pocket. I knew my only chance I had of surviving the night was Fiske and his team now. Thank God we knew the location. They'd better be there.

We crossed into Westchester County. I saw a sign for Yonkers. I figured we still had another half hour to go. I put my head back and tried to relax, tried to tell myself to calm down, when Willi suddenly pointed to an exit sign, McLean Avenue, and said, "Here."

Here?

Curtis put his turn signal on and moved into the right lane.

We were still twenty miles away.

"I thought we were going to Kensico?" I said to Bauer, as matter-of-factly as I could. Inside, my body was in riot.

"What made you think that?" Willi turned to me, mooning his eyes wide.

"I don't know. I just saw the map." I shrugged. "No big deal."

"Change of plans, Charlie." Willi looked at me and smiled. "The Hillview Reservoir is the last stop for water heading into New York City. The Kensico ducts feed directly into it. Besides, too many guards there."

"Hillview, huh?" Fiske and his team wouldn't be there. No one would. I was a dead man, I realized. Unarmed. No one backing me up. And Emma . . . No way to be sure she was ever released.

Not to mention that thousands of lives might be lost. I'd just have to do what they wanted, I said to myself. We pulled off. The road was dark. Virtually no other car around. I glanced in the mirror once again and didn't see anyone following us. My throat felt dry as sandpaper. "All the same to me."

42

It was only a short ride on pitch-black roads to a turn-off with a small white sign that read, *Hillview Water Facility.*

We stopped on the side of the road well up from the gate. This was a small facility. Lightly guarded. Not exactly a prime target in the first days of the war. The chances of any action coming here must be a million to one. Behind us, Friedrich and Trudi came to a stop in the Ford.

"This is where we're counting on you, Charlie . . . ," Willi said. "Switch seats." He opened the door and shifted over to the middle, and I prepared to jump into the passenger seat. "When we get to the gate, you get out and tell the guards precisely what we went over. That we're here to do some water testing. They won't have any choice but to believe you. Just remember, you're a captain with the Army Engineers. This looks like a military truck. Make yourself sound like someone in authority."

My eyes went wide as I looked over at Curtis and saw him take his gun out of his jacket and screw onto the barrel what I took to be a silencer. He cocked the action and the *ka-ching* sent a chill through me. "What's that for?" I asked.

"Eventualities," Willi said. "Just do your job. Hopefully, it will not have to be used."

I caught Curtis's eye. "Let's hope so."

I shut the door as Curtis stepped on the pedal and threw the truck in gear, and slowly we crept along the access road, a poorly paved single lane. I was now a participant in a plan to not only poison thousands of innocent people, but maybe cost a few soldiers their lives, soldiers who were now directly in front of me.

The truck bounced along the road at about five miles per hour. Friedrich and Trudi kept up in their car about forty yards behind. *This is it, Charlie.* There was no escape for me now, except to do what they said and pray that Willi and Trudi kept their word. No one would come to my rescue. I kept telling myself, hoping against fear, they had no reason to harm Emma once the job was done. But my eyes went to the gun in Curtis's lap. "Any eventualities," I muttered to myself again.

Ahead, I spotted a light, and then a wooden gate blocking the road came into view. Next to it, a small guard hut. Two flags, one the Stars and Stripes, the other on a blue background, which I assumed was New York state, hung limply on poles. At the sight of our headlights, someone stepped out of the hut, no doubt surprised that anyone was pulling up here in the dead of night. The country had been at war only a few days and this kind of target, which likely wouldn't even have been protected before then, was as quiet and backwater a posting as a freshly trained recruit could draw for himself.

We pulled up and came to a stop in front of the gate. A second guard came out. Both young, barely out of high school.

Carrying rifles. One was a corporal—I could see the two stripes on his arm—the other a private. In the darkness, our truck probably looked like any other military vehicle.

"Captain," Willi Bauer said, nodding to me, "it's your show now."

I looked back at him with ice in my gaze. I opened the door and stepped out.

"Corporal."

Both sentries snapped to attention at the sight of my bars. "Sir."

"We're from the 9th Engineer Battalion. We're going to be conducting some tests on the water supply here. You've been briefed, I believe?" I went around the front of the truck and came up to them directly.

"We have not, sir," the corporal said. He was young, twenty-one at most. Probably just out of basic training. Who knew, this might well be his very first assignment. The private looked like he was still in high school, barely even shaved. "No one alerted us to anything," the corporal said, clearly nervous at the rank standing before him and the events taking place at the odd time of night. "I was told to let no one in. May I ask to see your orders, sir?"

"Orders . . . ?"

"Please, sir," he said, clearly uncomfortable. "We were instructed to let no one in." His eyes glanced down and he seemed to fix on my brown shoes.

He looked back up at me.

I was about to tell him again that I was certain that they had been properly briefed, when I heard a dull *thud, thud,* and both sentries grabbed their chests with grunts and fell to the ground. Curtis stepped out of the truck, holding his pistol.

I shouted, "No! No!" Arm extended, he squeezed the trigger and each of their bodies jerked from two more rounds, an eruption of blood on their chests, and went still. Curtis faced his gun downward and put a final bullet into each.

"My God, what have you done!" I stared at the bodies in shock. "They were cooperating. They were just kids."

"They were soldiers," Willi said, climbing down from the cab. "And they saw your shoes." He waved at Trudi and Friedrich, in the car behind us, to come forward. "We are at war, Mr. Mossman. Get that through your head. At war."

I stood, gaping in horror at the two dead guards. The thought that they were at risk in any way, guarding a body of drinking water in Yonkers in the middle of the night, likely never entered their minds. I looked at Curtis, stuffing his gun back in his belt, and knew that in minutes, that could be me lying there with a bullet in my chest.

"Go help Curtis dispose of the bodies," Willi said to me.

"No. What did you even need me for if you were going to kill them from the start?" Then I knew. I saw Curtis take one of the guards' rifles and lean it on the side of the truck. That was for me later, to make it seem like I was shot by one of the guards.

"Help him," Willi Bauer looked at me impassively, "or I'll give Oberleutnant Leitner the nod and you'll never have a clue in the world what becomes of your daughter." Clapping his hands, he said to Curtis, "Schnell, schnell."

The black Ford with Trudi and Friedrich had driven up. Curtis dragged one of the sentries into the guard house. I took the other by the armpits, trying not to look at his face, and carried him in. Outside, Willi lifted the gate, and I was instructed to climb back in the cab. Curtis got behind the wheel and I noticed he had the dead sentry's rifle with him. We continued up the narrow road toward the reservoir. A high chain-link fence that circumvented the perimeter of the reservoir came into view. Friedrich jumped out of the sedan with a pair of metal cutters, ran up, and severed the chain that bound the gate. He threw the gate open and suddenly we were staring at millions of gallons of water to be pumped into New York City. Water that was about to become a carrier of gruesome death.

Willi got out and went through the gate, holding his map. Trudi followed. "Over here." He waved us on, heading onto the six-foot-wide concrete perimeter that encircled the water table. I could see the map was similar to the one I had seen of the Kensico Reservoir, where Fiske was likely encamped now with his team of agents, while I was here. Willi studied it a second, looking out over the edge. "The viaducts come in here," I heard him say in German, pointing. "Help them unload the cargo, Mr. Mossman, if you please," he said to me.

"You can't expect me to participate in this killing." I shook my head.

"We expect you to do what you're told, Mr. Mossman," Trudi Bauer interceded. "Oberleutnant Leitner, if Mr. Mossman hesitates again, kindly put a bullet in his brain."

"My pleasure, Frau Bauer," Curtis replied, leering at me.

Helpless, I slowly went back to the truck as Friedrich unlocked the rear door and rolled down the kegs to Curtis and me one at a time. We set them gingerly onto the ground. They were heavy, maybe around fifty pounds each, and when we put them down they each made a clang.

"Careful, careful," Willi Bauer said. "You're dealing with the most precious cargo of the German war machine."

In minutes, the four kegs were taken down from the truck. Curtis and Friedrich hurriedly wheeled them on their sides through the chain-link gate and up a series of steps onto the concrete perimeter to where the giant viaducts funneled water to the city.

What were they going to do with me? Kill me, as soon as they finished their task? That's what the sentry's rifle was for, I was sure. To make it seem that I was part of the party of saboteurs and had been killed by one of the guards. It wouldn't stand up, of course, once it was looked at, but by the time anyone figured it out, Willi and Trudi would be out of the country. I'd seen their packed bags. And I was left praying they'd live up to their word on Emma.

"Look, Mr. Mossman," Willi Bauer said with a gleam in his eye. Curtis and Friedrich had donned their protective gloves and were prying off the keg tops. "There you see the decisive first blow of the war, even more deadly than Pearl Harbor."

Curtis opened the first one. The keg contained what appeared to be a million tiny pellets. Like kernels of rice. Each containing the most lethal poison ever developed. A pinprick would kill a man. Able to remain potent in water without dissolving. It was as scary a sight as I had ever seen.

I was helpless, unable to do anything about what I was seeing. Even if I sprang forward and pushed a keg over, only a tiny part of the contents would fall out before I was shot.

"Friedrich, you can begin your work," Willi said. Then he looked at me. "Kurt, I believe it's time to show Herr Mossman the rest of the facility here."

My blood came to a stop. "What are you saying?"

"You've been a real asset, Mr. Mossman. And you will continue to be for us, well after tonight. The German war effort thanks you for your service."

"Willi." I looked at him, as now there was no doubt what they were going to do.

"We warned you over and over to stay out of our affairs, Charlie. It's a shame you did not listen. But now . . . Kurt . . ." He nodded, gesturing with his chin as if to say, *Get him out of here.*

"No one's going to buy this, Bauer. People know. Government people know. It won't make a difference whether I'm dead or alive."

"That only works once, Mr. Mossman. A shame."

Curtis took my arm and pulled me close to him. He thrust the barrel of his pistol sharply into my ribs. "This way, Mr. Mossman, please."

"What about Emma?" I said, panic throbbing through me. "You promised me she would be released. You owe me that at least. Tell me, Willi . . . Trudi. You owe me that."

"Don't delay, Kurt," Willi said, ignoring me. "Do it quickly, please, and come back. You're needed here." He turned and headed back to oversee Friedrich.

"You gave me your word, Willi." I fought against Curtis, who was trying to pull me away. "Please, Bauer. You don't need her. You promised me about Emma. I need to know."

"Well, I guess you'll never know, will you, Mr. Mossman?" Willi said, without even turning back. "If we make that call, or if we don't. But either way, it's nothing you'll need to worry about."

Curtis dragged me down from the reservoir level back to the truck, his gun in my ribs, me tugging against him. "You could just let me go, Curtis," I said. "All I want is my daughter back. I won't tell a soul about this for two days. For however long you need."

He didn't say a word, steel in his eyes. He just dragged me down the concrete steps, my legs barely cooperating.

"Curtis, please. You know Emma. You know she doesn't deserve this. You can do something. Please . . ."

He threw me against the side of the truck. My heart was almost clawing out of my chest. I was going to die. I looked in his eyes—cold and purposeful. He picked up the sentry's rifle that was leaning on the driver's door. For a moment I thought I could make a lunge for it—anything was better than just dying without a fight, no matter how futile. But then it was in his hands. He cocked the bolt back, *ka-ching,* satisfied himself that it was ready, and pointed it at me.

"Please," I begged one last time. "If I'm gone, make him do what he said for Emma. For the love of God, Curtis. . . ."

"What will you care?" was all he said, then leveled it at my chest. "You'll be dead. *Auf Wiedersehen,* Mr. Mossman."

"Curtis, please . . ."

Suddenly I heard a kind of *whoosh* in the air, and out of nowhere a spurt of blood erupted on Curtis's throat. His mouth fell open and he gagged. Then another *whosh,* followed by a loud crack, and Curtis took a step forward and, eyes wide, spun around. He dropped the gun and his hand went to his chest, blood all over them. He looked back at me, as if to say, *How? Who?* Then two more shots rang out. Curtis dropped to his knees.

Lights flashed on everywhere. Curtis was now face forward. Men in suits ran out of the darkness, enveloping me. On the reservoir perimeter, Friedrich had pulled out his gun and started firing wildly toward the lights. I heard a few short bursts in return and he fell back onto the beer keg and toppled into the water. Agents were streaming everywhere now. *How? From where?* Willi and Trudi had both pulled out guns, pointing them toward the advancing men. No one fired back at them.

"Put down your guns! United States government agents!" a voice shouted. "Put down your guns and get down on your knees."

Willi's eyes widened in panic. In a stumbling gait, he ran along the perimeter to the keg Friedrich had been attempting to empty, trying to finish the job. As soon as he got his hands on it, bullets clanged off the steel keg, forcing Willi to leap away from it. He looked into the lights, mouth agape. Then toward Trudi. They were trapped. The Feds had surrounded them. Out of the darkness, I saw Fiske run up to me. I looked at him, stunned, wobbly-kneed, ecstatic to even be alive.

"How?" I asked. How had they traced me here?

"You didn't think we'd actually let you go without someone following you?" he said. "It was a bit of a scramble to get here in time," he grinned, "but I told you we'd be here, right?"

"Right," I said, grinning in relief at the sight of him too.

The night was alive now, bright with light and radios crackling. Still holding their guns, Trudi pointed hers at any agent who approached, shouting, "Stay away. Stay away, or I'll fire."

"On your knees! Put down your guns! Now!" agents were barking.

I could see the Bauers trying to decide which was the better fate, to surrender or not be taken alive. They were surrounded. Escape was hopeless. They didn't move.

Fiske and I ran up to them on the edge of the reservoir. The agent shouted, "Willi and Trudi Bauer, I am Agent Harlan Fiske. You are under arrest for espionage, attempted sabotage, kidnapping, and plotting against the United States of America. Put down your guns. You can make what happens next either very hard or easy, and the first way to make it easy is to give us the whereabouts of Emma Mossman, who's of no value to you now. You have my word, we will make every effort that you and whoever is holding her will not be harmed."

Trudi stared at his face, her jaw agape, at the agent she thought was one of their own spies, and any fear in her eyes hardened into anger. *"You . . . ?"*

They closed ranks. There was a desperate pallor of fear on both their faces. Around them were the three unopened kegs of sarin. Willi kept eyeing them, like children he would never see again.

Fiske called out, "I'm asking you again, Herr and Frau Bauer, for your sakes and for the sake of an innocent girl, put down your guns and let us know where she is."

I stepped out of the bright lights myself. "Willi, Trudi, please . . ."

Willi spun in my direction, leveling his gun at me. I could feel the government agents about to drop him where he stood.

"Don't shoot! Don't shoot!" I screamed, throwing up my hands. Then I took another step to Willi and said, "It's over now, Willi. It's over. Where is she? Please . . ."

He and Trudi stood there for a moment, frozen, realizing that their grand plans of history had turned to dust, pointing their guns haphazardly into the headlights at the encroaching circle of agents. Finally Willi met my eyes.

"Willi, please . . . ," I begged. "I know you care for her. You both do. There's no point now in putting her at risk. Please, tell me where she is so I can bring her home. I'm begging you."

For a moment, he seemed to waver. I could see softening in his eyes. "Trudi, we should—"

"Willi, don't say another word," Trudi snapped at him in

German, "He betrayed us, Willi. Both these men did. Let our people do what they have to do."

"Trudi, please . . . ," Willi said, turning to her, "There's no point anymore. We're—"

"There is always a point, Willi. You mustn't waver. You must stay strong. They must know the will of the German Republic will not bend. Even in defeat. Whatever happens, we will be pawns of the U.S. government and then be returned one day. As heroes, Willi. It is not over."

"Trudi!" I took another step closer. "It is. It is over." Trudi swung and pointed her gun at me. "Please . . ."

Something seemed to crack in Willi's countenance—a tremor of regret maybe, or simply the recognition that this was no longer an act of war, just contempt now, breaking through the resolve. "Trudi, dear, he's right. It is over." He turned to her and lowered his gun. "It is."

"*Es ist nicht vorbei,*" she snapped back sharply. "It will never be over."

I took another step, only a few feet from them now; Fiske put up his hands to halt his men from firing. Willi swallowed and shook his head. Trudi kept her gun pointed at me, her hand quivering. Still, I never felt more sure of anything in my life.

"Willi . . . ," I begged him again. Tears in my eyes now. "It's Emma, damn it. Shoot me if you must. Do whatever you want to me. Just first, tell me where she is. For God's sake, Willi, it's not about the war anymore. It's my little girl."

I could see him shaking a little, and nodding, the reality of their fate sinking in. He glanced one last time at his precious kegs, all useless now. "Trudi, he's right, my darling," he said. "There is no point now."

"*Willi.*" Trudi cut him off. "Do not forget who we are. We are soldiers of the Reich, not cowards. He betrayed us. He turned us in." Her eyes came afire at me and she tightened the grip on her gun. "Let the little girl rot in hell, for all I care. Shoot him! Do your job."

For a moment, Willi raised his gun to the height of his waist, and Fiske yelled out, "Bauer, don't!"

Then Willi stopped. Swallowing, he seemed to find some certainty in his mind and dropped his gun. His eyes were not filled with anger any longer, but what seemed close to sorrow. He shook his head and put his hand out on Trudi's extended arm. "Mr. Mossman, you will find her at—"

"*Nein,* my darling—" Trudi cut him off. She raised her gun to his head and pulled the trigger. "*Nein.*"

Willi crumpled to the ground. His Alpine cap fell to the side, a pool of blood collecting around it. His kind, gray eyes staring glassy and lifeless back up at her.

"*No! No!*" I screamed out in horror, and sprinted toward him. "No!"

"I am with you, my love," Trudi said next. "*Heil Hitler!*" She put the barrel of her gun underneath her chin and pulled the trigger again. The blast blew her hat off the top of her head and she spun to the side and crumpled atop her husband.

"No!" I ran up and looked at them lying there. I yanked Trudi's body off of Willi and looked closely into his fixed, still eyes. "*Where is she?*" I screamed at him, on the verge of tears. I picked him up and shook him by the shoulders. "Where is she? Willi! Willi!"

Fiske came up behind me, kneeled, and pulled me away. "He's dead, Charlie."

He couldn't be dead, *Emma,* I was thinking, *Emma.* How would I find her? He was about to tell me where she was. "You said you would find her for me, Fiske," I said, worry metastasizing in me into rage. "You owe me that. You said we would find her, goddammit."

All around, Fiske's men spread across the scene, checking the bodies for life, surrounding the kegs of poison that were now the property of the United States government.

"They called her earlier," I said to Fiske in desperation. "From the brewery. I spoke with Emma. Were you able to trace it?"

"Not entirely." He shook his head. "The call was way too short. The only thing we were able to determine is it was placed to somewhere in New Jersey."

"New Jersey . . . ," I said, racking my brain. It didn't ring a bell for me. On anything. I shook my head in futility.

"You said Emma was being held by your housekeeper. Is there a chance she's from New Jersey?"

The only thing I recalled was Mrs. Shearer once saying she had to make her bus. "No, somewhere in the Bronx, I think. Not Jersey." That didn't help at all.

"We've got about an hour, maybe two, Fiske, until they suspect they won't be calling in."

"We could have someone at the other end of that call," he said. "At the brewery. But . . . Go back to anything Willi or Trudi might have divulged from the time they told you they had her. You said you spoke with Emma. Did you hear anything? Anything that might give you a clue? Background noise. Someone talking to her. Anything that could be helpful . . ."

I went back through my earlier conversation. *Daddy, I want to go home . . . I want to see Mommy.* I'd heard a voice, I thought.

Behind her. A woman's voice. I assumed Mrs. Shearer. But nothing. Nothing that might mean something. Nothing that might possibly be a clue.

All around me, government radios were crackling, agents were swarming over the scene.

I looked at Willi lying there with a hole in the side of his head. *You bastard. You never gave me anything. Anything I could use.*

She's fine, I thought of him saying again. Smiling at me at the apartment, trying to put me at ease. *Just look at it as if she was spending a day at camp.*

Silently, I went over those words again, something forming in my brain.

At camp.

"You said the call was to New Jersey, right?" I looked at Fiske expectantly, hope rising in me. "You're sure?"

He nodded. "Northern New Jersey. That much we're quite sure of. We just couldn't pinpoint it further. You weren't on long enough."

"Northern New Jersey . . ." I grabbed Fiske by the arm, exhilaration rippling through me. "You can take me, can't you? Now. With some men."

"I can organize a police unit at a moment's notice," he said. "But where?"

"Jersey. You said it yourself," I said, locking on his eyes. I looked at my watch. 3:21 A.M. We still had time. "I think I know where she is!"

43

We drove, siren blaring, speeding over dark local roads, back down Route 9 to the George Washington Bridge. Another car with four of Fiske's men kept up right behind us.

On the way I told Fiske, "The German American Bund has a camp in northern New Jersey, right? I've seen it in the news."

"Camp Nordland," he acknowledged. "I'm familiar with it. I was a part of the team that shut it down a few months ago. Why do you think she's there?"

"Because Willi Bauer told me just to think of it as if Emma was at a day at camp. *At camp,* Fiske. You said the call came from northern New Jersey. It has to be. It's the best chance we have."

We crossed over the George Washington Bridge to New Jersey, then onto State Road 15, heading north.

4:10 now.

Fiske radioed ahead and arranged for a team of local police to meet us and guide us in.

Willi and Trudi would have planned to return to the brewery

by now after the completion of their mission. Whoever was holding Emma—Mrs. Shearer, I assumed—would be awaiting their
call. Or possibly would have called in themselves by now.

"This housekeeper," Fiske said, looking over to me, "she's obviously one of them. But if she's taken care of your daughter she has
to have developed feelings for her after all this time."

"She's got the disposition of an iceberg," I said. "If she's even
who's in charge. I wouldn't count on what you say mattering an
iota."

After fifteen minutes we cut over onto State Road 517. At that
hour, we pretty much had the road to ourselves, our headlights
knifing through the darkness. There were virtually no other cars
anywhere.

4:20 A.M.

We turned onto Newton-Sparta Road, people on the other
end of the radio giving us instructions. "We're close." Fiske looked
over to me. "When we get there I want my team to lead the way.
You understand?"

"I understand," I said. I had no idea how many of the German
American Bund would even be there. Or if Emma was even being
held there. It was just a hunch. But everything racing in my heart
told me that she was.

In about five more minutes we drove through a highly wooded
area and came upon a sign and a dirt road. Two police cars were
parked on the side, lights off, awaiting us. Fiske pulled to a stop
and got out to confer with the local cops.

"We don't know what we'll find in there," he said. "And we
don't want to surprise the shit out of anyone and turn this into a
shooting incident. You stay behind me, you understand?" he said
to me. "I want your commitment on that."

"You have it. I just want to find my daughter, Fiske. That's all."

"All right. We're looking for a six-year-old girl," he instructed the other officers. "We don't know who we'll find inside. They might well be armed. I don't want any incidents to escalate out of control. So no guns except if absolutely necessary."

The state policemen nodded.

"Okay, let's go."

We took off up the road in the darkness. The only light was a streetlamp twenty yards down the road. A few of the Feds had flashlights. Who knew if there was a lookout posted somewhere. Or if Emma and Mrs. Shearer were even here. This was all just a big hunch.

The camp was built in 1936 by the German American Bund, one of the pro-Nazi organizations, whose volatile leader, Fritz Kuhn, had been convicted and jailed on tax evasion charges six months earlier. It was originally designed as a place where German-American families and immigrants might spend a country weekend in the summer remembering their homeland, but quickly morphed into a training ground for German Youth, celebrating Hitler and his annexations of Austria and the Sudetenland, and then his march through Europe. Swastikas were openly worn and anti-Jewish doctrines were taught. The Ku Klux Klan even held a rally here before I went to Auburn in 1939. We passed a sign. In German. It read, *WAS WIR IN DEUTSCHLAND ERREICHT HABEN, AUCH HIER.* "What we have achieved in Germany, here too."

We came upon a chained wooden gate blocking the road. A sign hung from it in English and German, *ACHTUNG. GESCHLOSSEN. CLOSED. PRIVATE PROPERTY,* it continued in English. *NO ADMITTANCE SUBJECT TO PENALTY BY THE NEW JERSEY DEPARTMENT OF REVENUE.*

Guns drawn, we squeezed around the shut gate. Crickets

chirped and the narrow road opened and we came upon a large white clapboard structure bordering an open field. The main clubhouse. It was completely darkened. Two of the men ran up onto the large porch, Adirondack chairs still lining it. The front door had a lock and chain securing it.

"No one here. Let's go on." One of them came back around, waving us on.

We went farther. There was a flagpole in the central field, from which I had no doubt a Nazi flag once waved prominently. There were several small white slate-roofed cabins situated around the field.

It was after four in the morning, and I didn't see a light in the entire complex.

My blood tensed. Could I have been wrong?

We kept on moving in the dark. One by one, we started checking the individual cabins. The first three were locked. Not even a porch light on. The whole place looked completely deserted. Fiske said it had been closed down eight months ago by the FBI and state authorities as the Bund's anti-U.S. propaganda grew more heated and the United States and Germany inched closer to war. It looked every bit of just that—shut down. No sign of life.

I began to grow worried.

Some of the cabins seemed to be set deeper in the woods. In the darkness, it was hard to even locate the trail. After checking six or seven of them, Fiske came over to me and gave me a frustrated shrug. *I'm sorry,* it said.

Nothing.

Maybe it was just a random expression Willi had used. *Just think of it as a day at camp.* Maybe it meant absolutely nothing. And I was banking all my hope on it.

Suddenly I heard one of Fiske's men who was ahead of us call, "Commander Fiske!"

We rushed up to the next cabin. Number 13. In the grass next to it was a vehicle. A Wagoneer. They flashed their lights all over it, all the while holding up a hand to remain quiet. It had New York plates.

Two of his men silently went up onto the porch to the front door. Suddenly a light went on. They knocked on it loudly.

After a second, we could hear voices and someone scurrying inside.

"Someone's in here," one of the agents said. "Federal agents!" he announced, continuing to bang at the door. "Open up. Now."

No one answered. But inside you could hear the faintest sound of hushed voices.

"Open the door!" the agent demanded again. Two drew their guns and put themselves on either side of the door. "We're federal agents. Open up or we're coming in!"

The cabin was tiny, maybe two small rooms. I couldn't tell if there was even plumbing. Everyone readied their guns. One of the burlier agents positioned himself to the side of the door, preparing to kick it in.

My heart jumped with anticipation, hoping Emma might be inside.

"*Komen! Komen!*" a voice suddenly called out from inside. Coming. A light went on. "Do not shoot! *Bitte. Komen,*" we heard again.

Slowly, the inside latch was thrown open and the door cracked. It was a man in bedclothes. Jabbering in German. The burly agent pulled him outside and the team of agents rushed in after, guns drawn, saying loudly, "Federal agents! Hands in the air! Everyone down!"

Fiske and I followed them in.

There were three other people inside. A woman. Another man, older. Their hands in the air. And a young boy. No more than three. Who looked sleepy and terrified. They all did. The man who opened the door was pushed back inside. Clearly the woman's husband. They were speaking only German.

I shouted, "Emma! Emma!"

The agents quickly went through the two rooms. It only took seconds. They came back out, shaking their heads. Empty.

It was just a family. Jabbering in German, frightened out of their wits. "Please, please, nein shoot, nein shoot," the father stammered. That seemed about the extent of his English. He dug into a leather pouch and took out some documents. Immigration papers. "Okay, okay," he said again, showing them.

"Where are they?" Fiske said sharply, handing the papers back. "The girl. A woman. Where are they?"

"Ich verstehe nicht." The man shook his head in terror, not understanding. *"Verstehe nicht."* The petrified mother held the boy and huddled next to the older man, likely his grandfather. They all seemed like they were just in hiding out here. In an isolated, German enclave.

"Where are they?" Fiske said again. He grabbed the father roughly by the arm and pushed him up against the wall. His wife let out a scream. "The girl. The woman. We know they're here somewhere. Where?"

"Madchen," I translated, stepping forward. A girl. I put my palm out to the height of my waist. *"Klein."* Small. *"Madchen,"* I said again. *"Mit einer frau."* With a woman.

They each looked at each other, hesitating a bit.

I couldn't tell if they knew what I was talking about or not. Or how much they even understood. Mostly it seemed they had simply camped out here with nowhere to go. Probably just off the boat a month or two, and with no job. Scared, with the war, they'd all be tossed in jail.

"*Madchen,*" I said one more time. They were a family themselves. With a child. Maybe they'd see my anguish. "*Mein tochter,*" I appealed to the father. My daughter. "*Mein tochter. Bitte . . .*" I looked at him, trying to convey my anguish. Please.

The father's gaze shot to his petrified wife and then to his boy. As if he knew he was about to give something up. Something they shouldn't reveal.

"*Bitte . . . ,*" I said again, the tiniest flame of hope lighting up in me that he knew where Emma was.

Please.

"*Sechszehn,*" the father finally said. He looked at me. He gestured toward the woods with his chin as if to convey, another cabin. Farther along.

Sechszehn.

I looked at Fiske. That flame had now lit into a fire.

"Number sixteen," I said. "Emma's here!"

44

Before anyone else could even react, I was out the door, in a full sprint. This was cabin 13. I leaped off the porch. A path continued from the field deeper into the woods. I tripped over a branch in the dark and steadied myself with my hand to keep from tumbling over.

Behind me, I heard Fiske shout, gathering his men. "Charlie, wait! Please!"

It was completely dark, the moon covered with clouds, but ahead of me, the shape of another cabin came into view—14. I kept on running. The cold was like daggers jabbing into my lungs. Stealing my breath. Another cabin appeared, tucked into the trees. Not a light on or any sign of life inside.

Cabin 15.

Emma was close. I felt it. Some things you could just feel.

"Emma!" I called out. I wanted her to hear me.

I saw the outline of another dwelling forming out of the darkness. White wood, shingle roof. It was small, just like the others.

But this one with a chimney. They could build a fire. And there was smoke.

My heart leaped. There was a light on inside.

I bounded up the stairs and onto the porch. "Emma," I called out. "Emma, it's me, Daddy."

I heard a muffled cry coming from inside.

Behind me, Fiske and three of his agents had almost caught up to me. "Charlie, wait for us. Don't go inside!"

I ignored him and jammed on the outer door. There was still a screen attached to the door and I pulled it open and literally threw myself inside.

A woman's voice said, "Don't come a step closer, Mr. Mossman."

In the corner, illuminated by the light of a single dim floor lamp, stood Mrs. Shearer, in a wool coat as if preparing to go outside, one arm wrapped around my daughter, in her sleeping gown, her hand pressed over Emma's mouth, keeping her from uttering a sound. In her other hand she held a gun, which she had pressed against Emma's head.

"Don't you even move a muscle, Mr. Mossman. I don't want to do it, but I will. She's just a piece of Jewish scum to me. Don't test my resolve."

"Mrs. Shearer," I said, putting up my hands to show I was unarmed. "It's over. Willi and Trudi are dead. Their plans have collapsed. There's no point anymore. Give me back my daughter. There's no reason to harm her now. No one else has to die."

I took a step, but her eyes narrowed in a threatening glare, and she pressed the barrel harder into Emma's head. Emma squealed. "Just stay back."

"Okay, okay. Emma, don't be scared, honey. I'm going to get you out. I promise."

Outside, Fiske and his team ran up the stairs and onto the porch. Mrs. Shearer's gaze darted to them, eyes dark and terrified.

I yelled, "Fiske, stay back! Mrs. Shearer, you can see now it's not just me. You're surrounded. There's no way out but to put the gun down and give me Emma. There's no point in scaring her any further."

Emma was whimpering, terrified, her eyes wide little moons. She twisted her head and momentarily freed her mouth from Mrs. Shearer's grasp. "Daddy! Daddy!" she screamed, trying to wrestle out of her grip and get to me.

"Honey, it's going to be okay," I said, as calmly as I could manage. Though inside, my heart beat feverishly. I held out my arms to show her how I wanted her. "Mrs. Shearer is going to let you go and it's all going to be over." I looked in the nanny's eyes, pleading. They didn't show much fear now, only the resolve to take this wherever it would go. There was no way out for her. Now it was just, how did she want it to end.

"Daddy, please, I want to go home now," Emma said, crying.

"I know, I know, darling. You're going to," I said. I looked at Mrs. Shearer. "Very soon. You will."

I heard a creak on the floorboards as Fiske eased through the door behind me, his hands protruding, showing he wasn't armed as well.

"Tell him to get out!" Mrs. Shearer barked. "Get out, or I promise, your daughter's brains will be all over this floor."

"Please, do what she says," I said, and spun around, my heart exploding with fear. "I'll be all right. Please."

He backed out, giving me a dart of his eyes to say, *My men are in position.*

"So it's only you and me now," I said, looking back at Mrs.

Shearer, taking another step toward her. "Let Emma go. I'll stay. You can do whatever you want to me. Let the child go, Mrs. Shearer. You don't have any issue against her."

"Willi and Trudi are dead, you say?"

"Yes. She shot him. Then she shot herself."

"Shot him . . ." Her lips creased into a wistful smile. "Shot the person she loved most in the world. A brave woman, that Trudi. She always did have more resolve than him."

"It doesn't have to end like that here . . . ," I said. "Look . . ." I took another step. "Just hear me ou—"

Her hand holding the gun leaped up and she jerked on the trigger. I heard a report and then a searing pain lanced into my shoulder. My arm went to it and I buckled in pain. Emma screamed, "Daddy!" and it took everything the old woman had to hold on to her by the collar as my daughter desperately tried to get to me.

I lifted my hand and saw a flower of blood had spread on my jacket. "I'm all right. I'm all right, honey," I said, rising back up. My knees were weak. I could barely stand.

"Are you all right in there, Charlie?" Fiske called out. Footsteps scurried around the side of the house.

"Yes. Yes. Just stay out. I'm okay." I put my hand to my shoulder and looked at the blood, then looked up at Mrs. Shearer. "Why?" I asked. "Why do you hate her so?"

Her eyes were fixed and dilated in her steadfastness and conviction. She tugged back at Emma, who was desperately trying to pull away. "Shearer is my married name, Mr. Mossman. My maiden name, you may know it, was McWilliams. My brother Joe, you may have heard of him."

McWilliams.

It took a second for the name to sink in. Joseph McWilliams.

The head of a group called the Christian Front. They were allied with Father Coughlin and the American Destiny Party. Trumpeters of Hitler. He was one of the speakers at the Madison Square Garden rally the night my life changed. "Joe McNazi" he was called.

"You're Joe McWilliams's sister . . . ?"

She slowly nodded. "You had a brother. I've overheard you talk of him. Did you admire him, Mr. Mossman?"

I looked at her and nodded too. "Yes. Very much."

"And I admired mine." She pulled Emma close and pressed the gun tightly to her skull. Eyes wide, Emma tried to wrestle out of her grasp. "Daddy!"

"So you'll tell him that I died a true sister in the cause," she said. "I'm sorry," she said.

She pulled the hammer back, gun pressed to the back of Emma's head.

Emma screamed. I took a lunge toward her. "Please. No!"

She paused on the trigger, just long enough that from behind me I heard two blunt pops, and Mrs. Shearer's head snapped back. Her hand let go of Emma and two red dots appeared on her forehead. She stumbled backward into the chair, her arms spread wide, her jaw slack, staring straight ahead. A trickle of blood ran down her face, zigzagging around her nose.

"Daddy!" Emma ran to me, in tears. I threw open my arms and hugged her as tightly as I'd ever held anyone without crushing them, almost afraid she would be taken from me forever if I let her go.

All around, agents rushed into the cabin. Shouting, radios crackling. They ran up to Mrs. Shearer. One checked her pulse and shook his head. "She's dead," he said.

Others came up to Emma and me.

"Here, let me check her, Mr. Mossman," one of them said. "Just for a minute."

"No," Emma said, crying, afraid to leave my arms. She shook her head. "No."

I looked at the agent and shook my head myself, and said back, "I've got her."

I picked up my daughter and rushed her out of the cabin. I pressed her face close to my shoulder, and when we got away from the noise and commotion, I wiped away her tears. "I've got you," I said. "I've got you, Emma. I won't let you go. Never."

She was crying, choking back heavy sobs. I held tightly to her small, convulsing body. "I've got you, baby. Daddy's got you," I said. "Everything's going to be okay." Suddenly I couldn't hold back myself. My eyes flooded and my face became wet with tears and I could only squeeze her tighter and tighter to keep from sliding myself. Thinking of Mrs. Shearer's glassy-eyed commitment at the end. Would she truly have pulled that trigger? She had hesitated just that much. The place became abuzz with police activity. Fiske came over, put an arm around me, and smiled at my daughter. "So this is Emma."

"Yes," I said. "Yes."

He patted me on the shoulder. "I have a car ready. She should be at the hospital." He glanced at my bloody shoulder, the blood seeping onto Emma's nightgown. "So should you."

I didn't even feel it. My shoulder was the last thing in the world for me. "First we're going to go home," I said. "We're going to go home now, baby. . . ." I hugged my daughter. I buried my face in her hair. She smelled so sweet. "Let's go see your mommy."

45

As the clock struck 4:30 that morning, Warren Latimer sat in the wood-paneled study of his home in Bethesda, outside Washington, D.C.

He'd dozed earlier on upstairs, then gotten up around two, anticipation rustling him from sleep, telling his wife that he'd be back up shortly, after he'd gotten the call from Willi that everything had gone as planned. He poured himself a glass of milk, checked the shelf clock one more time, opened his copy of Thucydides' *History of the Peloponnesian Wars*.

He put it down. The thought occurred to him, he hadn't set out to be what some might call a traitor. He'd been open to new ideas back at Yale. The Young Lions, they had called them. For a while, he'd even flirted with reading Marx. But then events in Russia and in the Depression here had changed him. He'd seen what power was like when put in the hands of the people, and it only led to bloodshed and chaos. The people, strengthened beyond their ability to govern, simply became a mob. Power, he began to feel, should always be in the hands of those who were best equipped to wield it, and our perpetual president—*dictator* some called him— did not understand that. The idea of a Fortress America became something in which he began to believe. America protected by its two great oceans. Protected from the real threat. The Bolsheviks. Communism.

The mob.

He wasn't a Nazi-lover at heart. Far from it. Just someone who was willing to use the Nazis as a guard against the future. To battle the real enemy. Once America saw there was no purpose in fighting a war they were not prepared to fight and that they were best served by staying neutral, they would quickly sue for peace.

And then a unified Europe under Germany's military might would be a true buffer against the Reds.

For the real war that was to come.

Fortunately there were many throughout the government who thought like him. The State Department. Clear thinkers. Not politicians. Students of history. He wasn't alone.

But by 4 A.M., Latimer began to fear something had gone wrong. Willi and Trudi should have been back by now—he checked his clock—preparing to leave. He should have been called. He heard a rustling sound outside. Latimer pulled back the shades. Two black sedans were parked across the street. When had they come? A feeling of dread came over him. He knew those cars. From his desk drawer, he took out the envelope Trudi had given him. In case something went wrong. Two tablets. Dabbed in the very substance they were to put in the water supply. Better to take the honorable way out, he resolved, than face the mob. He always knew this might be a possibility. His choice.

Around 4:30, no one had come for him but Latimer knew it

was over. The call he was awaiting never came. *Sad,* he thought, *for me and for the world.* He went to the bar and poured himself a rye. He heard a sound. A light went on outside. He peeked through the blinds again, and saw that four men had gotten out of the cars and were making their way across the street toward his house.

Too bad. It would have saved the country a lot of blood if they had only listened to him.

He clenched his robe and sat back down. He opened the envelope and took out the small, wrapped paper that contained two tiny pellets. So tiny he had to put his glasses on to even see them. He put one of the specks of white on the tip of his finger and put it to his tongue. He drank the last of his rye. *Too bad*, he thought. He heard the government men on his porch. Then he sat back.

"Warren Latimer," one of them called from outside. "FBI." There was knocking at his door.

He didn't move. He felt a tightness grip his chest. An acrid burning in his lungs. The beginning.

Too bad. He closed his eyes. He could have been useful. They would need him.

In the next war.

46

ONE WEEK LATER

"Daddy, why did Uncle Willi and Aunt Trudi have to die?" Emma said sadly. She put down her coloring crayon and looked up at me.

It was my first time back at the apartment after three days in the hospital. They had removed a bullet from my shoulder and my arm was in a sling. And then two days of being interviewed and debriefed by the FBI and various other government agencies known only by letters I didn't even know existed.

I let her have a few days with Liz.

"Because sometimes people who seem to be nice can do bad things," I said. I looked at Liz for help, but even she seemed unable. "I wish I could give you a better answer, honey."

After the nightmare with Mrs. Shearer at the camp, having the gun put to her head and watching her nanny be killed in front of her, Emma seemed to be okay. I knew one day it would be something she would have to deal with. Three people she had trusted like her own family had conspired to cause her harm. And they were dead now. "They did all love you though, Emma. They did."

She nodded, though maybe not entirely convincingly. "I know."

"They did, honey," Liz said. She came over and put her arm on her shoulder. "But in the grown-up world, everything isn't always clear."

"C'mon, how 'bout we work on that puzzle," I said, "in the time we have left." This time it was a pictorial of Africa. Elephants, lions, and zebras in the wild.

"Okay."

Liz—she hadn't gone back to work yet, nor Emma back to school, of course—was getting her dinner ready.

We played until about a quarter to six. I noticed Liz had taken out three dinner plates. Maybe it was her fella. What was his name? Not wanting to overstay my welcome, I said, "Well, maybe it's time I got going."

I got up, took my jacket, and ran my hand affectionately along Emma's hair. "I had fun, peach."

I looked at Liz. "Will I see you Thursday?"

From the moment I'd brought Emma back early that morning, like I'd promised, and put her into Liz's arms, safe, unharmed, I'd felt something different between us. She had come to the hospital without Emma, holding back a flood of things unsaid. But I could see it welling in her eyes. Taking shape. She even took hold of my hand to say goodbye and told me to get well as quickly as I could. The government men were making such a big deal of me, she barely could get more than a couple of minutes to even say something to me.

I said to Emma, "I'll definitely see you Thursday, peach. Maybe we'll go to the fudge shop and get something sinful we won't tell your mother about."

Emma giggled. "Yes, Daddy." The light went back on in her eyes.

"Around three," I said to Liz at the door, putting my arms through my jacket. "I'll—"

"Charlie . . . ," Liz said. She looked at me and gave me a shrug. "Maybe you'd like to stay for dinner this time . . . ? It's only a rump roast and some boiled potatoes. But there's enough. If that would be good . . . ?"

I stared back, startled by the invitation. My heart jumped a beat with hope and I grinned. "A rump roast sounds like the Ritz to me. I'd love to stay, if you'd like me to."

Liz looked at Emma and nodded. "We would."

Then Emma looked up at her and then back at me with what seemed a sparkle of anticipation. "Is it time to give it to him, Mommy?"

I looked at them. "Give me what?"

"Emma made you a present," Liz said. "I guess we both did." She shrugged. "I think so, honey. Go on, get it."

Emma ran into the bedroom and by the time I looked at Liz and said, "What's going on?" she had run back out and held out her hand. "Here, Daddy!"

It was a tiny box with pretty wrapping on it and a purple bow. No larger than a box that might hold a ring. And as I took it, looking at both of them, as light as a feather.

"It's not much," Liz said, putting her wooden spoon down.

I undid the bow and laid it on the table. I took off the wrapping and opened the box. I joked, "You know my birthday's not till March. . . ."

On a bed of tissue, there was a tiny piece of cardboard no more than an inch in length and a half inch high. The kind, I realized, you might affix next to the buzzer at the entrance to a building. And there was a single word written on it. In Emma's distinctive cursive.

The word was *MOSSMAN*.

"No guarantees, Charlie . . . ," Liz said, her eyes brimming. She shrugged. "But we could give it a try, right . . . ?"

Before I could even answer, I ran over and gave her a hug. Emma came over too. I picked her up. I had my arms around both of them, my face buried into them.

"It's not much . . . ?" I said, feeling everything I had lost in the last two years suddenly returned to me. "For me, it's everything."

EPILOGUE

NOVEMBER 1945

The war was finally over. At least in Europe.

Liz, Emma, and I were living in Brooklyn now. And two-year-old Gabrielle as well. The apartment in Yorkville was way too small for a growing family.

I was still working at the appliance store. Except that I was managing it now—and by that time it had doubled in size. The largest independent appliance store in New York City, our ads proclaimed. And we were opening a second one up on Fordham Road in the Bronx. With a million soldiers about to come home from the war and start families of their own, business was sure to boom.

Years back, *Life* magazine had done a spread on me. "The Hero Dad Who Saved His Family and Foiled a Nazi Plot." That made me a celebrity for a month or so. And because of it some teaching offers actually rolled in. At Boston University. And Ohio State University in Columbus. And even Columbia. Things had changed in the department once again. Rusk was out. But with a growing family, and another on the way, I decided maybe I would just stay where I was for a while. I discovered I had a knack for managing. The owner, Sol, whose own kids were in law and medical school, showed a lot of trust in me.

So I told them all I'd just think about it and get back to them. And never did.

That nagging voice on my shoulder told me I was a fool, of course. But I hadn't been listening to him for years now. I had a family to support. Funny how the paths in life unfold.

There was even a reward that came with what I had done. The government actually had a fund for the successful uncovering of foreign agents in the war. $10,000. I talked it over with Liz and we decided we'd keep half. Three thousand for us, and a thousand for each of the kids' college funds. The rest we gave anonymously to a family in New Jersey who had lost their son six years before to a drunken punch thrown outside a bar in Hell's Kitchen.

Anonymously, in the memory of Andrew J. McHurley.

It was rare now that I even thought about what happened back then. The Bauers, Mrs. Shearer, Latimer, they were all just memories to me now. Ones I had tried to forget.

And Noelle.

I rarely thought about her either, only how different my life might have been, our crossed paths, if I hadn't walked into that room with the Bauers and Latimer in it and seen how she betrayed me. After the incident, there was no trace of her anywhere. The investigators looked through her apartment. There was no sign of her there. Anywhere. It was like she had simply disappeared. And with that, vanished from my mind as well. I always remembered how sad she had looked that night at the Bauers' when it came out what she had done. *I had no love for any of this, Charlie . . .* And how Fiske had said that her parents were prisoners of the Nazis. How she was trapped into doing something she did not believe in, like me.

In war we all have to make choices. . . .

But one day that November, as I came home from a long day at work, I threw myself on the couch. The kids both wanted a piece of me before they went to bed. "Any mail?" I asked Liz.

"Just the usual," she said, tossing me a pile of bills and notices, which I started to sort through. "Oh, and this . . ."

It was an envelope addressed to me that had been forwarded from the brownstone on Ninetieth Street, where we hadn't lived in two years.

"Who do we know in France?" she asked, looking over my shoulder.

It was postmarked Rouen. To Charles Mossman. But there was no return address.

I opened it, shaking my head at her question. "Beats me."

There was no note inside. I dug around the envelope to be sure. Only a single black-and-white photo. I took it out and stared at it, and at first, didn't recognize a single person in it. "Who the hell . . . ?" A woman in a dark hat in front of a fountain, standing next to an older woman and man. Gaunt, their clothes rumpled. Only the thinnest and most inscrutable of smiles. If I could put my finger on it, the only word that came to mind was "proud." They just seemed proud to have taken the photo. To be alive. For a moment I thought maybe it had been sent to the wrong person and I checked the envelope again.

There was something beautiful about the woman in the hat. Then it hit me precisely who she was.

My heart surged. It was Noelle. After all these years. And the two others had to be her parents. Her parents who were in a Nazi prison camp.

There was a date written: *July 1945*. Two months after the end of the war in Europe.

They'd made it.

That's what the smiles said: They'd survived.

And there was an inscription on the back, in English: *None of our paths were straightforward, Charles. . . . But in the end, some led to good places. My hope is yours did too.*

Suddenly something rose up in me and I felt tears burn in my eyes.

I fixed on their smiles.

And then I noticed one more line, at the bottom. One that, as I read it, sent my mind rocketing back in time and explained so many things.

I had another American friend, Charles, Noelle had written. *His name was Fiske.*

Fiske.

My God, I suddenly realized, she had been his source. That's how he knew about Latimer. And that Emma had been taken. And about Prospero. But not what it was. And not the sub. In that moment I realized the path Noelle had truly taken. And just who had helped me get our baby back.

And why she was not to be found in the end.

"Who is this?" Liz asked, leaning over my shoulder.

"No one," I said. But my eyes welled up with emotion. I looked back at the photo, Noelle. Those proud, determined eyes.

My journey here was not straightforward either, Charles.

No, it damn well wasn't. I started to laugh out loud. Mixed with tears.

"Charlie, are you all right?" Liz asked. She saw the emotion on my face.

"Yes, I'm perfect, honey." I put the photo back in the envelope, slid it among the mail to be thrown out, and tossed it on the table. "I'm perfect. Hey, Emma, come here and give your dad a hug, peach."

ACKNOWLEDGMENTS

This book came about as far back as research for *The One Man*, where I came across a marvelous book, *Those Angry Days*, by Lynne Olsen, which dealt with the divisive and turbulent times in the run-up to WWII as America wrestled with getting into the war, as well as the ideological differences of the two most admired figures of their time: aviator Charles Lindbergh and President Franklin Roosevelt.

It was a time that reflected much of the rancor and polarization that is a part of life today: an intensely divided Congress, "isolationist" Republicans versus "interventionist" Democrats who were eager to come to the defense of Britain; the political saber-rattling that an all-powerful, populist president was circumventing Congress for his "imperial" ends; the fear of immigrants—in this case, not from Central America, but mostly European Jews. Not to mention that the whole idea of a "fifth column"—foreigners deeply embedded in the fabric of our daily lives—who would emerge in war to perform acts of sabotage and espionage—surely has a whole new meaning in today's reality.

The "fifth column," in this book, the spy network of Willi and Trudi Bauer, is based on what was known as the Duquesne Spy Ring, thirty-three mostly American citizens placed in key roles in U.S. companies who passed proprietary information back to Nazi Germany, which was uncovered in 1941. All either pleaded guilty or were convicted. It remains the largest American espionage ring ever uncovered.

But the most interesting aspect of the times, for me, in the years leading up the war, was the widespread tolerance for the Nazi cause and its leaders, whether in Congress, the State Department, the America First Party, or openly in German-speaking neighborhoods in New York City. It is a fascinating and largely unreported part of those times, famously symbolized by the February 1939 gathering at Madison Square Garden when over 20,000 people waved Nazi flags and cheered brazen Nazi propagandists, the very night this book begins. Yes, it was before images of the Holocaust came out. And yes, some of it was just to keep America out of another war. But the persecution of the Jews in Germany was well known here and somehow accepted in the highest circles of our government. It took Pearl Harbor to wake us from our moral sleep. One wonders what would have happened if Hitler had not declared war on us, and made events play out as they did.

Several people had a hand, as always, in strengthening this novel: Roy Grossman, for his insightful reading, and Herbie Mueller with the German (and with help on the Swiss foods!). And thanks as always to my team at Minotaur: Kelley Ragland, Andrew Martin, Madeline Houpt, Hector DeJean, as well as the group at Writers House, Simon Lipskar and Celia Taylor Mobley.

And to my family—Lynn and my kids—who have been there and supported me through several incarnations in life. My arms go around you. And to Martin and Louis, a new generation, who hopefully will have learned a little of whom they are in these books, and then carry it forward, which is the purpose, isn't it?